LISBON

To My Bro Joe;
Love ya, my Brother B,
JH, Jack

JACK DUARTE

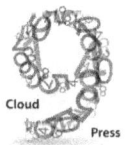

Cloud 9 Press

For information write to:
Cloud 9 Press,
634 Central Ave.
Lexington, KY 40502

ISBN: 978-1-7334597-5-4

Cover by Chris Inman, Visual Riot
Interior book and e-pub design by Chip Holtzhauer

Jack DuArte's
World War II Series

Dedication

*To my late aunt Izaura Duarte Gaillard
for her inspiration.*

*To my late grandfather,
João Berce Veigas Antonio Duarte,
for his unwavering love for his
native country that he passed on to me.*

*To Banning Lary,
for his exceptional suggestions
and attention to detail.*

*To John Duarte,
for his inspirational appreciation
for the plot.*

*To Steven Duarte,
for his excellence and dedication
in proofreading this work.*

Acknowledgements

In Portugal:
Manuela Romano de Castro

In England:
Ben Girdlestone

In the United States:
Ray Rizzo, Marcia Cone,
Courtney Turner,
Jay Philbrick,
Rock Daniels,
Deno and Jo Curris,
Ric Waldman,
Barb & Grant Mills,
Katya & Josh Lundberg,
Sandy Challman,
Jane & Tony Rabasca,
Billy King, Ricky Sins,
Dr. Marion Winkler,
Roger Barenz, Bill Snowden,
Ralph Gibbons, Festus Letzkus,
Walker Borders, Zach Doyle,
Tony Lacy, Kathie Maybee
Michael Harrison
and Rush Matthews

Portuguese Words

—A—

aguardente......................a type of Portuguese brandy usually added to Port wines.

—B—

bica ....coffee

Boca do Inferno.............the Mouth of Hell

bombilla........................a special metal straw used for making mate

borboleta.......................butterfly

—C—

campo............................field

carvalho.........................oak

chave ....key

—E—

e ....and

estabilidade economica...stable economy

estado novo....................New State name for Salazar's government

Exposição do Mundo Portuguese........Portugal's World Exposition of 1940

Eu I

—F—

falo ....speak

—J—

Jardim de Estrela............Star Garden

—L—

Licor Beirão....................Portugal's national liquor

Lisboetas........................inhabitants of Lisbon

leal................................loyal

lua.................................moon

—M—

Margaridas.....................daisies

Margaridas à beira-mar ..daisies by the sea

mártires da Pátria........... martyrs of the Homeland

mate ....a potent tea

meu..............................you

merda............................shit

Meu Amor.....................My Love

—N—

Não, obrigado.................no, thank you

nova ....new

—O—

O prazer é meu................My pleasure to meet you

O Século.........................Lisbon daily newspaper, in English "This Century"

ouro .... gold

—P—

PCP .... Portuguese Communist Party
perdoe-me .... pardon me
Polícia de Vigilância e Defesa do Estado (PVDE) ...... Portuguese Secret Police
petiscos .... the Portuguese culinary specialty that highlights
                       individual regions of the country portugues
Portuguese .... the language
pouco .... little;

—R—

recessão .... recession;

—S—

Sagres .... Portugal's most famous beer founded in 1928
Saúde .... Cheers
senhor .... sir or mister
senhorita .... miss
O prazer é meu sim .... the pleasure is mine
sim .... yes
sincero e leal .... sincere and loyal

—T—

tio .... uncle

—V—

verde .... green
vinho .... wine
volfrâmio .... wolfram, a vital element also called tungsten

German Words

Abwehr .... German Intelligence Service

Deutsche Mark .... the monetary unit of Germany equal to 100 pfennigs
Hauptman .... captain
jawohl .... yes
Kriegsmarine .... German Navy
Luftwaffe .... German Air Force
quatsch .... hogwash
Wehrmacht .... German Army

The Barcelos
Rooster Legend

The Barcelos Rooster that we use for our paragraph breaks is said to be the embodiment of the Portuguese love of life.

Legend has it that in 15th Century Barcelos, in Northern Portugal, a man was unfairly condemned to death. The prisoner demanded to see the magistrate who was at his home eating a meal that featured a cooked rooster.

The judge ignored the prisoner's explanation and sentenced him to hang. The prisoner pointed at the rooster and swore the rooster would crow at the hour of his hanging. When that time came, the rooster appeared and crowed as the prisoner said he would. The judge realized his mistake and saved the man's life. He later returned to Barcelos and sculpted a cross in honor of the Virgin Mary and St. James whom he believed responsible for the miracle. This cross still exists today and is called the Cross of the Lord of the Rooster and is displayed in the Archeological Museum of Barcelos.

Foreword

Monday, June 17, 1940
Portuguese Consulate
14 quai Louis XVIII
Bordeaux, France

His hand quivered as he held the document above the table lamp in his office. The movement did not go unnoticed by Aristides de Sousa Mendes, Consul General of the Bordeaux District of France for his beloved Country of Portugal. He attributed the shaking to the enormous pressure he and his staff were experiencing since the Nazis initiated on November 9th, 1938, the devastation and loathsome action known to the world as *Kristallnacht*. On that date more than a thousand Jewish synagogues were damaged or destroyed, along with thousands of Jewish businesses. Over 30,000 Jews were arrested and at least 91 were murdered.

The persecution and intolerance of Nazi Germany resulted in a mass exodus of millions of people. In southwestern France, the refugees only real hope lay in the hands of neutral Portugal, a smallish country of six million which shared the Andean border with its long-time rival, the Spanish State under Fascist Dictator Francisco Franco. But, Portugal itself was under the authoritarian regime of Dr. Oliveira Salazar who had seized power under the aegis of his *Estado Novo* or New State seven years before.

After Austria was annexed by Germany in 1938, neighboring countries began to take restrictive measures against emigration including Portugal. Salazar ordered the Ministry of Foreign Affairs (MNE) to produce Circular 14, a November 1939 edict that required Portugal's consular service to consult the State Surveillance and Defense Police (PVDE) and the Ministry before granting visas to

1

stateless persons, Russians and Jews expelled from their countries thus curtailing the flow of foreigners into his country.

Aristides de Sousa Mendes refused to accept this order, and issued visas to people he felt were in imminent danger or who had no other chance of escape.

It was now mid-June, 1940, a month after Germany had launched its offensive against France, Belgium, The Netherlands and Luxembourg. Thousands fled their countries, many refugees escaping through France toward Portugal.

Aristides de Sousa Mendes was soon overwhelmed with requests for immigration visas. Bordeaux and other smaller towns of Southwestern France were inundated with refugees. The greater portion of this calamitous group were Jews, bearing what little possessions, currency and precious jewels they had managed to bring with them.

The rooms inside the multi-storied, unpretentious Portuguese Consulate in Bordeaux were completely filled with refugees, as were the grounds located on a bend of the Garonne River at *14 quai Louis XVIII.* and many were sleeping on the consulate's stairwells or outside on the city's streets and in Bordeaux's numerous city parks.

Sousa Mendes' personal life contributed to his consternation. His mistress, French artist and singer Andrée Cibial, pregnant with his child, provoked a scandal in front of Sousa Mendes' family and wound up imprisoned for her effort. The diplomat finally caved and suffered a nervous breakdown. He took to his bed, was at odds with himself and the suddenly obstructed world surrounding him. In his absence his secretary, José Seabra, tended to the consulate's affairs as if his leader was still around and active.

That was three days ago and, suddenly this morning, Sousa Mendes invigorated himself, bathed, shaved and made his way to a door that separated the family's living quarters from the consulate's work area. He flung open the door and announced in a loud voice, "From now on I'm giving everyone visas. There will be no more nationalities, races or religions."

Several members of his family gathered around him. He explained he had heard a voice, of his conscience or of God, which clearly dictated to him what course of action he should take. 247

2

visas were issued this day, some to Portuguese citizens wishing to travel abroad but mostly to new emigres. The next day, 216 visas were issued. Each day between June 19ᵗʰ and 22nd, an average of 350 visas were recorded. Sousa Mendes directed Seabra to expedite the processing of all visas. It was further understood that the Consul General would personally sign each one.

The Lisbon government reacted immediately to the consul's actions and warned Sousa Mendes to cease his issuance. But by that time, Sousa Mendes had established an assembly line to process the visas and remarked boldly to everyone around, "I would rather stand with God against man than with man against God."

The stage was then set for the internal entry battle that would test Portugal's neutrality and exacerbate its fear of possible military action by Spanish authorities. Many felt Spain was eager to annex Portugal and its excellent ports. Dictator Oliveira Salazar quickly recalled Sousa Mendes and stripped him of his powers and consular title.

In effect, Sousa Mendes' removal did little to stem the tide of refugees clamoring to enter Portugal. What it did do was to signify the country's prime role as a humanitarian portal for anyone seeking protection from Nazi Germany. It also put the world's eyes on the country's unprepared capitol, the archaic and imperturbable City of Lisbon.

Chapter One

Tuesday, May 21, 1940
Along the Avenida de Liberdade
Lisbon, Portugal

Izaura Veigas Ribeiro strode purposefully up the *Avenida de Liberdade* in the direction of Lisbon's City Park. The beautiful street on this hot and humid late Spring day was Lisbon's finest and widest and tended to give the attractive 23-year-old light-haired woman a feeling of exhilaration whenever she had the opportunity to walk up its gentle grading. The avenue's perfectly spaced trees provided a small measure of relief from the sun's incessant shine and heat.

She left the top of the *Rossio*, passed a pair of theatres and noted the entrances of both the Hotel Aviz and Hotel Tivoli were crowded with the area's usual congestion. All sorts of people, locals and foreigners alike, scurried about going in and out of the hotels.

Business is certainly good for the hotels, there isn't a room available anywhere in the city. This war seems to be quite a boon for Portugal and her people. Almost everyone I know is working and the pay is better than before the war began. The people are all happy are living in the moment. When the war finally ends, they will no doubt be disappointed and be forced to return to their ordinary lives. she mused. *We Lisboetas should be very happy that Dr. Salazar, our country's prime minister, has seen the best and worst of our country. My uncle João says he is a gifted man who loves his country and its people above all and will lead it back to the greatness it once enjoyed.*

Isn't the Exposição do Mundo Português being constructed to show the world what we are capable of as a country? Everyone says it will be wonderful and will show our greatness as a nation. Most people I talk to hold the same opinion.

Izaura slowed her walk as she passed one of the sidewalk cafes along the *Avenida*. She leaned in to overhear some of the earnest conversations at the nearby tables. The thin young woman slowed her pace to a shuffle as the words *recessão* and *estabilidade economica* filtered out. Another word, *volfrâmio*, was unfamiliar to her. She made a specific note in her mind to discover its meaning.

A block later, Izaura turned westward toward *Rua Seculo* and her destination at the offices of one of Portugal's top daily newspapers, *O Seculo.*

Upon arriving at number 41, she stopped and pushed open the wooden doors. Only a tiny lateral sign announced to the world that this was the office of *O'Seculo,* and the domain of her favorite uncle, João Tomás Riberio, the paper's editor. She walked up the stairs to the top floor and waved to Dolores, her uncle's long time secretary whose desk was immediately outside the door that led to the editor's office. Dolores waved her in and returned to the paperwork on her desk.

Izaura opened the door and stepped in.

João Riberio looked up and smiled broadly. Izaura had been his most treasured relative her entire life. He greeted her warmly.

"What brings you here, my sweet *barboleta*," the name he called her since childhood.

Izaura strepped around the desk and bussed him in the Portuguese manner. "I am just here to see you and smother you with kisses," she replied as she pulled away. Haven't I done so in the past? I don't recall your ever objecting."

"I will never object my darling. You are a blessing to our family."

"Thank you, *Tio.*"

"Now that all the pleasantries are finished, why don't you tell me what precipitated your visit?"

"You always see right through me."

"It's just that I love you dearly, my sweet Izaura."

Izaura looked straight into her uncle's hazel eyes and began speaking in a soft and earnest tone.

"I've been thinking about what I want to do with my life, *Tio*. I want to do something important that will help our country, something that will make a difference. I want to be sure and do the right thing and I thought I would seek your advice. I wouldn't want to make a mistake."

"I am honored you think that much of me," Riberio replied. "I'm glad to help."

"It's like this, Tio, now that I have my law degree, I want to put it to good use. I'm not really interested in courts or the court system. I've grown wary of that scene. I want to do something more lively, more in keeping with the times we live in. I want my efforts to matter, if that makes any sense."

"It makes perfect sense, my dear. Not many people your age have such noble ideas. Many just want to make money and have fun."

"This is not the time for fun, *Tio*. Our country and the whole world are in real troubled times. Everything could be turned upside down in a matter of days or months."

"Quite incisive, Izaura. You have a good head on your shoulders."

"My parents can take all the credit for that, *Tio*."

"As well they should. Now, I just might have an idea for you."

Izaura leaned forward as her uncle began speaking.

"I was in a meeting the other day..."

Friday, May 24, 1940
Home of Duke and Duchess of Windsor
4 Route du Champ d'Entraînement
Bois de Boulogne
Paris, France

The Duke and Duchess of Windsor were seated at their breakfast table inside the fourteen-room mansion in Paris' elegant *Bois de Boulogne* section of the city. The couple rented the mansion for a small sum from the French government while he served as Great Britain's liaison officer with the French Army High Command. In reality, the former King of England was directly involved with British Military Intelligence. They wanted information on French defenses and specifically the Maginot Line the French military planned to utilize to hold off the Germans.

The Duke was displeased with his country's attitude toward his new wife, Wallis Simpson, and the Royal Family's strict attitude toward recognizing her in a proper manner. He was also in a quandary about the war and Germany. Since the Nazis had invaded France four days before and France seemed unable to stop the advance, he was even more wary of their marital situation.

He was engrossed in the morning newspaper when his wife noticed him frowning.

"What is it, my dear?" Wallis Simpson asked. "You seem troubled by what you are reading."

"Quiet, my love," he replied evenly. "This German paper tells a different story from the French ones. The French don't seem to be able to put up much of a defense even with the large number of soldiers in their army. The Germans have made huge advances since the beginning and the French have not answered their charge. The French papers report German advances, but nowhere near the actual figures."

"Maybe the French newspapers don't want to alarm the populace unduly," the duchess offered.

The Duke did not respond and continued to read. He finally lay down the paper and picked up his cup of Earl Grey. He sipped pensively and turned to his wife.

"We must be careful from now on," he warned. "If this onslaught continues, the Boche could be in Paris in a few weeks."

Wallis Simpson looked closely at her husband. "You really think so?"

"Absolutely. The French have put way too much faith in the Maginot Line and their army seems to be in dire straits. There is confusion at the highest levels and inattention to detail. In my opinion, this sort of behavior spells defeat and we are caught right in the middle of it."

"Can't we just leave if it gets too serious?"

"Yes, I have a contingency plan in mind. Depending on the circumstances, if we are unable to fly to England, we can take a car to Biarritz and then to Spain. I have spoken with the Spanish ambassador and his government has extended an invitation for us to stay as long as we wish."

Wallis Simpson didn't react to her husband's revelation but thought silently.

At least we have a place to go and I'm sure the Spanish will treat us nicely. I would prefer we go to America, but I'm sure that's out of the question. If England is invaded as many believe will happen, it certainly won't be any safer there.

I really like Spain and the Spanish throw really great parties. I will make the best of it and show complete support for his decisions. Yes, complete support...

The Duchess of Windsor finished her breakfast and solemnly prepared for the rest of her day.

Maybe the French will fool everyone and stop or at least delay the Germans; at least that remains a possibility. I will begin packing some things if it becomes necessary for us to leave at a moment's notice. Under any circumstance, I will be ready for any eventuality.

Friday, May 24, 1940
British Ambassador's Residence
Lisbon, Portugal

Sir Walford Selby was a proven British civil service official who was fundamentally sound in dealing with his typical consular duties. He had also developed a plausible working relationship with Portugal's head of government, Dr. António de Olivera Salazar. However, as his wartime duties progressed, Selby's deficiencies began to become more apparent. Selby was an old school consular official who was suddenly faced with new problems and decisions that were difficult for him to process. As the number of refugees fleeing Nazism swelled Lisbon's hotels and living spaces, so did the sudden increase of spies and clandestine activities on the part of both Great Britain and Germany. Selby was weary of such repulsive actions but continued his duties as best he could.

When he received a hand-written note from João Tomás Ribeiro, the hard- working editor of the Lisbon daily paper *O' Século* concerning the editor's young niece, he quickly agreed to accept an appointment for the young woman. It seemed a pleasant diversion from his continuing assortment of unpleasant consular tasks.

Izaura Veigas Ribeiro stepped into his ornate office and extended her hand.

"Thank you for seeing me so quickly, Ambassador," she offered in perfect English. "I'm sure you have more important things on your calendar than seeing me this morning."

"Not at all, my dear. When João's note arrived, I thought it only proper to see you. You know I hold your uncle in the highest regard," he replied.

"Likewise, Ambassador, he has much admiration for you and your country."

"Please sit down here, this sofa is much more comfortable than these chairs." He motioned to the well-worn Chesterfield sofa in pleated oxblood leather.

"Thank you," she said softly, sitting down next to the older man.

"Your uncle's note told me you are looking for employment and that you have a law degree."

"That's right, Ambassador. I want to find something to do that will make a difference during this war. My uncle said you told him you were adding personnel to the consulate. I hoped there might be something for me here. I've always admired England and made it a point to learn English as well."

"You've certainly succeeded, young lady. Your English is as good as any Portuguese I have encountered, even those who have lived in England."

Izaura blushed at the compliment and continued. "I'm also aware of the old agreement between our countries that binds us together for better or worse. I think that agreement is even more important given the present state of affairs. I hope it will never be broken."

"That agreement was undertaken more than 500 years ago and my country intends to live up to its substances. The Anglo-Portuguese Treaty is the oldest of its kind in the world and is taken quite seriously back in England."

"That makes me happy, Ambassador. I don't like the Germans at all. I find them rude and overly assertive. They act superior to the Portuguese and to the Lisboetas."

Ambassador Selby studied the young woman in front of him.

She is definitely a high-class person and should be able to help us in a number of ways. It will be good to have a Lisboeta in our ranks. She seems securely at ease and her looks will certainly act to her advantage. We have a new assistant military attaché coming here in a month or two and she would fit in nicely with him. What was his name? Oh yes, Jack Beevor, that's the chap they're sending. Izaura will have time to become familiar with the consulate before he arrives. Of course, our chaps here will have to vet the woman, but I doubt they will find anything wrong with her. She's too young and her uncle is solidly Anglo in his views. She might even be able to help us in that regard if the opportunity arises.

He returned his attention to Izaura and extended his hand. "I think you might just fit in here, Miss Ribeiro. Can you start tomorrow?"

Izaura flashed a broad smile and took his hand. "Thank you, Ambassador. You won't regret your decision."

"I certainly hope not young lady," he smiled.

Friday, May 24, 1940
Prime Minister's Office
10 Downing Street
Whitehall, Westminster,
London, England

The news of Germany's incessant march through the Netherlands, Belgium and now France threw Great Britain into a state of semi-panic since no one offered a strategy to stop the carnage. The war was all anyone talked about and even the most bullish of politicians remained silent in the face of such dire updates broadcast every few hours.

Among most Britons the real possibility that a German invasion on British soil was now a distinct possibility. Prime Minister Winston Churchill delivered on BBC a nightly address in an attempt to calm his countrymen and offer morale boosting in the face of the dire threat. Churchill decided to see the King and inform him that if the current French plans failed to stop the advancing Germans, he would have no recourse but to recall the British Expeditionary Force from France with a total loss of arms and munitions and possibly an extraordinary loss of life for both the French and British armies.

Such contemplations weighed heavily on the man who had been head of the British Government for only thirteen days. The trials and tribulations of his new office were such that he still worked, ate and slept at his residence at Admiralty House. His plan was to move into 10 Downing Street as soon as time permitted, but at this point in the war, no such time existed. The events in France had become more desperate with each waning hour and the prime minister knew his decisions during the next few days might well decide his country's fate.

As he sat in his study, Churchill reviewed several internal items that had been pushed aside due to complications of the failing war. A report from MI6 raised the real possibility that German parachutists would be part of the initial phase of a German invasion and that one of their main drop points would be Trafalgar Square due to its proximity to Whitehall. Churchill made a note to ensure guards were placed near Admiralty Arch if indeed they hadn't already been dispatched. Since he hadn't left his quarters or 10 Downing Street for the past few days, he admitted to himself he had little touch with the outside world.

This is all quite unbelievable and yet for some reason I feel a sense of confidence growing inside me. If the feeling is the same with the British people, we might well ride out this horrible scenario. The key is the French and their huge army. They simply must do something to halt Jerry's advance.

I've done all I can to support them, but it's beginning to look like our help won't be enough. I must write another note to President Roosevelt, the circumstances have become dire and I must make him see that we need his help badly. I must keep this correspondence with him secret, so it takes more than a day for him to receive my letter. Oh well, that's just the way it is, and I'll be damned if I can do anything about it.

He took out a piece of stationary and began composing a letter to the American president.

Friday, May 24, 1940
German Group A Wermacht Headquarters
Charleville-Mézières, France

Generaloberst Karl Rudolf Gerd von Rundstedt sat across from his country's leader, Adolf Hitler, at his headquarters in France's Ardennes Region. The general's Prussian roots spanned centuries of military service and his smallish 5-foot-7- inch frame belied the fact that he was top military commander and leader of Germany's Group A Army that had decisively defeated everyone and everything in its path for the last month.

Like his *Führer*, von Rundstedt sported a small mustache that at age, 64, had already turned grey. His piercing eyes cut through even the fiercest opponent. He listened attentively as Hitler began to speak.

"General, the Fatherland is extremely proud of what you have accomplished in so short a time. Your men deserve great praise for their heroic actions on behalf of the Third Reich. Their names will be recorded in our history books and children will tell of their exploits for years to come. You have made historic strides in our war against our enemies and your deeds will not be forgotten. Your mechanized units will be given special commendations and worthy individuals will be singled out for their accomplishments. The world will see what we Germans are made of, and you in particular."

"Me, my *Führer*," replied von Rundstedt, "I'm afraid I don't understand."

Hitler lowered his head for a moment then continued. "I intend to promote you to field marshal at the earliest opportunity, general. You deserve the honor and your troops will appreciate the respect the rank carries with it."

Von Rundstedt raised his head slightly and responded, "It will be my privelege, my *Führer*. I will accept it on behalf of all my men who have fallen so far. I know they will not be the last. I am honored you came all the way here to tell me in person."

"But there is more, general. I want to discuss with you exactly where we are at this point in our overall plan. I can hardly believe we have done so well in so short a period of time."

Von Rundstedt chose to remain silent, waiting for his leader's next words.

"I, along with my staff, am of the opinion that we might be going too fast in our efforts and that your mechanized units have outrun the infantry that is necessary to control the parts of France you have swept through. Boulogne is ours and Calais will be next. My latest reports have General Guderian within 15 to 20 miles of Dunkirk and his Panzers are encountering little resistance. Even though we have been successful, your losses have been high, am I correct?"

"You are correct, my *Führer*. I went over the numbers last night. We have lost close to half of our tanks and equipment."

"That is too much," Hitler scoffed. "Even with the successes you have enjoyed."

Von Rundstedt again chose not to reply as the tension between the two leaders increased.

Finally, Hitler spoke again. "My staff feels we have moved too quickly and have advised me to halt our advance for the time being and let the infantry catch up. Goering has promised me that his *Luftwaffe* can control the skies over the entire area and force the remaining cities into submission. I am inclined to believe him since his aircraft have proved to be superior to any the French or British have deployed."

Von Rundstedt was practically seething but managed to control himself as he spoke. "Are you serious? Stop our advance and let the enemy regroup when they are on their heels and practically giving up? I believe your advisors are wrong in this instance and we should be allowed to continue our advance."

"What if the enemy launches a counterattack and succeeds in breaking through your lines, General?" Hitler probed. "Our intelligence says that such a move is a real possibility. What do we do then?"

"Our intelligence always supports such a prospect, my *Führer*. It gives them something to do with their time."

Hitler chose to ignore the tank and infantry commander's retort and remained silent for several moments. He paced along the wall, head up, hands clasped behind his back. Then he turned and looked his general straight in the eyes.

"I have decided to follow my staff's advice, General. You will order your units to hold their present positions until the army and supplies catch up with them. Is that understood?"

Von Rundstedt fought to control his emotions but finally agreed. "Yes, my *Führer*, I will see that the orders go out immediately."

"Good. Then we are in accord. I must get back to my duties." He rose abruptly and offered the general his hand. Von Rundstedt looked at his leader and shook his *Führer's* hand. It was all he could do to control himself at what he considered this critical moment in the meeting and in the war.

Saturday, May, 25, 1940
Office of the Foreign Minister
Auswärtiges Amt
Wilhelmstraße 76,
Berlin-Mitte, Germany

Germany's *Abwehr* Intelligence Service paid close attention to the Duke and Duchess of Windsor's current trip to Spain since their agents first spotted the pair after their hurried flight from France. The Duke was received by Spanish officials and invited to several social gatherings. At more than one of these events, he displayed seemingly cutting remarks concerning the British Government's handling of the war. He also offered his unflattering opinions of the British Royal Family's treatment of him and his wife. Since the Duke made little effort to conceal his attitude, it immediately caught the attention of German diplomatic officials in attendance.

Moreover, it was also being rumored that the couple would visit Portugal, quite possibly as an addendum to their Spanish hiatus. This news was directly passed on to Germany's Foreign Minister, Joachim von Ribbentrop, who had already taken a keen interest in the couple. The German diplomat, along with other members of the Nazi hierarchy, had quickly interpreted the former King's personal viewpoints and actions as being favorable to their cause. If the former monarch was indeed pro-Nazi, this could provide an important *cause célèbre* for Germany in its attempt to dominate the free world.

A plan was soon developed by von Ribbentrop and coded as *Operation Willi.* The undertaking was seen as having several possible outcomes. Germany was actively planning an invasion of England later in the year and the Duke could return as head of a puppet government when Germany occupied England. The Duke was on record as opposing the destruction of his country and openly stated the war was unnecessary and that he was particularly unhappy with the way the war was being carried on. The present British government would not succeed in his opinion, and a change of some sort was needed. Also, the Duke was truly unhappy with the royal family's treatment of his wife and himself and their refusal to make her an official member of the royal family with the accompanying title, "Her Royal Highness."

Great Britain's Foreign Office had monitored the Duke's departure from Paris as Nazi forces approached the city. The Duchess of Windsor had priorly been sent to Biarritz and the pair then proceeded to Madrid where the Duke felt he would be safe. The British Foreign Office was satisfied with the couple's exodus. With the former king out of Great Britain for the moment there was little chance of any potential clashes with Prime Minister Winston Churchill or other members of the government. Von Ribbentrop saw this as a perfect scenario to woo the Duke and gave the order to initiate Operation Willi within the labyrinth of German intelligence.

If the Windsor's made it to Lisbon, as seemed more and more likely, his plan called for Germany to induce the couple to return to Spain where von Ribbentrop felt the former monarch could be more easily controlled by the pro-Nazi forces within that country. He believed with great conviction that the Duke of Windsor would give serious consideration to such a suggestion. *Operation Willi* would require intricate planning and a bit of luck regarding the exact timing, but the wily German foreign minister was even prepared to use force, if it became necessary, to persuade the Duke and Duchess to accept his proposal.

He realized the timing of the project was critical and hoped that German *Abwehr* intercepts would provide him the chance to put *Operation Willi* into effect.

Von Ribbentrop crossed his fingers and pushed a button to his secretary's phone. "Fraulein, get me Herr Schellenberg on the line at the *Abwehr*."

"Yes, Minister," came the reply.

A moment later, a buzz signaled the call was ready.

"Walter," von Ribbentrop spoke evenly, "What further information do you have about the Duke and his possible visit to Portugal?"

Schellenberg hesitated a moment and spoke authoritatively, "Nothing new, Herr Minister. I told you I would notify you as soon as anything new occurred."

Von Ribbentrop noted the hint of hostility from the *Abwehr* head, but decided to conceal his feelings. *I will take care of this know-it-all at some time in the future.*

"It's just that this is extremely important to the Third Reich," the foreign minister added.

"I am perfectly aware of that Herr Minister. You will be the first person I call if anything breaks." A click on the other end of the line signaled that Walter Schellenberg had ended the call.

Unfazed by his colleague's lack of respect, Joachim von Ribbentrop settled back into his oversized chair and contemplated his next move. He realized that if *Operation Willi* were to succeed, he would need a visit from Lady Luck to pull it off.

Chapter Two

Sunday, May 26, 1940
Cabinet War Rooms
Whitehall, Westminster
London, England

The daily meeting of Britain's 5-man War Ministry began with a startling announcement from Edward Wood, known as the Viscount Halifax, the country's foreign secretary. He addressed the group in his normal, controlled tone.

"My sources have indicated the Germans have stopped their advance in France, at least for the time being. No reason has been given but it appears they have stopped where they were a day ago. There is no activity on the front lines as far as we can tell."

"They could be waiting for supplies or petrol to catch up," offered Arthur Greenwood, a Labour Party member acting as minister without portfolio. "If that's the case, the halt could be extremely short-lived."

"Yes, I'm afraid so," Prime Minister Winston Churchill agreed. "No telling what Jerry is up to. The break in fighting might even give us enough time to get some of our chaps out of Dunkirk."

"How many can be evacuated, Prime Minister? Do you have any idea of a number?" Neville Chamberlain, lord president of the council questioned.

Churchill contemplated his answer for a few moments and spoke. "If we are lucky, maybe 40,000 to 50,000."

"Is that all?" Clement Attlee, lord privy seal asked. "That's only a fraction of our troops encircled around Dunkirk, not to mention the French Army."

"I am aware of the numbers, gentlemen. I have another plan that I have already begun implementing," the prime minister added. "It's too early to tell if it will be successful, but the hope it offers will be much greater than the numbers I just gave you. Vice Admiral Ramsay came up with the idea first and I fully support his view. I'm calling it *Operation Dynamo*. It calls for the accumulation of practically every ship or boat that can motor or sail to Dunkirk to be made ready to evacuate as many soldiers as quickly as possible. I will tell you more as the plan develops. We are a seafaring nation and we will put that expertise to work for our benefit."

There was no response from the assembled members as each one considered the possibilities of Operation Dynamo. The use of civilian ships and boats during wartime was almost unprecedented, but desperate times called for drastic measures. Only time would tell if this far-fetched scheme would succeed. The members silently prayed it would and their country's soldiers would be spared.

Monday, May 27, 1940
Prime Minister's Office
Rear of São Bento Palace
Lisbon, Portugal

Dr. António de Oliveira Salazar was born in 1889 into a modest family in the Viseu District of Central Portugal, the only such district that does not border either Spain or the Atlantic Ocean. His early schooling was at *Viseu's* seminary where he considered becoming a priest, but changed his mind after receiving holy orders. He attended the University of Coimbra where he studied law and developed a deep interest in finance. Salazar graduated with distinction with finance and economic development as specialties. He advanced rapidly through the university's law department and received his doctorate in 1918.

Portugal's *coup d'état* in May of 1926 vaulted Salazar into national prominence. Two years later, he became the country's finance minister and, in 1932, the struggling country's prime minister. He inherited a nation emerging from a deep depression, rife with corruption and incompetence and in dire need of direction and leadership.

Salazar took immediate action to turn his beloved country around. A new constitution was drafted along authoritarian lines highlighted by Catholic, nationalist and papal precepts. He termed Portugal's new status, *Estado Novo* or New State, a name that would stick for the next four decades.

In fact, Dr. António de Olivera Salazar became the smallish country's dictator. Portugal's National Assembly was composed of government supporters, with Salazar choosing his own ministers. He closely supervised their collective efforts and directed military police to repress any dissident activity. His sole aim was to focus his country towards regaining respectable economic status among the world's countries.

He sat at his sparingly furnished desk as he did on most Saturday mornings, studying a number of reports and articles placed on his desk earlier that morning. He noted the increase in size of the stack that was at least five inches high. Copies of his favorite newspapers topped the pile.

That's what this damn war has brought, he surmised. More reports and a good deal more to read. Nowadays I even get reports from some of my lesser departments; I guess everyone thinks they are covering their asses and I'm not sure this isn't for the better. I'd rather have the people in charge alert to new happenings than sit around drinking their bica and smoking cigars.

He thumbed through the reports and finally replaced them on his desk. He sat back and thought again.

Even the PVDE's reports are much longer than before the war, but I guess that's to be expected during these turbulent times. Our secret police have a difficult job, but I know they are in good hands. Captain Lourenço does a great job as their boss and I trust his loyalty to our country and to me.

Portugal's economic recovery and status depends on the loyalty of my people in important positions. I am blessed with their dedication or I couldn't succeed. Thank Our Lord for giving me the means to get through this incredible mess and to allow our country to emerge healthy once again.

He selected the top newspaper, *O Século,* and began to read the news of the day.

Tuesday, May 28, 1940
German Envoy's Office
Campo dos Mártires da Pátria 38
Lisbon, Portugal

Baron Oswald von Hoyningen-Huene was the Third Reich's Envoy to Portugal and a proven veteran of the German diplomatic corps. He was previously adjutant to German President Paul von Hindenburg in charge of foreign policy events and developments. Made envoy to Portugal in 1934, von Hoyningen-Huene proved to be an astute diplomat. He spent a good deal of his pre-war time developing close ties to both Portugal and a number of top officials of the Portuguese leadership. Interestingly, Hoyningen-Huene managed to evade being a member of the Nazi Party even though he was a career German diplomat. His mother, Mary Colley, was English and non-Aryan. He was born in Switzerland and was now in his 54th year.

Acutely aware of Germany's pre-war aims and goals, Hoyningen-Heune correctly assessed Portugal's increasingly important role in the course of coming world events. To that end, he poured himself into Portuguese culture, language and history. He lectured at the country's universities and was particularly versed in Portugal's former naval prowess.

He steadily built a force of German and Portuguese agents and even gave the okay to establishing a number of German-funded brothels along the Portuguese waterfront in an attempt to secure information on foreign seamen passing through the city. The ladies of the evening were all too happy to have extra German-funded escudos to add to their nightly take. The early successes of German military forces in Europe made it all the easier to secure funding for as many agents as the German ministry felt necessary. To many of the local *Lisboetas,* it seemed that Germany was definitely winning the war.

In the propaganda mills flourishing throughout the urban and rural areas of Portugal, the Consulate-General's well-polished techniques rose above those of the British. Wild stories lambasting the English and French were abetted by stories planted in Portuguese newspapers that supported the rumors. Of course, staff at the Germany ministry happily paid newspapers to print these speculations and, in most cases, utter falsities. Fake news flourished in the attempt to bamboozle the readers.

The daily consular pouch arrived at Sintra Airfield's grass runways on board a Lufthansa flight from Berlin and was met by a consular official in a black Mercedes-Benz touring car with several armed escorts. Sintra Airfield was a little less than 18 miles from Lisbon and landing was problematic due to nearby hills and soggy conditions following rainstorms. Both British Overseas Aircraft Corporation (BOAC) and Lufthansa used Sintra for their Lisbon-bound flights and often parked their aircraft next to each other. Sintra Airfield was also home to Portugal's Air Base No. 1., the Portuguese Air Force's basic flight training facility. The base contained a number of Italian Breda Ba-65Bis aircraft as well as an assortment of converted German Junkers Ju 52/3m medium bombers purchased from the two countries prior to the beginning of the war.

Pan American Airways, the American flag carrier, flew their famous Sikorsky S-42 flying boats to a conveniently-located float dock on the Tejo Tagus River near downtown Lisbon and were the frequent choices of wealthy Jews and European expatriates who fled Nazi Germany. These hearty means of flight, known as Clippers to the flying world, were able to make the Atlantic crossing in under thirty hours with stops for refueling. The Clippers' most important stop was in the Azores Islands, Portugal's tiny nine-island colony in the Atlantic Ocean since the early 15th Century and an increasingly important factor for both shipping and air travel during the war.

These facts consumed the mind of Envoy Baron Oswald von Hoyningen-Huene as he thumbed through Berlin's latest communication to his consulate,

Two items seemed of particular interest to the diplomat. The first was a possible visit to Lisbon by England's Duke of Windsor.

The other was an order to offer an opinion on a possible invasion of the Azores Islands.

I can understand the possibility of the past king's visit here, particularly with the attraction that Estoril offers. That would make sense and I will look into it at once. Some of our Abwehr agents have probably heard rumors of it from their sources, that's the way it works around here. They hear about things before I get the word. I don't really enjoy all this spying and intrigue, but if, it is necessary, I will do my part to see the Fatherland prevail in this situation.

About invading the Azores, that's another story entirely. Not only would it compromise Portugal's sovereign neutrality, but it would possibly mean we would have to invade Portugal itself or at least force the Spanish to do it. This would put those of us here in Lisbon in a true predicament. I hope it doesn't happen; I have made a number of delightful friends among the Portuguese. They are really good people and have been very respectful of Germany. Salazar himself is somewhat distrustful, but that's his job and he's proven to be very, very good at it.

A soft knock on the door to his office broke von Hoyningen-Huene's train of thought.

"Come in," he spoke calmly.

The door opened and a most attractive woman dressed in riding clothes stepped into the office. Baroness Gudrun von Hoyningen-Huene smiled and addressed her husband.

"Did you forget we were to go riding?" she asked softly. "After all, it is Saturday, isn't it? Why do you have to work so hard?"

"I just wanted to read the mail pouch from Berlin, my darling. I won't be long. Have a seat while I put these papers in the safe."

"I'll just stand, Oswald. You will finish sooner if I continue standing."

The German Envoy smiled and nodded affirmatively. "You are quite right, Gudrun. I'll hurry." He quickly dialed the combination and stuffed the papers into the safe. He closed the steel contraption and turned to his wife.

"There, I'm done. Now we can go and ride. It's still early enough that the heat won't affect the horses." The Baroness smiled at her husband and preceded him out the door.

Sunday May 26, 1940
Café Chave d'Ouro
Dom Pedro IV Square
Rossio, Lisbon, Portugal

Anyone who was anyone usually found their way to Café Chave d'Ouro located on the west side of Lisbon's ever popular *Rossio.* Built in 1916, it was home to the city's elite and opportunistic businessmen, the popular location for spies of all nationalities and most importantly, the place where refugees attempting to escape the Nazi horrors in their homelands could possibly find a market for jewels and valuables that might buy prized exit visas and boat tickets out of Portugal. The PVDE also maintained a large presence in the lively spot, mostly to keep tabs on each side of the never-ending battle for diplomatic supremacy within its borders.

The place was three stories, unusual for a gathering place in Lisbon. It afforded an open two-storied mezzanine with a panoramic view of the downstairs. A ten-foot clock kept track of the time for its customers, many of whom stayed until the small hours of the night. Café Chave d'Ouro had nine full-size billiard tables that were always occupied by the place's regular customers and small queues for anyone wishing to play.

It was also the principal hangout for Martim Alfonso Silva, the budding entrepreneur/jewelry buyer who occupied one of the prized ground floor tables he paid the staff to reserve only for him. To say business was good was a gross understatement.

Already tonight he had bought a pair of gold earrings and several necklaces from an Austrian couple for about a third of their actual worth. He paid that sum because he felt sorry for them after hearing their story. Silva usually offered only twenty percent of the jewelry's true worth, but sometimes a really heartbreaking story touched him and he relented. It also made him feel good that he had helped someone in dire need of assistance. This particular couple's story was compelling in that the family had already lost several members to the Nazis. Both of the couple's parents were gone along with one son and one daughter. Another son and daughter were in Lisbon, waiting outside a hotel with no vacancies. The people were Jewish, a compelling fact to Silva who was a non-practicing Catholic, but a person who respected other people's beliefs.

"*Perdoe-me, senhor,*" a middle-aged woman spoke in a thick accent as she approached his table.

Silva observed the woman, still attractive but obviously very troubled.

"*Sim,*" he replied casually.

"*Eu falo pouco portugues*" she replied stiffly.

"What about English?"

"Yes, I speak that a little. I was told you buy diamonds. Is that correct?"

Another customer. I hope this war continues for some time and Portugal remains neutral as well. At least this one is quite pretty and that's in her favor. If she wasn't so attractive, I wouldn't be that interested. But she did mention diamonds and diamonds are my favorite stones to buy. They never go out of style and hold their value no matter what.

"Please continue, Miss...?"

"Mrs. Rebecca Stoloff. And you are?"

"Martim Silva at your service." He bowed slightly, reached for her hand and kissed it. "How may I help?"

Sunday May 26, 1940
War Cabinet Rooms
Whitehall, Westminster
London, England

The initial reports on *Operation Dynamo* reached Prime Minister Winston Churchill and his War Ministry within hours of the beginning of the mission. Since Royal Naval Ships were playing a large part in the evacuation, their radio signals back to Admiralty tended to make the entire operation seem almost live.

Churchill and his ministers, seated around a table in the War Room in the early evening, couldn't believe the good news even when the first survivors reached the shores of Great Britain.

"I must hand it to you Prime Minister, *Operation Dynamo* seems headed for success," remarked Clement Attlee. "The numbers so far have been quite encouraging and it doesn't seem we've had many mishaps."

"Right," Churchill responded. "These first reports are mostly from the Royal Navy and don't include many of the civilian boats involved. We must wait for these vessels to make shore and report their numbers. In some cases, they are yachts and fishing vessels and will only carry a limited number of soldiers."

"What are the smallest boats we are using?" questioned Attlee.

"I am told that there are even some 14-foot skiffs and sailboats. Thanks to the fact the Channel is quite calm for the present, even these small boats are helping in the effort. It's a tribute to their owners and crews."

"Great British spirit, if you ask me," chimed in Arthur Greenwood. "Shows what we're made of. I bet Jerry is surprised as hell at what is happening."

"The bastard's trying to control the area from the air. His *Luftwaffe* aircraft are strafing the beaches and making it difficult for our men to board the boats. Our Spitfires and Hurricanes are giving the Nazis fits and have downed a number of German planes in the process. I don't think the Germans expected our aircraft to provide such cover. It doesn't seem they have added any extra air squadrons to halt our progress," injected Churchill.

A knock on the door interrupted the meeting. A Royal Navy admiral handed a folded piece of paper to the Prime Minister. Churchill opened the document and read the contents and settled back into his chair. His optimistic demeanor of the past minutes was replaced by a somber expression.

"Gentlemen," he began after a pause, "We've experienced some bad news concerning *Operation Dynamo*. It seems the Boche have succeeded in sinking two of our destroyers during the rescue operation. *HMS Grafton* was sunk today as well as *HMS Grenade*, the latter by an air attack. A third destroyer, *HMS Wakeful* was struck by a torpedo and is also in danger of sinking. I knew our luck was too good to be true and today we have proof of just that. We expected some losses during such a large operation, but losing three destroyers in one day wasn't part of the plan. I just hope many of the seamen on those ships were rescued. Details of that aren't yet available."

For several moments, no one at the table spoke. Finally, Churchill began again in a low voice. "What we seem to be accomplishing outweighs the loss of our ships. If this evacuation continues, we will have at least the remnants of an army to fight with. We will have the means to defend our country against our enemies and maybe even make him think twice about invading our island. We must all stand tall, for this could well be a turning point in our fortunes. It will also show the world that England is resourceful and intrepid, no matter what we face from our foes. I will go on radio as soon as possible later today and deliver this sort of message to our countrymen. I suggest we close this meeting and meet again tomorrow at 11:30."

Sensing no discussion, the prime minister rose and left the room.

Monday May 27, 1940
Café Chave d'Ouro
Dom Pedro IV Square
Rossio, Lisbon, Portugal

Her first days of employment at Great Britain's Consulate seemed a whirlwind to Izaura Veigas Ribeiro. In addition to meeting practically all the consular officials and employees, she had been given a number of printed articles and papers involving the embassy and Great Britain's historical ties with Portugal and its presence in Lisbon. Izaura found the reading interesting and was particularly intrigued by the ongoing linkage that had existed between the two countries for more than 500 years.

She also made a new friend, one of the few Portuguese women employed by the ligation. Pilar Soares Coehlo was several years older than Izaura, dark-haired and blessed with a ravenous olive skin complexion. When Izaura was first introduced to Pilar, the latter noticed a brief smile on Izaura's face. Once they were alone, she brought up the question of the smile.

"What made you smile when we met?" she posed.

Izaura grinned again and replied, "It's just that your name means rabbit and I've never met anyone with that name. I thought it a bit funny."

"I've had to deal with it my whole life," Pilar answered. "As I got older, I started telling people, mostly men, that it means I am hard to catch. Most of them laugh and we take it from there."

"I think it's a lovely name, Pilar. I really do."

"Thank you Izaura, I think your name is quite beautiful."

"Ribeiro? You really think so?"

"No silly, Izaura. The sound flows out of the mouth so smoothly."

"Thank you, Pilar. No one has ever said that to me before. I think we will become good friends. You can teach me all I need to know to survive here. I will be most grateful." She leaned over and bussed the older woman.

"I will teach you everything, even the bad stuff and who to avoid around here. Most of the staff are really nice and good at their jobs, but a few of the men seem to have their own agendas. When I can't read a person, there's usually a good reason for it."

Pilar seems to be a really smart person. I will learn a lot from her and maybe I can help her with her English. She's really not that bad, but I can make her better with her pronunciation. Hopefully we can be friends outside the embassy, I really don't have any real friends except a few from law school.

The two shook hands lightly and went to their jobs. For Izaura, it had been a fortunate meeting and something to build upon. She hoped that Pilar felt the same way about her.

Tuesday, May 28, 1940
Prime Minister's Office
Rear of São Bento Palace
Lisbon, Portugal

It had become increasingly apparent to Portuguese Prime Minister Dr. António Salazar that his country's attempt to occupy a side seat in the war had failed miserably. As summer wrapped its warm fingers around the country, the war was all that seemed to matter to his countrymen, and particularly the *Lisboetas*. Practically every report he read concerned the war and every meeting he attended featured an aspect of the conflict plaguing his country.

He called for Captain Agostinho Lourenço, head of the PVDE and one of his regime's staunchest supporters, to meet with him after lunch. Lourenço arrived on time and was seated in front of the prime minister as he finalized signing papers on his desk.

"Captain, sorry to have kept you waiting. It seems I sign way too many documents these days."

"I am happy to wait, Prime Minister. I realize you are a very busy man during these times," the police officer answered. "What is it you need of me?"

Salazar answered immediately and replied, "There are a couple of things that bother me, Captain. One is the large number of Jewish refugees in our cities these days and secondly, the reputation your PVDE seems to be getting as pro-Nazi."

"Prime Minister, the refugee situation is dire and is getting worse. I'm not sure what can be done about it. Many of the hotels have added additions and are still completely full. The Hotel Aziz now charges the equivalent of $6.00 a day for even the simplest room. Most of the refugees have brought ample money to cover such expenses. And jewels. I've never seen so many jewels in my life. The prices keep going down but the refugees continue to sell their precious stones."

"They have no other choice, captain. If they want to survive, they must sell anything of value they possess. Jewels and other valuables are of little value if you or your family are starving or dead."

Lourenço nodded his agreement and continued. "Yes, we are swamped right now, too many refugees and not enough staff to process the paperwork. We are all working long hours but the demand is simply too great. I'm afraid most of these people will be forced to wait here longer than they expected."

"I know you will do your best. Do you need more money to hire more people? That could be quickly arranged."

"I'm not sure we have the time to train any new people, Prime Minister. The paperwork must be filled out correctly and the facts verified to be correct. All that takes time and the refugees are quite insistent. The strain on my people forces them to make mistakes and I'm trying to not let that happen. Should any of them get sick and miss work, that would hamper our efforts even more."

Salazar looked into his close friend's eyes and offered some support. "I know you will all do your best, Agostinho. You always have. You will come out of all this and things will return to normal. Wait and see..."

Again, Lourenço nodded affirmatively.

"Now, about the other matter. It is equally important to me and our country."

The PVDE head lowered his head and spoke softly. "Prime Minister, I know you are aware I fought with the British during the last war. I came to appreciate their values and have many friends within their ranks. They trust me and I would never betray that trust."

"What about your top people? Do they feel the same?"

Lourenço considered the question for a moment and answered, "I have no doubt some of my people are taking money from the Germans. They are also taking money from the British, if that makes any difference. This is a game we play, one with extremely high stakes. Our world is filled with lies and falsehoods and one side constantly tries to outdo the other. I don't pay a great deal of attention to most of it and that seems to work for me. If I got rid of all the officers, I suspect of taking money, both sides would immediately try and bribe any new officials I would appoint. I like my present people and I believe they are all doing their jobs at a high level."

Salazar measured the policeman's answer for a brief moment and replied. "I'm sad to say I suspected as much, Agostinho. We live in trying times and the end is not in sight. We all must do what seems correct to us and we will be judged for our actions at a later time."

Captain Agostinho Lourenço did not reply and waited for his leader to gesture. Salazar nodded, Lourenco rose and offered his hand to the Prime Minister. The two friends smiled and the PVDE leader turned and exited the room.

Tuesday, May 28, 1940
War Cabinet Rooms
Whitehall, Westminster
London, England

The mood inside the War Cabinet meeting was gloomy and represented the feelings of most of Great Britain. There was also disagreement between Great Britain's leadership as to what direction the country should take from this point on. Former Prime Minister Neville Chamberlain was on record as favoring a possible agreement between his country and Italy and even a potential arrangement with Germany should circumstances permit.

Winston Churchill was adamant his country should fight no matter the circumstances. Churchill still clung to his belief that 50,000 troops could be rescued from the beaches of Dunkirk but the matter was downgraded to the more important fact that Italy was about to enter the war on the Axis side. France was about to fall and the only aspect of interest was whether or not the country would become neutral.

Three hundred thousand members of its army were caught in a German trap in Northern France with little prospects other than surrender. Belgium's surrender earlier that afternoon came as no great surprise to anyone in the ministry, but the British people were aghast at the news. Many were just beginning to realize the true depth of Great Britain's plight and the ensuing consequences of actual armed aggression on their sacred isle.

Churchill was also determined to keep the morale of his countrymen positive and mentioned that fact to his ministers.

"I am extremely pleased with the work of Minister Hugh Dalton regarding our countrymen's confidence during this crisis. His radio broadcasts are just what the country needs and have been warmly received by practically everyone in all parts of Britain. His chats are well-chosen and speak to the very heart and soul of our cause. I'm told his words are greatly appreciated for their content and candor and that they give a sense of truthfulness to our mission. I feel Dalton is an excellent minister of information."

The other ministers nodded in agreement, a rarity in the five-man war cabinet. Now it was back to business as usual.

Thursday, May 30, 1940
Aboard the TS/RMS King George V
East Mole Pier
Dunkirk, France

The popular Clyde passenger turbine steamer *King George V* had been built fifteen years before to provide passenger service to Inveraray in Scotland from her home port at Southampton. She was fast, sleek and offered excellent accommodations for her passengers. At the outbreak of war, she was outfitted as a troop carrier and was one of the first ships designated to provide help for the thousands of British, French and Belgian soldiers trapped on Dunkirk's crowded beaches.

This trip between Dover and Dunkirk was *King George V's* third and Captain Robert McCallum McLean was the ship's master. The *King George V* had already survived several aerial strafings by the *Luftwaffe* with only minor damage, but the veteran skipper realized his luck might not hold much longer. He offered encouragement to his crew as they assisted the mixture of soldiers climbing aboard his beautiful vessel.

At least we are tethered at the end of the pier and can get underway at a moment's notice. He reasoned: The water is deeper here and easier to maneuver in. That's the advantage of being one of the larger ships in this evacuation. Poor blokes must walk a mile to get to us but no one's complaining. Wonder how many we'll get on board this time? You'd think after so many trips over and back they'd start running out of soldiers, but that's not the case. From the looks of it there are still plenty more waiting. The Beachmaster has his hands full, but it's been orderly so far and that's the reason we have saved so many. I hope this is our last trip, that Jerry airplane nearly got us last time. I heard from some of the other skippers that several destroyers and some other ships have been lost, but these little boats have been the difference. Problem is with so many boats in the water, it's hard not to hit one of them. Most are good sailors and obey the rules, that's the key to it all.

Captain McLean's mind returned to the present as his chief steward reported the *King George V* was nearing its full capacity. He spoke to the chief steward. "We have taken on quite a load today; there's probably no standing room anywhere on the ship, am I correct?

"Aye, Captain, the steward replied. They're standing back to back everywhere there's room, I had all the chairs stacked to make more room. Some of these blokes haven't had a bath in weeks and it smells 'orrible down there. The ones on the outside have a better smell, but I think that's due to the sea air."

Captain Mc Lean chuckled and spoke again. "As soon as you are ready to haul in the gangplank, call me right away. I want to get us moving before any more Nazi airplanes get the idea to bomb us."

"Aye, Captain," the man returned. "As soon as we've loaded, I'll call right away." He offered a quick salute and departed the bridge.

Chapter Three

Tuesday June 4, 1940
Cabinet War Rooms
Whitehall, Westminster
London, England

The prolonged period of pessimism that had permeated the War Cabinet had abruptly changed earlier that day. At their usual 11:30 meeting, Prime Minister Winston Churchill was set to announce the final numbers related to *Operation Dynamo.*

With a hearty voice that could barely conceal a widening grin, the grandiloquent British leader addressed his ministers. "Gentlemen, I am proud to share some incredible figures with you. I am sure some of you have guessed this operation has been wildly successful, far beyond anything I would have imagined.

"According to my latest figures, some 335,000 of our allied troops have been plucked away from right under the noses of the Boche."

"Jolly good show, PM," offered Clement Attlee. "Everyone I've met and talked with is engrossed with the results." The other ministers murmured their approval.

Churchill nodded and continued as the ministers quieted. "These numbers include some 220,000 British troops, almost 110,000 French troops and around 8,000 or so Belgian army members. These numbers are not exact and I feel there might be some duplications. I will have a more assured number in a few days."

"The Royal Navy deserves most of the credit, they performed masterfully," declared Minister Without Portfolio Arthur Greenwood."

"Quite so, Arthur," Churchill agreed. "But the civilians who came to our aid are the real strength behind our success. They risked their boats and their very lives to save our army. We couldn't have done it without them. They are England and their legacy should be cherished."

"The people and newspapers are already calling it the 'Miracle at Dunkirk.'" another minister chimed in. "I think that phrase will stick for some time."

"Gentlemen," Churchill continued. "We must not forget another important fact---the way the French fought to keep the beaches open and allowed the evacuation to continue. My reports say many French soldiers made heroic stands which made the Germans pay for every inch of French ground they acquired. That's why so many Frenchmen were rescued. I felt we owed it to them and their countrymen. I also feel they will return to fight the Nazis at a later date. Many of them have scores to settle with the enemy.

"We must now turn to other tasks ahead and how they may affect our homeland. We are still in a crisis and one slip could prove disastrous. If Italy enters the war, we must be ready to deal with that. The Germans still have numerous barges and ships in place that could easily be used to transport their armies for an invasion of our island. To do that they would have to control the skies and I do not intend to let that happen no matter how great their number of aircraft.

"As you know, I recently appointed Lord Beaverbrook as minister of aircraft production and he has assured me we will have a great many more Spitfires for our use in the near future. The plants have already geared up and the numbers are encouraging.

"I share all this with you because it is necessary for us to be ready for any eventuality. The success at Dunkirk is but the first step in the process to gain the upper hand over the Boche and its devilish intentions. I will call upon each of you as the situation becomes necessary. We are still in a critical segment of this war and I fear the worst is still ahead. It is necessary we all keep our morale at a high level and this filters down to the common people of our country.

"It will get worse before it gets better and, in the near future, we may very well be fighting by ourselves against Germany and its allies. I have had little encouragement from President Roosevelt as to the intentions of the United States and Ambassador Kennedy has been little or no help. I feel he is a defeatist at heart and no real friend of Great Britain. But he is the U.S. Ambassador so we must put up with him for the time being.

"While all this dire likelihood is facing us, I urge you to continue your dedicated efforts to ensure our country's well-being. I thank you for your support during *Operation Dynamo* and ask for your continued counsel and assistance.

"If no one has any objections, let us continue this meeting at a later hour. You will all be notified as to the exact time."

Sunday June 9, 1940
Café Chave d'Ouro
Dom Pedro IV Square
Rossio, Lisbon Portugal

While it wasn't entirely unusual for two single ladies to frequent the Café Chave d'Ouro, Izaura Ribeiro and her friend Pilar Coehlo decided it was worth the chance and stepped into the packed café and restaurant. Both were nattily dressed and wore French aslant hats that were popular at the time. They had no trouble getting a second-floor table overlooking the main part of the interior building.

"I've been wanting to do this for some time," confessed Pilar Coehlo. "I couldn't get anyone to come with me until you arrived."

"It's no big deal, Pilar. I asked my father and he said it would be okay as long as we were properly dressed. The world is changing, even here in Lisbon. Women are allowed to do things they haven't been able to do before," Izaura explained.

"Well, it's certainly exciting to be here, isn't it? This is the liveliest place in the entire city. Maybe even the country, although I haven't really seen anywhere else to compare."

"You are probably right, Pilar. I hadn't really thought about it."

A waiter came and the ladies each ordered a glass of *Dão Vinho Verde* to drink. "My father said the wine is really good, from the north of Portugal."

"I've had it before at my house," Pilar commented. "It's not sweet but it's easy to get down. Here's to a fun time tonight..." She raised her glass and clinked Izaura's glass.

The pair slowly sipped their wine and peered down into the mass of people who gathered on the ground floor of the Café Chave d'Ouro.

Moments later, something caught Pilar's attention. She pointed downward and spoke, "Isn't that the nice French couple from today at the embassy?"

Izaura squinted and agreed, "Yes, it's them, seated and talking to a man at that table. I wonder what they're doing here? They seemed upset at the embassy."

"I'm going down and find out. I know the man they are talking to; he is kind of a friend of mine," Pilar announced. "I'll be back in a few."

Izaura was surprised when Pilar suddenly arose. She followed her friend's progress down the stairs and saw her arrive at the table. Pilar sat down and an animated conversation between the four took place. This lasted for about ten minutes when Pilar suddenly stood. She shook hands with the couple and came back upstairs.

"So, what was it?"

"Let's order another *Vinho Verde*, I'm going to need it," replied Pilar.

They summoned the waiter and ordered more wine. Izaura waited for Pilar to start speaking, but she was deep in thought.

The wine arrived and Pilar took a large swallow. "First of all, my friend's name is Martim and I think he really likes me. I met him a while ago in the *Rossio* and have run into him several times since. He is always quite charming and asks if he can take me to lunch or dinner. I've always said no, but he still asks."

"What about the French couple? Why are they here?

"Well, it seems that the lady needs some sort of special operation that is only available in the United States. They are Jewish and had to leave their country because of the Nazis. Luckily, her family had money and she left with some valuable jewels. They are trying to sell the jewelry to be able to get out of Lisbon. They want to go to a place called Boston if I understood correctly. There is some sort of special hospital there that can help her."

"But why are they talking to your friend?"

"Martim is in the business of buying and selling jewelry. When I heard their story, I asked Martim to help them. They seemed to be such a nice couple."

"Will he help them?"

"If he wants to take me to dinner he will," smiled Pilar. "I made him understand that before I left the table."

Pilar took a notepad from her purse and began making some notes. Izaura looked questioningly at her friend.

"Why are you making notes?" she asked.

"I need the details to give to someone," Pilar replied quietly.

"Someone who? Who would want to know?" Izaura sat back and crossed her arms impatiently.

Pilar considered the question, took another sip of wine and began.

"Listen, Izaura. You and I are becoming friends so I'm going to share something with you. It is important that you keep it to yourself. I could be in big trouble if anyone finds out."

"Find out what, Pilar? You are starting to scare me."

Pilar sighed and continued, "It's quite simple I'm afraid. Some months ago, a horribly dressed person approached me at lunch and asked me if I wanted to make some easy money. He had a thick accent and spoke terrible Portuguese. I told him to leave but he sat down and stayed. He produced some money and told me it was mine to keep. It was a good deal of money so I listened. He said he was an agent of the German intelligence agency and offered me twice the pay I get from our embassy to keep my eyes and ears open about any information I thought would be valuable. He told me what to look for and how to get the information to him. At first, I said no and then he offered me even more money. I thought about it and realized I might be able to supply him with useless information and still keep the money. I enjoy working for the British but the pay I receive isn't very much. As long as the Germans want to pay me, I can't really see any harm if the information I give them is useless."

Izaura tried to digest what she was hearing and finally replied. "Pilar, what you are doing isn't right. What if the British find out? You would be out of two jobs and be branded a spy by the people you know and trust."

"I don't think they will find out. We are much too busy with the evacuees and besides, I'm not doing anything all that wrong. The information is quite useless and I intend to keep it that way. I'll take my chances; the money is just too good to miss out."

"I'm afraid for you, Pilar. You're taking a big chance."

"I'm a big girl, Izaura. I know what I'm doing. Thank you for caring, that's what friends do for each other."

Izaura didn't reply but her face displayed deep concern. Pilar noticed her and suddenly stood up. "Come on, Izaura. I want you to meet my friend Martim. I already told him about you." Pilar gestured to the waiter to bring the check with them.

The two proceeded down the stairs and wound their way toward a nearby table.

"Izaura, this is my friend Martim Silva. Martim, Izaura."

Martim looked at the beautiful young woman and extended his hand. Izaura did likewise and Martim guided her hand to his mouth. He kissed her hand slightly and raised his head. "It is always a pleasure to meet a gorgeous woman, *Senhorita. O prazer é meu.*"

Izaura smiled and acknowledged the greeting. "Any friend of Pilar's is a friend to me also," she replied. 'So you're in the jewelry business I'm told."

"Unfortunately, the war has forced many of us to do something we wouldn't ordinarily do, Izaura. I'm simply providing a service for people in need."

"Did you help that French couple," Pilar injected. "They were very worried."

"Of course I did, Pilar. You made it clear that I should help them so I did. It might have cost me some money, but your wish was my command."

Pilar smiled and touched his hand. "You will be repaid in heaven, Martim, for your good works."

Martim looked back at her and grinned. "I think it will take more than a simple courtesy to get me to heaven, Pilar."

"Nonsense, just be sure to add more goodness to your total. That will help."

"Whatever you say. Let's toast to the French couple and to the war."

"I won't toast to the war," Izaura asserted. "That would be ridiculous."

"Then let's toast to a fun evening and another round of *vinho verde.*"

"Perfect," Pilar agreed.

The three raised their glasses and clinked them together. The sound was lost in the unrelenting noises of enjoyment that the *Café Chave d'Ouro* always offered.

Tuesday, June 11, 1940
Legal Offices of Slaughter & May
16 Fleet Street, Temple
London, England

John Grosvenor Beevor was working hard at Slaughter & May, one of London's top law firms and was considered a rising star among the firm's cadre of young lawyers. He had already achieved junior partner status and his keen intellect and fervor marked him as a major player in the future of Slaughter & May. Known to all as Jack Beevor, the young lawyer had been educated at Winchester College in Hampshire and New College in Oxford where he was considered an outstanding student as well as a born leader.

He joined Slaughter & May in 1931 and was sitting in his office when a secretary dropped a letter on his desk. He noted the War

Department reference on the envelope's outside and quickly opened the document. A smile emerged as he read that he had been offered a commission and given the rank of lieutenant in the British Army.

No more sitting around waiting for things to happen, I can finally do something that will help my country. I am indeed a fortunate person and I hope this commission will lead to something even greater. The Nazis are a formidable enemy and my country needs everyone to step up. If what I have read about them is even half true, they will stop at nothing to achieve their goals. We must all be equally driven, nothing else will suffice.

He pulled a sheet of paper from a drawer and began composing a letter to his father Henry Beevor. It was important to let his family know of his new status and impending duties. His family would be proud of his actions and Beevor was excited to express his own feelings to them. After a few minutes of writing, he realized that one piece of paper would not be sufficient for his message. He retrieved a second sheet and continued writing. It was important that he voiced his true feelings on the matter no matter how much time and paper it involved. Satisfied he had made his feelings known, he folded the pages neatly and placed them in an addressed envelope. He summoned the secretary and handed her the envelope.

"Please post this immediately," he directed. "It's quite important to me."

"Of course, Sir. Right on it."

Jack Beevor sat back and contemplated.

Tomorrow I will be in the army and who knows what will happen. It's all for the best and it's what I really want. I just hope I don't muck up things, that would be quite unfortunate.

He returned to the present and looked at his desk. There were still some loose ends to tie up and he only had the remainder of the day to complete his tasks. He would work into the night if necessary and would leave his firm as up to date as possible.

The paperwork that accompanied Beevor's entry into the British Army caught the attention of one of Great Britain's newly conceived organizations, the Special Operations Executive or simply, the SOE. His scholastic achievements and his curriculum vitae stood out even though the SOE was still in its formative stage. As the implementation of the unit was considered forthcoming, the hiring of a person with proper qualifications as one of its first operatives became a real priority.

Jack Beevor was delighted with the attention given by the SOE but readily admitted he knew nothing about spying or any of the clandestine activities his new affiliation was assigned to. He knew the SOE was recently formed at the bequest of Prime Minister Winston Churchill and that activities were confined to locations outside Great Britain, but little else. He poured himself into the crash courses he received and it was soon decided by the SOE's hierarchy that Beevor possessed the necessary organizational skills that a field officer needed for the SOE. All that remained was to find a spot that could utilize the young attorney turned officer's particular skill set and the bright young man would be cast into the growing fracas of the world war.

Wednesday, June 19, 1940
Testing Laboratory
Rua Padre Manuel Vaz Leal 2
Barroca Grande
Covilha, Portugal

Early summer was particularly enjoyable for Dr. Gerhardt Schoenfeld in his hilly laboratory located just two miles from Portugal's Panasqueira Wolfram mine, the largest mine of its type in the world. During Roman times, the area had been explored for tin. At the end of the 19th Century, a shiny black stone was found that proved to be wolfram, also called tungsten, an important element used in manufacturing armor-piercing shells and bullets. Wolfram is a strong and dense metal and is placed inside the shell that is then surrounded by the explosive or incendiary charge. Wolfram had become increasingly important to Germany and other militaristic countries during the 1930's when those countries sought to make their weapons as lethal as possible.

Dr. Gerhardt Schoenfeld was a full professor of chemistry at *Munich's Technische Universitat Munchen* when he was tapped by the National Socialist Government to begin work on wolfram with the goal of improving its effects within the shells and ammunition used by the German *Wehrmacht, Kreigsmarine* and *Luftwaffe*. His early work was well received and in 1938, he was designated to relocate to Portugal, the source of almost all of Germany's wolfram purchases. He was ordered to move to Central Portugal, the site of the largest wolfram mine in the world to continue his research.

Since Schoenfeld was embedded in a repugnant relationship with his domineering wife, the idea of relocating was appealing to the 46-year-old scientist. He asked and was granted permission to bring his top assistant, Hans Pfeffer, along with him. After some discussion, the Nazi Government agreed. Upon arriving in Portugal, Schoenfeld selected the small city of Barroca Grande for his lab, some two miles from the great Panasqueira Mines. That was almost two years ago, and Schoenfeld felt his work was nearing a breakthrough as the summer of 1940 continued its slow progression.

Whenever the duo needed equipment or more money, Schoenfeld simply made the trip to Lisbon and the German Embassy. The emancipated chemist thoroughly enjoyed the City of Lisbon and some of its features that Barroca Grande lacked, including the city's excellent selection of hotels, restaurants, cafes and, most importantly, high-caliber brothels of the Alcântara section of Lisbon's waterfront area. Schoenfeld delighted in the company of several ladies and soon became one of the brothel's preferred customers.

Thursday, June 20, 1940
Ritz Hotel
Plaza de la Lealtad 5
Madrid, Spain

The newly-appointed British Ambassador to Spain paced the floor of the smallish suite he occupied at Madrid's finest hotel. Sir Samuel Hoare was now 60 and had held numerous positions in various British governments since 1922. His Conservative Party ties had cost him his latest post, Secretary of State for Air, but high contacts within the government allowed his being awarded the Spanish ambassadorship. He had left London immediately for his new post.

Finding no suitable living quarters anywhere, he was forced to stay at the Ritz Hotel in the very heart of the city. The place was a grand example of Belle Époque architecture and the social and political center of the country.

Hoare was appalled at what he found upon arrival. The hotel was full of Germans, many outfitted in Nazi uniforms and ill-fitting suits and outerware. A number of Spanish officers and officials were also present. Animated conversations filled the crowded hotel lobby and spilled into the adjoining halls.

You would think we were in Germany for all the flaunting I see, he ruminated.

What the foreign secretary feared seems to be a reality. No doubt the Germans are trying hard to push Franco and the Spanish into the war on their side. This will all be quite tricky for me and the ligation staff but that's the job I've been given. Good thing I checked the suite for listening devices, I already found two. No use letting them know I know about the devices; they would just place new ones that might be harder to find. I'll just keep my words to myself and be careful of what I say on the phone. They are undoubtedly monitoring my phone, the immediate click when I pick up the receiver is surely evidence.

Tomorrow I meet with General Franco and from what I have perceived, he is quite a handful. We'll see how that goes. This situation seems to become nastier with each passing day. My people at the embassy are on edge and the fact that the Duke keeps shooting off his mouth doesn't help matters any. I've already let London know something specific must be done in his case and I'm not really sure what that something is. You don't exactly tell a former king what he can or can't do, can you? Sticky wicket it all is and I am in the middle of it all. He and the Duchess are only two floors up but I've yet to see them in person. Maybe that's for the best, or until I have my meeting with Franco.

A knock on the door signaled the daily delivery of English newspapers and the mail pouch from a member of the legation's staff. Sir Samuel Hoare walked to the door and peeped through the hole. He recognized a junior staffer and opened the door.

"What have you for me today?" he asked pleasantly. "Any good news?"

The man frowned and shook his head negatively.

"I feared as much, nothing really upbeat is there?"

Again, the man nodded. He turned and left the room as Hoare unfolded the stack of newspapers and opened the pouch.

Thursday, June 20, 1940
Palacio de El Pardo
Just outside Madrid, Spain

Generalissimo Francisco Franco stood near a window of his office and observed the splendid surroundings that the 16th Century Renaissance buildings of the Palacio de El Pardo offered. He did this as often as time permitted as the sights reminded him of his country's great past glories. The current leader of Spain was absolutely determined to lead his beloved country back to the elevated levels he felt it deserved.

At 48, he had survived a bloody civil war that had cost half a million lives and had ended a little over a year ago. His Nationalistic Falangists outlasted a Republican consortium of communist and socialist groups for control of the country. Franco and his cohorts also had the support of both Germany and Italy in the form of munitions, soldiers and air support that eventually swung the pendulum toward the nationalist side.

Franco was weary of war and decided on a position of neutrality for his country despite both Germany and Italy's insistence that Spain come into the war on the Axis side. He felt his country needed time to mend from its costly war and that his military needed even more time to recover from its internal wartime tribulations.

Ramón Serrano Suñer was Spain's Minister of the Interior and a close friend of Germany who had lobbied on their behalf during the Spanish Civil War. His wife Ramona was a sister to Franco's wife Carmen, making him Franco's brother-in-law. He had been summoned to the Palacio de El Pardo by Franco and arrived five minutes early for the meeting as was his habit.

"*Mi Caudillo,*" he exclaimed after being shown into the office. Suñer made it a practice to use his favorite name for Franco both privately and publicly. He genuinely liked his leader and the title, *Caudillo*, was the most respectful he could imagine. The two shook hands firmly and Franco gestured for the minister to take a chair.

"Ramón, I have several important jobs for you that must remain very confidential. Suñer nodded once and leaned forward.

"First of all, I want you to plant several stories in various newspapers about the Duke of Windsor and the remarks he has been making about the British Government and the British Royal Family. Also, tell some of our top agents to leak these stories to British businessmen and anyone within the British colony here who has any influence. Many will have already heard about the Duke and these stories will only help our propaganda.

Next, I want you to start working on a plan to invade Portugal should it become necessary to do so. This shouldn't be anything too elaborate, the Portuguese Army has only 30,000 soldiers and these are poorly trained. I also want you to go over the correspondence for the past year from our Foreign Ministry. I am not completely satisfied with General Beigbeder's work or his attitude toward some of the countries we interact with. I might have to replace the foreign minister and you would be my choice for that position. It would be good if you were familiar with what is going on in that ministry."

"Thank you, *Mi Caudillo;* it is my honor to serve you."

"And, Ramon. It might be necessary for you to travel to Berlin and Rome again in the near future. I have received cables from both Hitler and Mussolini and they want answers to their proposals. This is something to be done in person, don't you agree."

"Definitely. I have had good rapport with each man in the past."

"Excellent. We need time for our country to heal and that point must be made at all costs."

"Yes, *Mi Caudillo*. I will see that they understand."

"Get on with it then, I know you are quite busy these days. Please give my regards to Zita and your family."

"And you to Carmen. We talk about her quite often."

Franco returned to his desk and paperwork while Suñer made his way out of the office.

Chapter Four

Sunday, June 23, 1940
Praça do Império,
Belém, Lisbon, Portugal

The day all Portugal had been hoping for had finally arrived. The *Exposição do Mundo Português*, or Portuguese World Exposition, was formally dedicated and opened to the world's eyes. Two dynamic sculptures of Hippocampus seahorses by António Duarte graced the front part of the huge square meant to showcase Portuguese history since its inception. At the exposition's back stood the Monastery of the Jerónimos, the country's near perfect architectural masterpiece that was completed during the Manueline period in the 19th Century.

Prime Minister António Olivares Salazar and practically every Portuguese official was in attendance. His Royal Highness the Duke of York, the King of England's younger brother, led a large British mission intent on strengthening its relationship with Portugal and highlighting the Anglo-Portuguese Treaty initially signed during the reign of British King Edward III in 1373. The treaty proposed "perpetual friendships, unions (and) alliances" between the two countries who were the great sea powers of the 14th Century. It is the oldest surviving agreement in the entire world.

Representatives of all Portuguese colonies were present with exhibits which showed the world Portuguese colonization. Portugal's former colony of Brazil, the only other nation invited to participate, featured its own exhibit.

Portuguese President Marechal Carmona inaugurated the exposition on a warm June afternoon to the delight of the large crowd. Most officials wore bowler hats or top hats that offered protection from the sun. Many men in the crowd wore morning tails which provided an air of formality and reverence to the important event.

Prime Minister António de Olivera Salazar chose a dark grey suit and was the centerpiece of the occasion since his *Estado Novo* was the showcased *cause célèbre* for the country and the exhibition.

Among the Portuguese royalty in attendance was the 5th Duke of Palmela, educated in Great Britain at Cambridge and an avid supporter of Salazar and the Estado Novo. The pair shook hands warmly then the Duke spoke in an even tone.

"This is such a great day for you and our country, my dear friend. The world will now take notice Portugal has returned to its former status as a world leader. And Portugal has you to thank for it all."

"You are too kind," replied the Prime Minister. "I got the idea in 1935 after New York announced it would have a World's Fair. It took a great deal of planning but I believe it has achieved its objective. Portugal is back in the world's eyes and it's up to us to keep our country moving ahead."

"Yes, it's true. I'm particularly delighted to see the large British Mission who accompanied the Prince. Added the Duke, "I believe it's the largest such delegation to be here. It shows the intent of their leadership in these troubling times."

"You are probably correct," Salazar conceded. "We have been friends with England for an extremely long time. And, I understand their war is not going well for them. If the reports I have received are correct, they have their hands full even with their incredible success in evacuating the beaches of Dunkirk."

"I have not heard such specific news, my friend. I am delighted you receive such news before our country does."

"It is quite important for me to be well informed; don't you agree?"

"Most assuredly. That way you can stay on top of things."

Salazar nodded and prepared to take his leave. He thought of something else and turned back to the Duke. "Oh yes, Domingos. One more thing. You must remember that during the Napoleonic Wars, our country was the only one in Europe that fought on the English side. Our alliance goes back for many centuries.

Many Portuguese tend to forget some of the more important circumstances of our two countries' partnership. It is possible they need reminding; don't you agree?"

"Yes, Prime Minister. I most certainly do."

"Then enjoy the exposition. It will help you recall some of our country's past glories. I think you will appreciate it."

Domingos Maria do Espírito Santo Beck, 5th Duke of Palmela, nodded his agreement as Salazar departed. He had no doubt many of his countrymen would also agree.

Friday, June 28, 1940
Office of the Foreign Minister
Auswärtiges Amt
Wilhelmstraße 76,
Berlin-Mitte, Germany

The information from Spain puzzled Nazi Foreign Minister Joachim von Ribbentrop. Seated behind his ornate desk, he reread the cables and documents he had carefully laid out before him.

This doesn't make sense. I keep getting reports from Abwehr agents the Duke of Windsor keeps spouting off about the British Government at social events and the like and the accounts seem well-founded. It can't be that several agents get the information wrong, so I must feel they are accurate. On the other hand, our ambassador in Madrid hardly mentions such matters and states there is only a rumor the Duke and Duchess will go to Lisbon. If they were serious about the visit, they would have made arrangements by this time.

I need correct information! It's too important to the Third Reich. What should I do? Maybe I should send someone who will cut through the quatsch and get things done.

He thought for several moments and finally verbalized.

"Schellenberg!"

He's the perfect official to send. Even though he doesn't like me, he follows orders well. He's also very smart and can adapt to extraordinary situations if necessary.

Von Ribbentrop pushed a button on his desk and spoke into an intercom. "Call the *Amt VI* office and ask Chief Schellenberg to come to my office. Make it a priority, there's no time to lose."

"Jawohl, Herr Minister," came the earnest reply.

Friday, June 28, 1940
British Ambassador's Residence
Rua São Francisco Borja 63
Lapa, Lisbon, Portugal

British Ambassador Sir Walford Selby was seated behind his desk but gazed out the large window overlooking the immaculate garden which adorned the British Embassy's grounds.

His diplomatic career spanned more than three decades and he considered his accomplishments to be successful. Over the past few weeks, he had become disheartened by notes and letters from several of his friends in Whitehall about his possible replacement as ambassador. He recently celebrated his 60th birthday and realized his duties in both Austria and Portugal had taken a heavy toll. He was tired of the struggles and the current political problem with refugees was all that Selby and his staff could handle.

His current dilemma was the impending visit of the former King of England, Edward VIII and his wife Wallis Simpson, the current Duke and Duchess of Windsor. As he stared out the window to the garden below, he pondered what could happen next.

Why are the Duke and Duchess coming here now? Lisbon is bursting at its seams and I'm not sure I can get a room for them even if he is the former King of England. Planning their visit shouldn't be too difficult, there are always a plethora of people wishing to rub noses with royalty. Also, he's a pretty decent fellow who has always been good to me. I can't say the same for his wife, but that's another story altogether. I wish I hadn't received the notes about my being replaced, I don't fancy being a lame duck diplomat. Not much I can do about it if the decision has been made and from the tone of the notes I've received, it seems that's the case.

I shall continue here until relieved and then I will retire and write my memoirs. I've been involved in a number of high-profile situations and my tenure in Austria should make really good reading. I'd better get onto finding a suite for the Duke and Duchess, no time to waste.

He pushed a button on his desk and instructed his secretary, "Have Marcus Cheke come right in."

A few moments later, Press Attaché Marcus Cheke arrived. Ambassador Selby explained the salient facts to him and the need to prioritize the couple's upcoming visit. He also told Cheke to make a reservation for the couple at the Hotel Palacio in Estoril, a setting he knew the Duke would favor due to its proximity to the marvelous Estoril Casino, now Europe's last surviving gambling establishment. The casino was the preferred haunt of most visiting well-healed business exiles, as well as displaced royalty from all over Europe. He knew the Duke's former status would guarantee a reservation for the couple.

Friday, June 28, 1940
Prime Minister's Residence
10 Downing Street
Whitehall, Westminster
London, England

While the pressures of his office had abated to some degree following the Miracle at Dunkirk, Prime Minister Winston Churchill still faced the daunting prospect of a German invasion of Great Britain. He was also faced with an internal problem in the form of the Duke of Windsor and his current behavior in Spain.

Churchill had always been a proponent of the former king, but the Duke's current status and his location in Madrid raised the

PM's concerns over possible political scenarios that could endanger the couple. Spain was decidedly pro-Nazi and the prospect of the Windsor's being in German hands was unfathomable to the still green prime minister. He sent a cable to the Duke reminding him that he was still in the British military and needed to be back in England where he would be offered an official residence.

Churchill received a phone call from British Ambassador Sir Samuel Hoare that the Duke was definitely considering a trip to Portugal as soon as his younger brother departed the country after attending the opening of the *Exposição do Mundo Português* the past weekend. Hoare also stated he had informed the couple that a Royal Air Force aircraft would be waiting for them in Lisbon to return them to England. Hoare indicated the Germans, at every opportunity, had stepped up their efforts to persuade him to stay in Spain, but the Duke had politely refuted their efforts.

The Prime Minister considered his options and thought to himself.

We really need to get him back on British soil, no matter what it takes to accomplish the feat. A visit to Lisbon is well enough and it's the only place where we can get an aircraft to pick them up. Bloody nasty scene, but something we must deal with at once. I wonder what else we can offer him if he refuses to return to London. Perhaps a governorship at one of our colonies might work if it's the right setting.

He reached for a folder on his desk that contained the list of colonies and any current vacancies. He began reading the list and suddenly a name literally jumped out at him.

Bahamas. I know he is fond of the place; he's even discussed the spot with me before. It's a bit out of the way but it might be just the right fit for him. I'll put out a feeler and see what comes of it.

Saturday, June 29, 1940
Sintra Airfield
Sintra, Portugal

The *Lufthansa Junkers Ju 90A-1* passenger aircraft touched down on Sintra Airfield's grass runway and slowly taxied to the terminal serving passengers arriving in Lisbon. One of the first travelers to alight was *Brigadeführer* Walther Schellenberg, Germany's leading spymaster. He was the officer chosen by the country's foreign minister. Joachim von Ribbentrop, to execute the details of *Operation Willi,* the Third Reich's attempt to influence the Duke of Windsor into returning to Spain.

Schellenberg was none too happy with the assignment. He mused his chances as the Mercedes W150 staff car wound its way toward the German Legation in Lisbon.

The more I think about this scheme of von Ribbentrop's, the more I am convinced it has little chance of success. The former king is too widely known and will undoubtedly have a large number of British agents guarding him, not to mention the Portuguese PVDE who will have responsibility for him and his wife.

This is a ticklish situation with Portugal being a neutral country. We cannot afford to do anything that might provoke its government or the whole scheme might backfire on us. Maybe our ambassador will have some insight into all this. I really can't fathom our success unless something extraordinary occurs and he falls into our hands.

The limousine finally arrived at the consulate and Schellenberg stepped out. He entered the building and was immediately pointed to the ambassador's private office.

Baron Oswald von Hoyningen-Huene rose to greet the well-dressed intelligence officer. "*Heil Hitler.* I hope you had a comfortable flight *Brigadeführer.* Welcome to Lisbon."

"I hope I am not wasting my time, Ambassador," Schellenberg replied curtly. "*Operation Willi* seems a bit far-fetched to me, but I will follow orders like everyone else."

"Please sit down, this sofa is quite comfortable," the diplomat offered.

Schellenberg acknowledged the offer and settled into a corner of the divan as the ambassador continued speaking.

"I have come to a similar conclusion, *Brigadeführer*. If and when the Duke travels to Lisbon, he will constantly be in the spotlight. Neither the British nor the Portuguese will allow us to get anywhere near him during his stay. One of our spies at the *Hotel Palacio* in Estoril has reported a reservation for the couple and that's worse than having them here in Lisbon. The setting there is much less congested and much easier for the authorities to control."

Schellenberg considered what he had just learned and finally replied. "Just how effective is the PVDE in all this? What can we expect from them?"

The veteran diplomat considered his answer and spoke. "They are quite adept at their job. They have an excellent leader, Captain Agostinho Lourenço, and the full authority and confidence of Dr. Salazar. I can't see them making any mistakes. The Duke's visit will be an important event for the country and I am sure extraordinary precautions will be in force."

Schellenberg nodded and thought to himself.

Our ambassador is considered an excellent diplomat and knows Portugal and its people on a firsthand basis. I must respect his thoughts. I will poke around and see for myself. Our only hope is that Estoril might offer a small chance, but I'll know when I see it.

The pair continued to talk amiably and Schellenberg shared his views on Germany's recent successes in France. The ambassador was delighted to gain first-hand knowledge of the occurrences and invited his visitor to dinner later that evening.

Saturday, June 29, 1940
Prime Minister's Office
Rear of São Bento Palace
Lisbon, Portugal

When Dr. António Salazar received information that a reservation had been made for the Duke and Duchess of Windsor at the Hotel Palacio in Estoril, he quickly set in motion a plan he had conceived over the past few days. He ordered his secretary to call the hotel and ensure the reservation was cancelled due to non-availability. At the same time, he put a call to his old friend, Lisbon banker Ricardo Espírito Santo who owned a large, palatial home in close proximity to Estoril in the small town of Cascais.

When Espírito Santo came to the phone, the Portuguese prime minister greeted him warmly. "Ricardo, my friend, I have a small favor to ask of you."

"Most certainly, Prime Minister. You know you have only to ask."

"Ricardo, the Duke of Windsor is coming to Lisbon in a few days and I understand he has had a problem in securing a place to stay during his visit. The hotels are all full and I thought it would be nice to offer him accommodations of both a personal nature and are somewhat unique. The Duke enjoys visiting the Estoril Casino and your house is quite close. I would consider it a favor if you would allow the Duke and Duchess to stay with you at your home when they arrive."

"I would be delighted, prime minister. It would be a great honor," Espírito Santo replied. "I will also host a grand welcoming party when they arrive. I know everyone will want to meet them."

"We must be careful of who we invite, Ricardo. Security during the visit will be extraordinarily tight. I will have Captain Lourenço call you to set up the important details."

"Excellent! I've dealt with him before."

"And, Ricardo, one more thing. I know your bank handles a great deal of money for the Germans and you have many friends within the consulate, but this is an entirely different situation. There can be no involvement with the Germans on this, the circumstances are just too critical. I hope you understand."

"Of course, Prime Minister. I'll act accordingly."

"Thank you, Ricardo. I knew I could count on you."

"Always, Prime Minister. Always."

Monday, July 1, 1940
Palacio de El Pardo
Just outside Madrid, Spain

Spanish Foreign Minister Colonel Juan Beigbeber stood in front of Generalissimo Francisco Franco as his country's leader finished his rant on the status of the Duke of Windsor. It was obvious to the diplomat that his superior was very displeased with what was happening.

Beigbeber offered another solution to his country's de facto dictator.

"Mi Caudillo," he began, "I offered a week ago to detain the Duke so the Germans could send someone to talk to him, and my offer still stands. I would be willing to do whatever is necessary to keep him and his wife here in Madrid."

"Your offer is well meant, Colonel, but I believe it would be unwise to force a former King of England to do something against his wishes. If he intends to leave, then so be it. I will send Javier Bermejillo to accompany the couple and he will report back to me."

"I would be happy to also accompany them, *Mi Caudillo.*"

"That will not be necessary, Colonel. One watchdog will be sufficient."

"As you wish, *Mi Caudillo.*"

"Thank you for coming here Colonel. If you have any additional ideas on this horrible situation, feel free to reach out to me."

Monday, July 1, 1940
Room 107
Hotel Atlántico
Estoril, Portugal

Brigadeführer Walther Schellenberg was pleased when the news reached him that the Duke of Windsor would be staying in nearby Cascais, at the home of Portuguese banker Ricardo Espírito Santo. After his arrival, he had been thoroughly briefed by the German ambassador and Espírito Santo's name had come up in several instances as a true friend of the Third Reich. He had immediately taken a short ride to the house located at *Boca do Inferno* on the very edge of Cascais. The town itself was nothing more than a small fishing village, remote save for the cluster of large houses facing the Atlantic Ocean. These houses were strikingly similar, each set more than 100 yards apart and each containing high walls and heavy hedges that offered protection for the wealthy homeowners from any unwanted visitors. An unlit road ran along the cliff tops. It led to the center of Cascais in one direction and, in the other way, directly to the famous Cabo do Roca, the location of Europe's most westerly point.

Schellenberg considered his options.

This is not an ideal location to attempt to penetrate; any visitors would stand out like a sore thumb. I would have preferred the couple had stayed at a hotel, where there is a good deal of activity. Our only option might be an armed attempt at capturing the Duke, but that is certainly out of the question. That leaves the Estoril Casino. It's certainly large and busy enough, but getting in there would be difficult. Good that I brought some fake papers and a Swiss passport with me, but I'm not sure how much good it would do to get inside the place. Our local agents will be well-known to the PVDE and I don't have enough time to send for more agents to assist me.

Unless our ambassador comes up with something more concrete to work with, I can't see Operation Willi coming to fruition. Von Ribbentrop won't be pleased with my news, but that's his problem. I'll stay here until the Duke arrives, maybe something extraordinary will turn up, like their taking a side trip or visiting a place that isn't well-guarded.

In any case, I'll go to the Casino this evening and see how it's set up. I might even wager some of the Third Reich's Deutsch Marks. I haven't had any leisure time since the war started, and this might be my last chance for a bit of relaxation for some time to come...

Wednesday, July 3, 1940
Espírito Santo Mansion
Cascais, Portugal

The agreement British Ambassador Sir Walford Selby made with the government regarding the Duke and Duchess of Windsor's visit was that Ricardo Espírito Santo, owner of the property, would not be in attendance during the couple's stay at his home in Cascais.

That agreement was negated when Espírito Santo stepped down and opened the door of the touring car that brought the pair from Spain at just past six in the evening. After the pair alighted, the charming Portuguese banker welcomed them in the name of his country's elected leader, Dr. António de Oliveira Salazar. He then added, "Your Highness, I will make every attempt to insure your enjoyment during your stay here in Portugal. My staff and I are at your service and our PVDE is here to ensure your safety and privacy." He pointed to a number of well-dressed individuals in lightweight dark suits and brim-edged fedoras standing around the two-story house and gardens.

"I know you must be tired from your journey and I have arranged for you to be shown to your rooms. I hope you will be able to join me later this evening for dinner, say around nine."

The Duke looked at his wife for conformation and nodded, "That will be fine. Thank you ever so much for your hospitality and kindness."

A number of servants appeared and attended the couple's large amount of luggage affixed to the top of the car. The entire procession then entered the house and moved to the bedrooms located at the rear of the dwelling.

Wallis Simpson surveyed the rooms and remarked to her husband. "This will do nicely, my dearest. This is much better than a stuffy hotel room. I noticed an outdoor swimming pool and a lovely garden. There was a pleasant breeze when we arrived and I'm sure it will be present during our stay."

"I'm glad you are pleased, my dear. You never know what to expect in these situations. But I agree. Some tend to work out better than others."

"And our host is simply enchanting, don't you agree?"

"I am told he owns the largest bank in Portugal. The rich can afford to be both amiable and appealing at the same time."

"You're always weary of people," the Duchess added.

"I learned that art when I was King. Most people want something from you and most of them don't want you to know it. I'm just being realistic, my dear."

"Whatever you say, dearest. I want to take a bath and get a little rest before dinner."

"I'll be right here when you finish. I want to study some maps of the area. It's always best to know what's around you when you travel."

"Good thinking," she trailed off and entered the bathroom.

The Duke picked out an old, seemingly comfortable Chesterfield Chair with an ottoman and settled in to peruse his assortment of maps.

Chapter Five

Wednesday, July 3, 1940
British Ligation
Rua São Francisco Borja 63
Lapa, Lisbon, Portugal

When Jack Beevor was initially informed of his first duty station as a Great Britain's Special Operations Executive operative, he was none too happy his destination was the neutral country of Portugal. Beevor had hoped for an assignment in one of the German-occupied countries of Europe as an undercover agent where his actions might prove immediately definitive to his country's cause in the war.

Nevertheless, the former barrister decided he would make the best of ant assigned duty and would dedicate himself to improving Great Britain's standing within Portugal and the entire Iberian Peninsula.

Upon arrival in Lisbon, Beevor presented his credentials to Sir Walford Selby as the Assistant Military Attaché. Selby looked at the documents and announced, "We need a security officer in this Embassy, and, as I gather you will have nothing to do unless the Germans cross the Pyrenees, I want you to take this in hand. I also want you to oversee the use of diplomatic bag facilities, and in particular the transmission of currencies."

Beevor considered the ambassador's statement and thought to himself.

He clearly has no idea of what I am to do here nor the fact that I work directly for the SOE even though he has been informed of my status with the SOE. Perhaps the SOE is simply too new and few

realize its true mission. This could prove to be a two-edged sword for
me. While I need to work independently of the embassy and its staff,
I need their cover and help in doing my job. I will have to walk a thin
line around here and hope my new boss, the Military Attaché, is a
person who will understand my role in all this. I'll just wait it out and
see what happens. This is going to be more complex than I imagined,
but I guess it comes with the territory. The advantageous aspect of all
this is I will be able to build my own SOE group here to ensure my
prime objectives are accomplished.

Jack Beevor's attention returned to Sir Walford Selby when the
newcomer realized the ambassador was still talking to him. He
waited until the older diplomat finished and extended his hand.

Sir Walford Selby was pleased with the answer given by his new
assistant military attaché. He had no way of knowing the clever
young man standing in front of him had little intention of adhering
to what he had just said.

Thursday July 4, 1940
Room 107
Hotel Atlántico
Estoril, Portugal

It was almost midnight when *Brigadeführer* Walther Schellenberg
returned to his room at the Hotel Atlántico. He had spent most of
his evening scouting the Estoril Casino and its grounds. Earlier
that day, the German Embassy notified him that one of their spies
had gleaned information that the Duke of Windsor would visit the
casino sometime that evening. It was Schellenberg's first opportunity
to glance at the former British King and the security that would
undoubtedly surround him. Schellenberg decided the visit was worth
the distant possibility of him being exposed, so he decided to arrive
around 9 o'clock. He was stopped at the entrance and his passport
carefully examined by one of a number of men who he immediately
identified as policemen from the PVDE. Another man who seemed
to be the leader of the group was summoned by the first policeman

who handed Schellenberg's Swiss passport to his boss. The second officer studied the passport and finally spoke to Schellenberg.

"Senhor Gisler," he began, reading from the passport. "I see you have traveled extensively out of your country for several years. Exactly what sort of business do you do?"

Schellenberg was prepared for the question and answered, "Chocolates, Officer. The world loves our Swiss chocolates. Selling is an easy business for my company."

Captain Agostinho Lourenço again studied the passport and replied, "And I suppose you speak German as well as Swiss."

"Practically all Swiss speak excellent German, officer. The language is quite similar to our own."

Lourenço nodded and handed the passport back to Schellenberg. "You may go, Senhor Gisler, I wish you luck at the tables tonight."

"I will certainly need some, officer. I wish you a good night also."

Lowrance nodded and turned away. Schellenberg replaced the passport in his suit pocket and entered the casino.

An hour later the Duke of Windsor and his party entered the casino with the accompaniment of at least a dozen uniformed police officers. A way was cleared for them and they were shown to a private gambling room located on the casino's second floor.

Schellenberg thought to himself.

There is no way of even getting near the Duke, much less talking with him. This plan, Operation Willi, was ill-advised from the start and I am just wasting my time by going through the motions. I'll cable von Ribbentrop from the embassy and wait for his reply. Then I'll make my way back through Switzerland to Germany where I can actually contribute to the Third Reich. I must admit the Portuguese police are really on top of this and are much better trained than I expected. I'll also inform the Abwehr of my feelings for their records. This could possibly be useful sometime in the future.

Friday, July 5, 1940
Testing Laboratory
Rua Padre Manuel Vaz Leal 2
Barroca Grande
Covilha, Portugal

The fact that Dr. Gerhardt Schoenfeld was in an unusually jovial mood was not lost on his assistant in Barroca Grande, Hans Pfeffer. As the pair shared their morning mate, Pfeffer decided to probe his superior as to why his mood was so upbeat.

"Herr Doctor, is it the *mate* that makes you so spirited today? You are certainly in a good frame of mind, of that I'm sure."

Schoenfeld considered the question and replied, "Hans, I'm always in a good mood when I return from a trip to Lisbon. Haven't you noticed before?"

"I thought it might be the *mate*, Herr Doctor. After all, everyone says I make the best *mate* in this whole area."

"Your *mate* is indeed the very best, Hans. Where did you learn to make it so perfectly?"

"An old Portuguese woman showed me how to do it. It must be done precisely to get the best results."

"And what is it made from?"

"She said the tea contains berries and twigs of the holly yerba mate plant that are ground up and dried over a fire."

"Fascinating. What comes next?"

"Well, first you must simmer some water; but do not boil the water. If you want a sweet *mate,* add two spoonfuls of sugar like I do for our *mate.*"

Schoenfeld nodded as his assistant continued. "Then you place the ground leaves into a gourd and stir softly with a special bent instrument called a *bombilla*. Tilt the gourd and be sure the *bombilla* touches the bottom without the yerba around it so it won't get clogged up. Then straighten the gourd and make sure the *bombilla* is still touching the bottom. Stir for about five minutes and your *mate* is finished."

Schoenfeld took another swig of the *mate* and smiled at his assistant. "It certainly beats coffee in the morning, it gives me something of a jolt."

The old woman said that mate is many, many centuries old, and came from the prehistoric Guarani natives of South America. Portuguese sailors tasted the mate and brought it back with them."

"A good story, Hans."

"But you didn't tell me why you are so happy this morning, Herr Doctor."

"Let's just say that I found a certain place in Lisbon that makes me exceedingly happy, Hans. I'll leave it at that. Now, let's get back to work. Where were we on our latest experiment?"

Friday, July 5, 1940
Cabinet War Rooms
Whitehall, Westminster
London, England

The question of what to do with the Duke of Windsor had bothered Prime Minister Winston Churchill for the past week. The former monarch seemed adamant about returning to England. British intelligence had intercepted German Enigma cables and were acutely aware of *Operation Willi* and its perceived value to the Third Reich. Foreign Minister von Ribbentrop's reference to the use of force to return the Duke to Spain weighed heavily on the British leader as he sought an alternative for his country.

His weekly meeting some three days ago with King George VI might just have produced a viable alternative for the Prime Minister. The King was keen on keeping his brother out of England during the war. "We must keep him at all costs out of England," the monarch stated, arguing that such a stance would be better for all involved. The King then offered a suggestion. "Make him the

Governor and Commander-in-Chief of the Bahamas, we can still keep an eye on him without the problems his closeness with the tabloids might cause."

Churchill mulled the idea and became convinced the Duke of Windsor might just take to the idea. Living in the tropical beauty of the Bahamas with its perks and simple ceremonial duties might appeal to the former King and his wife. He called his secretary and dictated a short cable offering the post to the Duke.

If he accepts, this will bloody well put the problem to rest. Too bad it has come to this; I genuinely like the former King. We'll just have to wait and see how it all develops, but I have a rather good feeling about it...

Friday, July 5, 1940
Prime Minister's Office
Rear of São Bento Palace
Lisbon, Portugal

Captain Agostinho Lourenço of Portugal's PVDE secret police waited as his country's Prime Minister finished dictating a letter to his secretary. He was pleasantly surprised when Dr. António Olivera Salazar completed his dictation, dismissed the secretary and turned toward him.

"Captain Lourenço, what news do you have for me regarding the Duke of Windsor?"

"Only good news Prime Minister. He is enjoying his stay and I know for a fact the Germans have not been able to get close to him. He even went to the casino a few times, but there were no incidents. Our security measures worked perfectly."

"Excellent, my old friend. This could have easily turned quite nasty for us if your protection hadn't been so complete."

"My people are well-trained, Prime Minister. They understand their jobs and act as true professionals."

"Have you heard anything about their plans for the future?"

"Only indirectly, Prime Minister," answered the PVDE head. "One of my men who speaks English thought he overheard the Duchess asking the Duke if he was really interested in the governorship of the Bahamas. My man didn't know the meaning of what was asked and wasn't entirely sure he had heard correctly."

Salazar considered his captain's words and reflected.

If all this is factual, the British have offered the Bahamas to the Duke to keep him out of England. Funny how these things work out. If the Duke takes the offer, he will probably be leaving Estoril sometime in the near future. I hope he doesn't take too long to decide, all the security surrounding him takes a lot of manpower and those agents could be doing something other than standing around guarding the couple.

Then the country's leader changed the topic to another matter. "Have your agents heard anything about the possibility of Spain invading our borders? The British told me certain officials within Franco's government are pushing for such a scenario at the urging of the Germans. While I discount what the British say regarding their enemy, it makes sense for the Spaniards to extend their reach. That would give them the right to argue against their joining the Axis, something I don't feel General Franco wishes to do."

"I haven't heard anything, Prime Minister. I know there are many German agents in Spain and they do their best to make the British look bad in the newspapers. Public opinion there is mixed as far as the war is concerned and their leader doesn't seem to put much stock in their opinions," answered Lourenço.

"What about our own people, Agostinho? What do they think about Spain and her possible actions?"

"That's another story, Prime Minister. I believe ordinary people are afraid Spain will act against us, and the upper classes are even more apprehensive since they have more to lose. The cafes are all abuzz with rumors, most invented by the Germans. The *Abwehr* has increased its agent base here and propaganda seems to be one of the top objectives. The major newspapers don't pay much attention to their propaganda, but some of the lesser ones give the Germans plenty of space."

"Yes, Agostinho, I read the papers each day and see it for myself. I wonder if we shouldn't make an example of some of these German agents to show them, we are in complete control."

The PVDE head considered his leader's question and replied, "That might just work for us. Arrest a couple of the agents and have them deported for some minor transgression. The German Consulate will object, but that will be mostly for show. It will demonstrate to the intelligence community we mean business. I'll see to it as soon as I get back to my office."

"Excellent, Agostinho. Keep up your fine work."

Lourenço saluted and turned to leave the office. A wide grin covered his face indicating his personal approval of the plan. He had disapproved of the Germans since he fought with the British in the Great War and was delighted with the prospect of putting the Nazis in their correct place.

Friday, July 5, 1940
German Envoy's Office
Campo dos Mártires da Pátria 38
Lisbon, Portugal

It was necessary for *Brigadeführer* Walther Schellenberg to visit the German ligation in order to use a secure line for his call to German Foreign Minister Joachim von Ribbentrop. The capable German officer had put off making the call until he was completely convinced that *Operation Willi* was a failure before it actually began. He also knew that von Ribbentrop would react negatively to the information he would pass on.

When von Ribbentrop came on the line, Schellenberg chose his words carefully. "Herr Minister, I'm afraid I must inform you that *Operation Willi* has proven to be quite difficult to implement. I have spent several days attempting to communicate with the Duke of Windsor with absolutely no success. The British have kept him secluded and the local PVDE has provided excellent security since the couple first arrived in Lisbon. I even tried to see him at the Estoril Casino and my passport was carefully checked before I was let in. It was totally impossible to get near the Duke regardless of any plan I devised."

Von Ribbentrop became incensed and shouted into the phone, "You are supposed to be the cleverest officer we have in German intelligence. That seems not to be the case here. I can't believe you haven't been able to figure something out. I might have made a mistake sending you in the first place."

Schellenberg let the comment slide and finally replied, "That's most certainly up to you, Herr Minister. You do whatever you think best. I will be returning to Berlin on the first Lufthansa flight I can find and get back to my regular duties."

Von Ribbentrop slammed the phone down and exclaimed, "*Scheiße, was für ein Idiot. Muss ich alles selbst machen?*

Schellenberg replaced the phone and allowed himself a grin as he thought.

Good thing Hitler favors von Ribbentrop. The pompous arse is definitely a detriment to the Third Reich and everyone but our Führer doesn't seem to know that. Oh well, the way things are going for our Wehrmacht, no one will really give a damn about Operation Willi. It might be best in the long run that it failed; no telling what might have happened if we forced the Duke to go back to Spain...

Thursday, July 18, 1940
Jack Beevor's Flat
Rua de São Miguel 155
Alfama, Lisbon, Portugal

The small furnished flat in Lisbon's Alfama District that served as Jack Beevor's residence was the perfect meeting place for the members of SOE's Lisbon group that was now in its formative stage.

Only four agents were involved at first, two established journalists and a financial expert along with Beevor himself. Both journalists were engaged in black propaganda intended to fend off the current similar propaganda efforts of Germany's *Abwehr* in the country. Both countries deemed it vitally important to win the opinions of the Portuguese people to their sides and a great deal of effort went into the propaganda labors of each country.

Initially, Baker Street had given their new SOE agent a number of goals, some quite easy and others more difficult. First and foremost was a plan to demolish the SACOR government oil refinery located in the Tagus River estuary in the event of either Spanish or German invasion of Portugal. Portuguese authorities had decided to deny the oil to any invader but lacked the technical expertise to develop such a plan.

Additional areas of concern included penetrating the more established Lisbon *Abwehr* intelligence network by whatever means possible and coordinating his group's activities with Britain's SIS group that had its own set of directives to accomplish. Throw in the fact that the British Ambassador and the existing military attaché expected Beevor to spend time in the embassy on mostly clerical issues, Beevor had little time left in his days for other activities.

Beevor scheduled a staff meeting for this evening, to learn more about Germany's local intelligence efforts within the country. His small staff was happy to share their insights with their new leader.

Beevor's financial expert was the gem of the team. Michael Terestchenko was from one of Russia's wealthiest families and served as Russia's last finance minister prior to the Bolshevik Revolution. He had fled his country rather than face a firing squad. He was internationally respected in European financial circles and brought a wizened attitude to his job. He spoke seven languages and his English was flawless.

Jack Beevor probed his staff on the local *Abwehr's* activities. The question brought a smile to Terestchenko's face.

"The *Abwehr* here are not well run and have many more informants in the country than we do," he began. "They seem to have unlimited funds for their efforts and are willing to do just about anything to get results. They are fairly easy to spot, their heavy clothing gives them away in many cases. A number of their agents are young, fresh from the Hamburg *Abwehr* school and not very shrewd in their efforts. They don't seem to pay much attention to us, but concentrate on getting information on British convoys and shipping. Their leader is a fellow named Ludovico von Karsthoff who holds the rank of major. Von Karsthoff is something of a playboy, enjoys fast cars and socializing."

Beevor was impressed with Terestchenko's reply and asked again, "Are you aware of how they get this information?"

"Of course," the confident former Russian answered. "They have operated several brothels down by the waterfront since the war began. The girls are briefed on how to extract information from visiting sailors. If the information proves correct, the girls are given rewards. It's a neat little system."

"And are the Portuguese, and the PVDE in particular, aware that the *Abwehr* has set up these places?"

"That's harder to confirm. Since the brothels provide a service of sorts, I believe the PVDE turns an eye about their activities. It is entirely possible the state police are not aware of the brothel's ownership."

Jack Beevor made a mental note to himself. *It might be quite interesting to a neutral country like Portugal to discover that a major foreign power owns and operates an intelligence gathering service in the form of several brothels under its very nose. I will check on it and see what comes from my efforts.*

The conversation turned to black propaganda and Lisbon's SOE unit's efforts to combat the same disinformation and deceptions used by Germany. It would take several hours for the journalists on Beevor's staff to explain their efforts and those of their enemies...

Wednesday, July 31, 1940
Hotel Aviz Private Dining Room
Rua Duque de Palmela 32,
Lisbon Portugal

The evening meal at Lisbon's Hotel Aviz's posh restaurant was nearing its end when the Duke of Windsor stood and addressed his friends who were seated around a large table.

With a moderate tone and amiable face, he made the following brief announcement. "My dear friends, I'm afraid this will be our last dinner in marvelous Lisbon, a place the Duchess and I have come to love. I have decided to accept my government's offer of the post of Governor of the Bahamas and we intend to depart tomorrow on the *SS Excalibur*. I want all of you to know that we have enjoyed this country's incredible hospitality and that it holds a most special place in our hearts.

"With this blasted war continuing at full bore, I am unsure of what lays ahead for my country and the entire world. I trust the almighty will guide our efforts and bring us eventual victory, for that would be good for the entire planet.

"Please keep us in your thoughts and prayers and hope that everything goes our way."

He raised his glass and toasted, "To Portugal and its leader, Dr. Salazar."

A resounding chorus of "Portugal and Dr. Salazar" filled the room.

Most of the men present approached the Duke and offered him their best wishes. It was a fitting end to the former British king's visit during a particularly trying time for everyone concerned. One of the gentlemen excused himself and immediately sought out a hotel telephone. He dialed the number from memory and waited for a response.

When he heard a familiar voice on the other end, he began his conversation. "Captain Lourenço, I have just finished dinner at the

Hotel Aviz with the Duke of Windsor. You will be interested to hear what he just announced..."

Friday, August 2, 1940
British Ligation
Rua São Francisco Borja 63
Lapa, Lisbon, Portugal

While it wasn't one of his favorite jobs within the British Legation, SOE group head Jack Beevor fulfilled his role as assistant military attaché by conducting interviews with displaced refugees seeking a means out of Portugal to any country that would take them. Most were Jewish and were interested in getting to various South American countries or the United States. Beevor listened patiently to their sorrowful stories and offered solace and help whenever possible

When the door opened for the third time this morning, Beevor looked up to see the face of an unusually attractive young Portuguese woman handing him a folder with papers inside. In near perfect English, she introduced a man and woman to Jack Beevor. "Major Beevor, this is Hanna and Ezekiel Cohen from Antwerp, Belgium. I have told them you might be able to help them on their journey. I'm not sure they have slept in days and have many questions I was not able to answer."

Beevor observed the woman and replied, "I'll most certainly try, Miss...?"

"Izaura Veigas Ribeiro, Major."

"Thank you, Miss Ribeiro." He gestured to the couple, "Please have a seat."

After a half hour, Jack Beevor completed the necessary questioning and showed the couple to the embassy door. He felt he could help these refugees and left them with an uplifting assurance that the embassy would contact them in the near future. He returned to his desk and weighed a thought which occurred to him during the interview.

What was her name? Izaura I believe, beautiful name and a beautiful young woman. I wonder if she could be of help to our group. She is only doing entry-level work at the embassy and I would hope the ambassador would look favorably at my snatching her for my work. If she is as intelligent as she seems, she could really help us in outdoing the Germans. I'll ask the head of chancery about her and see what he says. I'm in dire need of additional people for my mission and being stuck here in the embassy doesn't afford me much chance of finding new people to help the SOE.

He picked up the phone and dialed the number for the head of chancery. When a resonant voice answered, he spoke "Mr. Charles, this is Jack Beevor. I have a question and I hope you can help ..."

Monday, August 12, 1940
German Envoy's Office
Campo dos Mártires da Pátria 38
Lisbon, Portugal

The fact that two of his agents had been banished from Portugal and sent back to Germany did not sit well with the German Envoy to Portugal, Baron Oswald Theodor von Hoyningen-Huene. He immediately summoned Major Ludovico von Karsthoff, head of the *Abwehr* contingency in Portugal to his office for an explanation of the recent events. Von Karsthoff was accompanied by his second-in-command, *Hauptmann* Ernst Holtzhauer.

Von Hoyningen began abruptly, "This is totally unacceptable, Major von Karsthoff. In fact, something like this has never happened to me during my service to the Fatherland. What do you have to say about it? Why were your men singled out?"

Von Karsthoff looked at his deputy and then at the senior diplomat and replied, "I have no idea why the PVDE suddenly decided to expel my agents. The charges were quite trivial and applied to nothing other than what we have been doing all along. I have tried to contact my sources within the PVDE, but they haven't answered my calls. Maybe the government has decided to tighten their grip on foreign intelligence operations and this event is meant to warn us about our future operations. I really don't have any other ideas." Holtzhauer nodded his agreement but remained silent.

Von Hoyningen-Huene looked at his intelligence chief and sighed. "I want you to be very careful from this point on, Major von Karsthoff. We don't need this kind of notoriety at this time. Things are going quite well for the *Wehrmacht* and the newspapers seem to be swinging to our side for once."

"I know that all too well, Herr Envoy. It is because of our efforts that the newspapers are doing so. We have paid them well for the stories."

"Well, the top newspapers haven't swallowed your input, they have remained neutral like this entire country," von Hoyningen-Huene replied.

"No, they haven't," admitted von Karsthoff. "Hauptmann Holtzhauer has spoken to our agents about this and told them I expect better results in the future."

"You must be very delicate in your approach, Major. I don't want to piss off the PVDE anymore. They could make my job here much more difficult."

"You have my assurance, Herr Envoy. Holtzhauer will speak to all of them again about the need for complete discretion. You have nothing to worry about."

"I'd better not have more problems or you will be held accountable," the German envoy warned. "You must take this seriously, very seriously."

Von Karsthoff stood and saluted. "*Heil Hitler*," he uttered in a pitched voice. Holtzhauer seconded the exclamation and raised his arm stiffly.

The envoy nodded toward the door and the *Abwehr* leaders turned and left.

Von Hoyningen-Huene watched the figure as he departed. *Fatuous, driven men who act before they think, I've about had my fill of some of these types. I have worked hard to have a delightful relationship with Dr. Salazar and the Portuguese Government and I will not see it ruined by these impulsive fools and their infantile antics. I will call my source in the government and see if I can find out what motivated the PVDE to act against us...*

Chapter Six

Thursday, August 15, 1940
Café Lua
Rua da Rosa 158
Bairro Alto
Lisbon, Portugal

Several Cinzano umbrellas served as adversaries to the relentless sun that beat down on the three tables outside the tiny *Café Lua* in Lisbon's *Bairro Alto* neighborhood. Izaura Veigas Ribeiro and Pilar Soares Coehlo ordered two *Licor Beirão* and slowly sipped the delicious concoction that was Portugal's national liquor. Made from a family recipe of herbs and spices, the drink was originally a medicinal aid for stomach pain but its popularity as a slightly sweet but tasty beverage made it Portugal's favorite casual drink.

Pilar was in the process of answering her friend's last question: exactly who was Jack Beevor and what is his job?

"I really don't know much about him, Izaura. He doesn't come to the embassy every day, maybe once or twice a week. I know he is a major and his title is the assistant military attaché, but that's all. He never wears a uniform and he nods to me when we pass in a hall but it's nothing more than a polite nod. I believe he's a little older than me, but not that much. He's been here a month or two, but we've never had two words to say. He's quite handsome but he never looks at me that way."

Izaura took a moment to consider what her friend said and commented, "I can't for the life of me figure out why he wants to see me tomorrow morning in his office. I only met him once when I took some refugees into his office, but I didn't think anything of it. As you said, he was polite and very business-like."

"Whatever it is, you haven't done anything wrong so it can't be anything negative," assured Pilar. "Let's finish our drinks and make a night of it."

"Sounds good to me, but I wish I knew what was going on. I don't enjoy being in the dark about things, particularly about my job."

"No one enjoys not knowing, but sometimes that's just the way it is. I have a feeling your meeting might turn into something good for you."

"Why do you say that?"

"No real reason, it's just a feeling."

"I hope you're right," Izaura added. "It would be nice to have something good happen."

She raised her glass and clinked with Pilar. "*Saúde!*" Izaura proclaimed.

"*Saúde*" answered Pilar. "To us both."

Tuesday August 20, 1940
Testing Laboratory
Rua Padre Manuel Vaz Leal 2
Barroca Grande
Covilha, Portugal

The German testing laboratory near Portugal's wolfram mining area was silent as Dr. Gerhardt Schoenfeld bent over his counter littered with a variety of flasks, jars, vials and various test instruments.

He was just finishing the final phase of his most recent experiment when he exclaimed, "Hans, I believe we've finally done it! The experiment is a success! Let us inform Berlin of our results."

"You are to be congratulated, Herr Doctor," returned Hans

Pfeffer, his dutiful assistant. "Our Fatherland's war efforts will now take a new turn. Our shells and ammunition will now be able to penetrate anything that gets in the way."

"There are still the field tests to consider, Hans. Before production can begin, the new material must be thoroughly tested. On paper everything looks fine but only testing can determine its long-term usefulness."

"So, how will that happen? Must we go back to Germany to test the discovery? I was just beginning to enjoy Portugal and what the country has to offer."

"I'm not really sure of what comes next. I will notify Berlin and wait for their reply."

"That might take a week or so," Pfeffer replied impatiently.

"You are quite right, Hans. This area is quite remote and I certainly can't trust the telephone. No telling who's listening in."

"So, what do we do now?" questioned the assistant.

"I don't know about you my dear and loyal assistant. I am going to Lisbon as soon as I send off the news to our superiors. I have some unfinished business with a certain young lady there and I intend to address that situation."

"You mean the whorehouse, Herr Doctor?

"Most certainly, Hans. It's the finest establishment of its kind and my Louisa is the most beautiful woman in the entire place."

"I would never call a whore beautiful, Herr Doctor."

"You have never seen her, Hans. And, you have a lot to learn about women and life."

"That's probably true, Herr Doctor."

The esteemed scientist turned and ended the conversation. He began writing his notes to send to his superiors in Berlin. While he concentrated on his composing, his mind tended to drift toward a thought of Lisbon... and, of course, his Louisa and her many charms and talents. He decided to leave tomorrow and to stay as long as possible.

Thursday August 22, 1940
Prime Minister's Office
Rear of São Bento Palace
Lisbon, Portugal

Portuguese Prime Minister Dr. António Salazar listened with feigned interest to the story German Envoy Baron von Hoyningen-Huene was relating. Salazar realized the visit was a matter of form and that the German diplomat was forced to relate the story to keep up the diplomatic façade of his country. He had numerous visits in the past from the senior diplomat and admired the man's cool and clear approach to sometimes difficult situations.

When von Hoyningen-Huene paused, Salazar took the opportunity to reply to his visitor. In a soft and even tone, he began. "Baron, we have both experienced a number of difficult situations since you became your country's envoy to my country. We have always managed to find a solution to these problems and I hope this time it will not be different."

Von Hoyningen-Huene nodded but did not reply.

Salazar continued, choosing his words carefully. "I realize your country is involved in a major war and that you are winning. For that, you deserve the credit. But, since Portugal is a neutral country and I will do everything I can to preserve that neutrality, there must be some limits to what your intelligence people can do to influence my countrymen. The British have large investments in our country and have been honored visitors here for hundreds of years. They have many influential friends among the Portuguese elite and some of these people are unhappy with your government's approach. In their eyes, it's bad enough that you are winning at this time, but when you add smoke to the fire in the form of false claims and innuendo, they feel disinclined to join forces."

The German envoy replied in a low voice, "But we have many friends here and do business with a number of the people you just mentioned."

"That might be true, my dear Baron. But, enough is enough. I ask that you instruct your *Abwehr* agents to refrain from any further attempts to discredit the Anglos with made up stories and false claims."

Again, the German diplomat attempted to explain "You mentioned *Abwehr* agents, Prime Minister. I am not aware..."

"Please, my friend. My PVDE estimates there are at least 75-100 *Abwehr* agents active in my country. I can get you exact numbers if you prefer."

Von Hoyningen-Huene hesitated and began, "I don't..."

"There will be no further discussion on this matter. I will expect you to do as I ask as soon as possible. If you do, there will be no further expulsion of your agents from my country."

The veteran diplomat nodded and rose. "As you wish, Prime Minister. Is there anything else?"

"Not at this time, my friend. Thank you for taking time to come and meet with me. I'm happy that we see eye to eye on this matter."

Von Hoyningen-Huene turned and started for the door. He was sure to conceal the look of discontent that engulfed his face as he departed the room. His superiors in Berlin would not be happy with the Portuguese Prime Minister's edict and would demand he find additional ways to deride their enemy. It would take all of his diplomatic expertise to fend off the repercussions that could arise from this fateful meeting. It was up to him and his staff to provide alternatives to please Berlin's. That would not be an easy task to accomplish.

Friday, August 23, 1940
British Ligation
Rua São Francisco Borja 63
Lapa, Lisbon, Portugal

With great trepidation, Izaura Veigas Ribeiro stepped into the room occupied by an intent looking man who was seated behind a small wooden desk. Jack Beevor looked up and smiled as he indicated to the nicely dressed young woman to sit in a chair across from him. She took her seat as Beevor began.

"I expect you might be worried about this meeting, Izaura. Is it okay to call you Izaura?"

"It's my name and you're welcome to use it. And, yes, I have no idea why you wanted to talk to me or what it is all about. No one seems to know what you do here, Major Beevor, except your title is the assistant military attaché."

Beevor leaned back on his chair and smiled as he answered her. "You are correct about my title and as far as my job is concerned, only two other people here in the embassy actually are aware of what I do."

"That sounds a little ominous, Major. And perhaps a bit secretive."

"Very observant, Izaura. And, you are nearly correct."

Beevor had decided to take a factual approach with Izaura and quickly got to the point. "What I do here is top secret and this conversation is for your ears only, Izaura. Am I clear?"

Izaura balked at the statement but quickly recovered. "Yes, I understand I'm to tell no one."

"Good, then we are in agreement." He paused and continued. "My mission here is to disrupt the flow of information from Germany's intelligence service that is called the *Abwehr*. They employ numerous agents, both German and even some Portuguese. They secure information on ship movements and report back to Berlin with the information. They are also responsible for planting false or misleading information in a number of the daily newspapers. They are, in fact, spies for their country and perform a great deal of secretive work."

"So, are you also a spy for your country?" Izaura interrupted.

"In a manner of speaking, yes. I report back to London on a regular basis to get instructions on how to do my job correctly. I am aware of the political implications of my work and the fact that Portugal is a neutral country in the war."

Izaura looked earnestly at Beevor's face but did not comment.

"The reason I have asked you here is simply that I have a need for a female agent in my group, preferably one of Portuguese descent. I am aware that you have earned a law degree and I was surprised to see that you had not pursued a career in law."

"I found it quite boring near the end of my studies. I was close to graduating and finished my studies, but I decided to find something else to do. My uncle got me this job with the British Consulate and I have enjoyed helping people in my work. The pay isn't all that great, but I have made a number of friends here and I intend to stay as long as I can."

"If you accept my offer, your pay will increase substantially. My group is not paid out of the embassy's funds, and I have a rather large budget to work with."

Izaura's face brightened as she considered Beevor's last statement.

"If you accept this job, you will tell everyone you have been reassigned to other duties that will keep you out of the embassy on most days. You can say you are doing research or some other innocent toil. You will meet me whenever necessary at my flat in the *Alfama* where my other group members meet me. There is a certain element of danger in what we do, but I will try and keep you out of potentially dangerous situations."

"Why would you do that, because I'm a woman?" questioned Izaura.

Beevor produced a big smile and answered, "No, not at all. We have a number of female agents in our organization and everyone is treated equally. Same pay, same danger, same problems."

Again, Izaura chose not to respond. She waited as Beevor continued his explanation.

"You might be expected to do things you aren't particularly keen on doing, Izaura. Whatever it takes to get the job done, you will be expected to act accordingly. By the way, I neglected to ask how you feel about the Germans."

Izaura paused for a second, then responded. "In the beginning, I neither liked or disliked them. In fact, I had little contact with Germans, not even in school. But once I began work at the embassy, I began hearing what the Germans had done to so many people in their own countries and I realized that it was the intent of the Germans to subjugate the entire world. I've also heard rumors that the Germans want the Spanish to enter the war and invade my own country. This cannot be allowed to happen and I am willing to do anything I can to help put an end to all this fear and suffering. The

British seem to be the only country willing to stand up to the Germans and they undoubtedly need a good deal of help to accomplish their aims. If I can help, I'd be delighted to get the chance. You seem to be doing something specific to end this madness and I'm the person to help you if you want me. I'm not sure I have the correct training for your group, but I am a quick learner."

For one of the few times he could remember, Jack Beevor was rendered almost speechless. He cleared his throat and addressed the young Portuguese woman. "Well, Izaura, that about says it all. You are correct in your outlook and I hope many of your countrymen and women feel the same way; if so, our task will be that much easier. Welcome aboard."

"Splendid. I have one more question."

"Certainly, Izaura. What is it?"

"What is your group called?"

Beevor hesitated but responded, "We're called the Special Operations Executive."

Izaura thought for a second and replied, "Sounds like a law firm to me."

Beevor smiled at his new agent. He nodded and thought, *she's smart as a whip and isn't afraid to say what she feels. She will fit in nicely with my group. I'll get her started with some easy jobs and see how she does.*

Sunday, September 22, 1940
Small Flat
Barrio Alta
Lisbon, Portugal

At nearly 28 years and five months, Juan Pujol Garcia realized he was at a crossroads in his life. Born in Barcelona to a wealthy family who owned a dye factory, Pujol had already experienced enough discouragement and dismay to last his entire life. He was conscripted by the Republicans during the Spanish Civil War but his values were more oriented to Franco Nationalists. He deserted and became a Nationalist until his views again got him into trouble. He wound up hating both fascism and communism and became determined to help the British in their fight against Germany. He attempted to join British intelligence on three occasions but was denied due to lack of experience.

Using forged identity papers, he then managed to interest one of Germany's *Abwehr* agents in Spain into accepting him as an agent and training him in the organization's current spy methods. He finished the schooling and sought a method of offering his services to the British as a double agent. As a trilingual, his German handlers instructed him to move to Britain and establish a network of sub-agents for their cause.

Pujol disobeyed his orders and instead moved to Lisbon. He cleverly utilized a number of reference books he found in Lisbon's main library along with a tourist guide to Great Britain and newsreel reports he viewed in local cinemas to deceive the Germans into thinking he was in Britain setting up his network of spies. His reports were very detailed and happily accepted by the *Abwehr*.

He continued to pester the British until they finally gave in. At this point, the British were eager to use him on their side and Juan Pujol was made a double agent in the service of Great Britain. He eventually met with Jack Beevor who was astonished by the brazen simplicity of Pujol's scheme and the fact the Nazis had fallen for his elaborate charade. While Pujol wanted to take a part in Beevor's local activities, he was told to keep on doing his deception and the time would come when he could manage field work for Beevor's small group.

Juan Pujol Garcia was finally in a position to do good for the causes he believed in. He began feeding a steady stream of misinformation and diluted facts to his German handlers, much of which was provided by the British. When Germany expended a great deal of resources and time trying to locate a phantom convoy Pujol had created, Great Britain's intelligence system realized Pujol was an incredibly important asset to their cause of disinformation and gave him the code name of the leading actress of the time, Greta Garbo.

From now on, Pujol would be referred to as Garbo and great care was given to his assignments and ploys and to protect his real identity.

Thursday, September 26, 1940
Jamaica Bar
Rua Nova do Carvalho 6 – 8
Lisbon, Portugal

For many decades, the bars and clubs of Rua Nova do Carvalho had served the rudimentary needs of Lisbon's seagoing individuals. Conveniently located just off the River Tagus between the Rua de S. Paulo and Rua Ribeira Nova, the short street contained a series of four and five story buildings that offered their patrons the earthly delights they had missed during their voyages. While prostitution was illegal in the Catholic country of Portugal, Lisbon city authorities turned a blind eye to the area that added to the city's reputation as one of Europe's leading port cities.

One of the foremost establishments was the Jamaica Bar located in the middle of the first block and considered by many of its patrons as Lisbon's best brothel. The ladies of the Jamaica, as it was called, were beautiful and talented in their profession. While the clientele paid a few escudos more for their services, it was generally agreed the additional dosh was definitely worth it. Few customers quibbled when it came to price.

For Jamaica's *Abwehr* owners, the place was Lisbon's top producer of information regarding ship schedules, routes and general information that was routinely passed on to *Kreigsmarine* wolf packs operating in the nearby Atlantic Ocean. These U-boats were controlled by U-boat Command at Kernevel along Brittany's coast in Northwestern France and operated with much success harassing British and other nations' supply and shipping convoys.

It was almost by accident that Dr. Gerhardt Schoenfeld had stumbled onto the Jamaica during one of his earliest visits to

Lisbon. He was looking for a specific dock on the Tagus and happened to walk down Rua Novo do Carvalho when he spied a pair of attractive ladies entering the Jamaica. He followed them into the building and was greeted in a fashion he was unaccustomed to, but one the German scientist immediately identified with. After an hour of exchanging pleasantries with several of the ladies he made an arrangement with the Jamaica's Madame Estella for the services of one Louisa Flores, the young woman he considered the most beautiful in the luscious harem.

Louisa was twenty-two and possessed incredibly beautiful brown eyes that sparkled when she looked at him. She wore her jet-black hair pulled back and in a bun with a bright pink ribbon affixed to the rear. Her smile completely fulfilled the German who had never encountered a woman with Louisa's looks and charm.

For the rest of the night and into the next morning, Dr. Gerhardt Schoenfeld experienced pleasures he had never thought possible. He lay in the bed next to Louisa and studied the ceiling where he noted some cracks in the plaster. He put the minor discrepancies in the ceiling aside and let his mind wander.

This is what I've been missing my whole life. This is what men of the world talk about and what I have never experienced. Yes, I've had several women, but never one like this. Her mission is to please me and she does that in a remarkable manner. I don't feel as if I'm making love to a prostitute but to a woman who appreciates what I have to offer.

That encounter was several months ago and had been repeated on every visit to Lisbon the German scientist could manage. He would call ahead and reserve a room for Louisa and would marvel more at each succeeding visit. The last was as fulfilling as the first and it became apparent to Schoenfeld his relationship with Louisa was becoming more than just a business experience. His Portuguese had improved to the point that he was able to talk to her in her own language.

She stirred in the bed next to him and opened her eyes. "Good morning, Gerhardt," she said softly. "What time is it?"

"Almost nine, Louisa. Why do you ask? Do you have someplace to go?"

"No, my love. Your time is my time and you always pay for as long as you like."

The reference to money annoyed Schoenfeld, but he chose to ignore it.

"I want to take you to the best restaurant in Lisbon for breakfast or lunch; you decide which," he proposed. "We have something to celebrate and I want to make the meal something special for you."

"What is so special?" she replied, "this is the first time you want to see me outside of the Jamaica."

"It has to do with my work, Louisa. I'm sorry but I can't tell you any more than that. Let's just say I am near a breakthrough in my research and I might even have to go back to Berlin."

"You mean you will be leaving Lisbon? That doesn't sound very good to me."

"No, it will be a short visit to Germany and then I'll return to Portugal. I shouldn't be gone for more than a few days; a week at most."

"You better not leave me," she cooed as she snuggled close to him. I have become very fond of you since we met."

Schoenfeld looked at her and believed what she was telling him. It was the first time in his life a hard-to-get woman had paid him much attention and Schoenfeld was pleased. *This is something special, he thought. I am a truly fortunate man. I don't want to mess this up under any circumstances. I must be really careful...*

Friday, September 27, 1940
Reich Ministry of Armaments and War Production
Minister's Office
Viktoriastraße 11,
Berlin, Germany

Formed in mid-March by Adolf Hitler to control the administration of military arms and supplies for the German *Wehrmacht*, the Reich Ministry of Armaments and War Production was run by senior Nazi *Reichminister* Dr. Fritz Todt. The minister was a civil engineer and was previously responsible for the construction of the motorways system in Germany called the *Autobahnen,* a feat that Hitler considered a personal triumph. Two years earlier, Todt formed an economic vehicle named *Organisation Todt* that effectively utilized more than 800,000 forced laborers to build the Siegfried Line that was meant to defend Germany from any attackers.

From his ministry's headquarters on *Viktoriastraße* in southwestern Berlin, Todt adeptly controlled Germany's wartime armament efforts. When news of Dr. Gerhardt Schoenfeld's breakthrough reached the minister, he was quick to realize the eventual effect the discovery would have for his country's military.

He called his secretary into his office and excitedly dictated a laudatory message to Schoenfeld that also ordered the scientist back to Berlin to discuss his wolfram findings in person.

"How should I send this message, Herr Minister?" the secretary asked.

"We don't want to waste any time; this is too important. Get him here as soon as possible," replied Todt. "Have it encrypted and send it on the *Enigma* machine as soon as it is coded."

"Most certainly, Herr Minister. I will see it is done immediately."

"Good. Let me know when it is acknowledged and when he will be in Berlin."

"*Heil Hitler,*" the secretary barked as she left.

Reichminister Fritz Todt did not answer the secretary's salute. He was already engrossed in a series of reports he was preparing for his *Führer.* He was intent on not making a mistake in his details. Hitler demanded exact facts and figures and Todt did all he could to provide correct salient facts. He also realized what would happen should he fail in his mission.

Wednesday October 2, 1940
Hut 6, Sherwood Drive,
Bletchley Park, Milton Keynes,
Buckinghamshire, England

Bletchley Park Hut 6 was one of a number of designated structures that housed the Government Code and Cypher School in Buckinghamshire, miles away from the bustle and glare of London and its cluster of intelligence agencies. These organizations attempted to keep Great Britain on an intelligence gathering level with other top countries, mainly Germany. The stately complex that comprised Bletchley Park was established before the outbreak of war when it became evident that Great Britain and France were on a collision course with Adolf Hitler and his band of thugs who formed Germany's ruling National Socialist Party.

As far as Bletchley Park was concerned, its mission and work were considered so secret few Britons even knew of its existence. All staff personnel were sworn to absolute secrecy; this trust would be broken only under penalty of treason. Germany had its own experts attempting to break Allied codes, but considered its Enigma machine unbreakable. This proved to be a great advantage for the Allies in their never-ending quest to stop the German onslaught that threatened the entire free world.

Unknown to the Germans, a Polish mathematical team had broken the code in 1938 and had managed to get the details of their discovery out of their country and then to England. British authorities quickly prioritized their work and managed to develop the first computer machines that allowed them to break the codes in a matter of minutes. Alan Turing, another top Cambridge University mathematician and logician, provided a great deal of the original reasoning that led to the construction of the cryptanalytic I believe this to be most important. It was intercepted on its way to the German embassy in Lisbon and seems to refer to a Dr. Schoenfeld, a name on our list of active German scientists. He works with wolfram and our MI5 blokes aren't sure of his present location. I thought you might want to see this.

Bombe machines that were instrumental in eventually breaking the naval *Enigma.* Their work was termed Ultra and gave Great

Britain a huge advantage in intelligence gathering and determining the correct military decisions and procedures to defeat their enemy.

Hut 6 was but one of the units on the Bletchley Estate grounds that provided cryptanalysis of Army and Air Force *Enigma* messages. It was considered one of the top priority units within the complex and contained some of Bletchley Park's most qualified staff and personnel.

Some thirty minutes after *Reichminister* Todt's secretary handed his message to the *Enigma* clerk for transmission, a Wren sergeant walked into the office of the commander of Hut 6, 34-year-old Cambridge mathematician Gordon Welchman. Welchman was the unit's founder and had developed the means of dealing with its most sensitive information.

Welchman sported a neat mustache and was dressed in civilian clothes. He looked up and took the paper from the Wren who stood before his desk.

"Something important, I hope," he bantered.

"Yes, sir, I believe so," she answered. "Otherwise, it wouldn't be marked for you now, would it?"

"Carry on, Sergeant. I'll take it from here." Welchman suppressed a grin at the woman's reply, then opened the envelope.

A handwritten note was attached that the youthful scholar read first.

I believe this to be most important. It was intercepted on its way to the German embassy in Lisbon and seems to refer to a Dr. Schoenfeld, a name on our list of active German scientists. He works with wolfram and our MI5 blokes aren't sure of his present location. I thought you might want to see this.

Welchman peered at the signature scribbled at the bottom to no avail.

Another one of our diligent staff looking out for his or her country. The dedication here is quite fantastic. Our people work long hours and never complain, unlike other branches of our military. Maybe it's the fact that so many of our staff are really gifted, above average in intelligence and filled with keen commitment.

He then examined the decrypted German message that congratulated Schoenfeld and ordered him back to Berlin as soon as arrangements could be made.

This is undoubtedly an important intercept, he posed. *Anything to do with wolfram and armaments is special and we now know this Schoenfeld fellow is on to something. I can't believe the Nazis could refer to this in a message, but then, they are not aware we have broken their Enigma code, are they? I must see that this gets to the proper hands as soon as possible, and that means right now.*

He reinserted the message into the envelope and redirected the address to Brigadier Oswald Harker, the current head of MI5. Welchman figured this personalization to the section head would guarantee immediate attention. He called for a Wren runner and handed her the sealed envelope. "Please get this to MI5, will you? It's quite important."

"Certainly, sir," came the reply. "I'll see to it right away." She saluted and left.

Gordon Welchman returned to his desk that was stacked with messages and interceptions, and began redirecting them to the proper authorities. He was pleased his operation within Bletchley Park's top-secret undertaking was running so smoothly. In his mathematical world and to his exact way of thinking, it was the way things were supposed to work.

Chapter Seven

Friday, October 4, 1940
Jack Beevor's Flat
Rua de São Miguel 155
Alfama, Lisbon, Portugal

The whirlwind introduction to the SOE's Lisbon operation was a godsend to Izaura Veigas Ribeiro. She found herself continuously busy learning the codes and routines that Jack Beevor had laid out for his group. She had already participated in several minor missions and wasn't totally surprised when her boss described his next assignment.

"The Germans are getting most of their live information from the places on Rua Novo do Carvalho and London wants us to have a piece of it," he began. "I immediately thought that you might be able to help on this one."

Izaura looked at Beevor with a blank look. She had never visited the Rua Novo do Carvalho, but knew it was the city's red-light district.

"You don't mean," she replied weakly, her voice trailing off.

Beevor realized his mistake and corrected himself. "No, Izaura, you misinterpreted my meaning. I would never..."

Izaura took a deep breath and let him continue.

"What I meant was I intend to infiltrate some of the places and attract ladies to serve as *our* agents. There are plenty of ladies serving the Third Reich and I want to turn the tables to our side. We need to find a way to turn some of the sharper ladies into double agents and provide them with false information to pass on to their *Abwehr* handlers, while at the same time, extract information from the Krauts.

Izaura quietly digested Beevor's new plan and asked, "How am I to infiltrate these places? I have never been to one and wouldn't know how to act. Are you sure you want me for this task?"

Beevor answered quickly, as if he knew she would ask. "Because of who you are and how you act, I think you are the best person for this job. You must find someone who is familiar with these places, Oslo, Roterdão, and Jamaica for instance. The person you find might even know some of the ladies and be able to recommend them to you."

A light flipped on inside Izaura's head.

The only person I know that might be aware of such things is Pilar's friend, Martin Silva. He's a man of the world and would be familiar with such things. I will go see him tonight and I will take Pilar with me. She told me that story about a girl she knew who was spying for the Germans, so this should be right up her alley.

She returned her attention to Jack Beevor who was listing details he hoped he could obtain from the ladies Izaura would compel into joining his team.

"And, lastly, we would expect them to share any information they extract regarding the actions of anyone that might cause harm to Great Britain or any of her allies."

Izaura knew this assignment was the most important she had been given as an SOE agent and was determined to make the most of it. As soon as the meeting with Beevor was finished, she immediately headed for the British Consulate to speak with Pilar. The excitement of her new task was already beginning to affect her, a sensation she knew she must control to be successful. She had wished for excitement and intrigue in her new career and was delighted that it had taken a turn in just that direction.

Monday, October 7, 1940
Special Operations Executive
Iberian Desk
64 Baker Street, Westminster
London, England

The same day that Bletchley Park codebreakers successfully decoded Germany's *Enigma* message concerning Dr. Gerhardt Schoenfeld's wolfram activities, a second copy of the message was delivered to the Special Operations Executive's Iberian Desk for analysis and evaluation.

The section's head was 28-year-old Harold Adrian Russell Philby who was known to everyone as Kim Philby. A graduate of Trinity College, Philby had been recruited by MI6 after witnessing the Battle of France as a reporter and returning to England. When MI6's Department D was absorbed into SOE, Philby was made head of the entity's Iberian Desk due to his familiarity with Spain. He had worked as a journalist for *The Times* during the Spanish Civil War where he covered the war from the pro-Franco headquarters.

Philby studied the intercepted message and called for his assistant.

"Have this message sent to Lisbon and mark it *Most Secret* to the attention of Jack Beevor. Include a message from me and instructions that he is to monitor this person as closely as possible, but from afar. Dr. Schoenfeld is not to know we are interested in him or that we are aware of the fact that he is operating in Portugal. The German embassy will undoubtedly know his location, so that might be a starting point for Beevor. If we have a double agent inside the embassy, they might even know of this Schoenfeld and what he is doing in Portugal. Is that all clear?"

"Certainly, sir. How should we send it?"

Philby thought a moment and replied, "In the diplomatic pouch. That's the safest and surest way of sending something as delicate as this. Can you make tomorrow morning's BOAC departure?"

The man considered for a few seconds and answered, "Yes, that will not be a problem. If necessary, I'll run it out to the airfield myself."

"Good show. I knew I could count on you."

"Thank you, sir. I'll be on my way."

Philby acknowledged the departure and thought to himself. *This is the first really important piece of work we have sent Beevor's way. It will be interesting to see if he comes up with something.*

Wednesday, October 16, 1940
Prime Minister's Office
Rear of São Bento Palace
Lisbon, Portugal

The flowing red robe that signified the patriarch of Lisbon Cardinal Manuel Gonçalves Cerejeira was promptly shown into Prime Minister António de Oliveira Salazar' private office.

Even though the two had been friends for more than two decades, Salazar chose to kiss the Cardinal's ring as the prelate extended his hand.

"It was good of you to come on such short notice, old friend," Salazar spoke as he firmly gripped the cardinal's hand.

"When you need me, I am always available, António," returned the prelate. "I have no fonder memories of when we were students at Coimbra. I remember staying up all night when we found a particularly engrossing subject. I also remember we didn't always agree on what was right or wrong."

Salazar smiled broadly at his long-standing acquaintance and touched his shoulder as the pair approached a large sofa, the only piece of furniture besides his desk and chair in the unpretentious room.

"Let's sit here, the sofa is the most comfortable piece of furniture I own."

"I don't understand you at all António. You are our country's

Prime Minister and could surround yourself with whatever you wanted. Yet, you choose to lead a Spartan existence with only essential necessities. I recall our surroundings in Coimbra were quite meager, just like your office here. Then we had no money for anything but study and food, and no one cared about our surroundings. But why you live this way now, that's a mystery to me."

Salazar chose to reply to his friend's words using his first name. "Manuel, I have given this matter a great deal of thought. First of all, I consider myself frugal and that speaks of my surroundings. I have what I need to fulfill my job and that is what is really important. I am also aware that the Portuguese people as a whole have very little and yet are able to survive and be productive. When they read about me and my surroundings, I believe they are convinced that I am one of them and I hold their values at a high premium. Their loyalty is extremely important to me and therefore to our beloved country. If my people see me in a setting that is similar to their own, I believe they identify with what we are trying to accomplish. It's as simple as that."

"I already knew your answer, António. I just wanted to see if you had changed the wording a bit."

Salazar produced a full laugh, something that had become a rarity for him of late.

Cerejeira joined in the joke. Despite their positions of prominence, the two old friends were allowed to tease each other whenever they liked.

Salazar looked over at the cardinal and spoke in a direct tone. "Manuel, I have just reread the Pope's *Saeculo exeunte* document that he provided for our *Exposição do Mundo* celebration in June. At the time I was pleased with the Pontiff's praises of Portugal's gloried past and his hope for our country's future. But, at the time, I felt there was another tone to the encyclical and promised myself to go over the document whenever I found time. That time is this week and I have studied the document very closely."

"And what did you derive?" asked Cardinal Cerejeira. "Did it not meet your expectations?"

Salazar thought for a moment before answering. "This encyclical is a direct result of the Concordat of 1940, an agreement you participated in writing, negotiated its terms and eventually signed for the Holy See. I felt at the time everything we agreed upon was fairly obvious to all. I intend to live by the letter of the agreement and so will the citizens of Portugal.

"But I honestly feel the tone of the Pope's later message seeks to give the church a stronger position within our country than is laid out in the Concordant, and there is where my fears lie. I am adamant that no religion, including our beloved Roman Catholicism, be allowed to intervene in the workings of the Portuguese government. I have held that belief since the beginning of the founding of the *Estado Novo* and feel strongly about it to this day.

"I seek absolute neutrality for our country and this neutrality seems to be providing a welcome economy for most of our citizens. The only way this good fortune can continue is through a strong government that is unhampered by civil and religious morays that are unproductive and sometimes expensive.

"Manuel, I know you want what is good for our country as well as what is good for our church. You have done an amazing job as patriarch of Lisbon and you are loved by all our brothers and sisters. I wish they held me in the same esteem, but that is not meant to be. I must accept their thoughts and opinions for what they are---the voice of the people."

"You, too are loved, António, but in a different manner. Perhaps there are a few dissenters, but I believe the people of Portugal are thankful for your love and leadership."

"Always the statesman, my dear friend. I appreciate your opinion and hope you are correct. Now, what about the encyclical?" he asked, getting back to the subject of their discussion.

"I do not agree with you on the underlying meaning of the document," the cardinal responded. "I think the Pope merely wanted to restate the intention of the concordant and its effect on the Catholics of Portugal."

Salazar considered his friend's words, lowered his head and said softly, "I want you to make it clear to Rome there is a limit to the church's authority and that such authority is governed by the Portuguese Government. As long as the church accepts that premise, there will be no problems. If it oversteps its authority in any manner, I will be forced to take action that might become unpleasant for both sides. Is that understood?"

"Yes, António. I'll see to it that Rome understands your meaning. You can rest assured there will be no problems as long as I am Patriarch of Lisbon. You have my word."

"Then we can leave on a favorable note," Salazar concluded. "It is always my great pleasure to see and talk with you."

"I feel the same way, António. It was good of you to meet with me in this manner."

"Go with God," Salazar offered.

"That's supposed to be what I say, old friend."

Both figures laughed and shook hands. Before he left, Cerejeira extended his hand again. Salazar bowed slightly and kissed the Cardinal's ring.

Tuesday, October 22, 1940
Café Chave d'Ouro
Dom Pedro IV Square
Rossio, Lisbon, Portugal

It was just before nine when Izaura and Pilar made their way into the crowded confines of the *Rossio's* most frequented bar. The high noise level and the varying degrees of animation added to the place's allure. This was Lisbon at its social best and the *Lisboetas* who crowded into the place were involved in all sorts of bantering and mingling.

At first, the young ladies were unable to locate Martin Silva. His usual table was filled with a bevy of Germans, easy to identify by their clothes and voices. At least seven men were seated around the table and a string of German songs boisterously bellowed forth. Distaining looks from the Portuguese seated at surrounding tables had no effect on the intensity or fervor of the intoxicated Germans.

Pilar finally spotted Martin at another table and pulled Izaura through the mass of humanity that was the *Café Chave d'Ouro's* ground floor.

When they finally arrived, Pilar was forced to almost yell to be heard. "We almost couldn't find you, Martin. You weren't at your usual table."

"I know," Martin answered halfheartedly.

"I was a bit late tonight and the Germans forced their way to my table by threatening the waiter who was saving it for me. The poor fellow was upset, but was unable to do anything about it. Those people are bullies and know they can get away with just about anything."

Both women nodded their agreement as a waiter approached their table. "Two glasses of Dão white," Pilar ordered. Izaura nodded her agreement.

"What brings you ladies out tonight?" Martin asked. "You haven't been here in weeks."

"It's too crowded to really enjoy," Izaura offered. "But, tonight, we had a reason to come. You."

"I am honored," he quipped. "And what might you want with me? Are you selling some jewelry or possibly even buying?"

Izaura moved closer to Martin and spoke in a lower and leveled tone.

"Martin, you are a man of the world, right?" she began.

Martin Silva looked dubiously at the young woman and replied, "Yes, you can say that. Most men in my position would say yes to that question. Why do you ask?"

Izaura fumbled for words and looked directly at the man in front of her. "Martin, do you know anything about the brothels on *Rua Novo do Carvalho?*"

Silva was surprised at the question but suppressed any facial indication.

"Possibly, my dear. Why do you ask?"

Again, Izaura chose her words carefully.

"My job requires me to get to know some of the ladies in those establishments, particularly the really smart ones. I am looking for people who don't care for the Germans or their harsh methods. These ladies should be able to handle themselves under certain circumstances and will be well paid. Is that clear enough for you?"

"So, you want to make them spies for the British," Silva responded with a sly grin.

Izaura hesitated at his immediate grasp of the situation. "I guess you could say that. And, I need it done quite quickly if at all possible."

Martin Silva looked at the two women, shook his head and asked, "And exactly what do I get for helping you with this? After all, you wouldn't be able to find anyone without my help."

"You will get into our extremely good graces," Pilar interjected with a knowing smile.

Silva smiled and acknowledged the meaning. "Okay, ladies. I'll see what I can do after I finish my business here tonight."

"Martin, one more thing," Izaura added. "We need a lady from each of these places; Roterdão, Oslo and Jamaica. These are the best places, right?"

"Yes, they employ the highest quality women."

"Good, then you know what to do."

"I'll get back to you in a few days with some names," concluded Martin Silva. "You won't be disappointed with my choices."

The ladies finished their wine and stood up to leave. Martin touched Pilar's arm and whispered, "Don't forget about your good graces."

Pilar scoffed and pulled away. "Get something useful for Izaura and we'll see," she said coyly...

Friday, November 1, 1940
German Envoy's Office
Campo dos Mártires da Pátria 38
Lisbon, Portugal

The head of Germany's legation in Portugal, Baron Oswald Theodor von Hoyningen-Huene, was pouring through the daily diplomatic pouch that had just arrived at his embassy via the morning *Lufthansa* flight from Berlin. A number of regular messages were included and one caught his eye from the Reich Ministry of Armaments and War Production under the imprimatur of its head, Dr. Fritz Todt.

The message was simple and straightforward. Dr. Toth mentioned some new developments regarding wolfram and the Reich's decision to greatly increase its purchase of the raw mineral from Portugal. The message also pointed out the need for swift action on von Hoyningen-Huene's part in securing the additional wolfram and ensuring its immediate shipment to Germany.

The German diplomat pondered how to approach the Portuguese government about obtaining increased quantities of wolfram and knew this would be a delicate topic.

This wolfram thing must be handled with care or else it will backfire. Portugal is insistent on remaining neutral in this war and everyone knows what wolfram is used for. I will have to point out our invasion of Russia has increased the need for more wolfram, particularly since the Wehrmacht is doing so well in the operation. They can't argue with that since the newspapers are filled with accounts of our victories and the progress of our armies. They will probably give the British an opportunity to increase their wolfram shipments at the same time, just to remain neutral in the process. That's probably accurate since we will ultimately get what we want. I also expect the price to be higher since the war has had an incredible effect on the price of the ore.

He pushed a button on his desk and summoned his secretary. When the woman arrived, he told her. "Set up an appointment with the Prime Minister at his earliest convenience. Do not say what it concerns but just that the details are important. Is that clear?"

"Perfectly, Herr Envoy. I will see it is done immediately."

He again considered his position.

When I took this station, I never expected it to become so difficult. Portugal has become the key country in Europe for a number of reasons. I don't care for all these Abwehr agents running around with their cloak and dagger methods, but as long as we accomplish the goals of the Fatherland, I will do whatever is necessary to see our objectives are fulfilled...

He returned to his desk and continued sifting through the assorted communications and messages from the diplomatic pouch. He also made a mental note of how the volume of messages in the pouch had increased and how much harder he and his staff at the legation have worked since the war began.

Saturday, November 2, 1940
Café Chave d'Ouro
Dom Pedro IV Square
Rossio, Lisbon, Portugal

More than a week had passed since Martim Silva's last visit with Izaura Ribeiro and Pilar Coehlo at the *Café Chave d'Ouro* in Lisbon's Rossio. The place was as crowded as usual, but Silva had regained his favorite table on the Café's ground floor. Pilar received a message from Martim asking that the pair meet him that night. His message stated that he had good news.

Izaura saw him first and waved in his general direction. Martim Silva sat alone drinking his favorite Portuguese brandy called *aguardente* in a miniature snifter. He was taking a sip when the women arrived at his table. He smiled at Pilar and then at Izaura and motioned for them to sit down.

"What are you drinking, Martim?" asked Pilar. "I've never seen a glass like that."

Silva offered her a taste she eagerly accepted. A sip later and her face contorted in horror from the high alcohol content."

"That's terrible, Martim. What is it you are drinking?"

"It's called *aguardente*, my dear Pilar. It's sort of brandy made here in Portugal and it's what makes our great ports last so long. I like it by itself and this glass is called a snifter. You can roll the brandy in the glass and release its essence."

"It tastes quite awful if you ask me," Pilar offered.

"It's an acquired taste, Pilar. Brandy is usually enjoyed after a meal and helps with your digestion."

"I don't need that kind of help, Martim. Oooh!"

"Order what you want. Here comes the waiter."

"We will have two glasses of *Dão* white, please," Izaura directed.

"*Sim senhorita,*" the waiter responded.

The drinks arrived quickly and Martim turned toward Izaura. "I have been successful in finding some ladies to help you," he began. "These are all exceptional women and quite smart. I didn't go into what you want them to do, but they are eager to earn extra money in a way other than on their backs."

"So, who are they and where do they work?"

"Well, there are two ladies from the *Roterdão*, and one each from the *Jamaica* and the *Oslo*. I have arranged for them to meet you tomorrow so you can explain the arrangement. You must also tell them what you will pay them and it will always be in cash."

Izaura nodded her agreement and asked, "Where and at what time, Martim?"

"I picked a place where no one will notice. It's a park called *Jardim de Estrela*. It's a huge park and there are benches near the park's entrance and I told them to meet you at 10 o'clock. I think you will be able to pick them out quite easily and I have informed them of your appearance. Wear scarves, possibly tied, around your neck. I have also written down their names and their work places on this paper." He handed the paper to Izaura who looked down at it with great interest.

Sensing the information was complete, Izaura looked at Pilar and smiled. Pilar returned the smile and glanced at Martim. "You have done well, Martim. Our thanks to you."

Martim nodded knowingly and sipped the last of his *aguardente*. He glanced at Pilar who looked straight back at him with no hint of recognition of her promise.

After their glasses were empty, Izaura and Pilar got up to leave the *Café Chave d'Ouro*. Martim took Pilar's hand and squeezed it roughly. Pilar looked at him with a look of disbelief.

"You are hurting my hand, Martim. Let me go."

"You now owe me, Pilar. It's time we settle our debts."

"What are you talking about, Martim?"

Izaura noticed the exchange and came closer. "Is there a problem, Martim?"

"No, no problem. Pilar and I were merely discussing something."

"We have to go, Pilar. It's getting late."

"I am ready," Pilar answered. "You lead the way."

She turned to Martim and scowled, "I'll talk to you later."

Martim shrugged but said nothing. It was a strange ending to an eventful night.

Saturday, November 2, 1940
Cabinet War Rooms
Whitehull, Westminster
London, England

British Prime Minister Winston Churchill surveyed the plethora of messages and dispatches that crossed his desk daily and kept him abreast of the latest happenings within his country, the military, and the deadly war they were waging against the Nazis.

He paused a moment when he opened a *Most Secret* message from the Special Operations Executive Iberian Desk detailing the Bletchley Park intercept of a German *Enigma* message that concerned wolfram, a mineral with which he was thoroughly familiar and vitally important to any warring nation. He scribbled a note to himself and dialed his secretary's extension.

Grace Hamblin answered the phone and was met with a gruff, "Miss.." on the other end. She replaced the phone and rose to attend to the Prime Minister. She grabbed her notepad and gently knocked on the door of Churchill's office.

"Come," was the response and she quickly entered the room.

"Grace, I want you to take a special message. *Most Secret*, of course, to Philby at the SOE's Iberian Desk."

"Yes, Prime Minister," she replied. "Go ahead, I'm ready."

"Mr. Philby, your report on Portuguese wolfram caught my attention. I consider this to be of prime importance to our country and every effort to find more about this discovery should be made by your agents. I would expect ongoing reports on this matter as soon as anything develops on your end.

"Keep up the good work your people are doing. With your perseverance, we will eventually prevail in this woeful war."

He paused and added, "That's all for now, Grace. Thank you."

"Not at all, Prime Minister. I'll see to it at once."

Churchill returned to his pile of messages and puffed on his Romeo & Julieta and sipped a glass of Gonzalez Byass Amontillado sherry. He glanced at his watch and saw it was nearing midnight. He made the decision to sleep in the War Rooms instead of going back to Downing Street. He knew his work wasn't finished and didn't want to waste time walking home. He sipped the sherry again and returned to his reading. It was a typical night for the indomitable government leader. He also considered that he was currently unaware of what day of the week it was and didn't care...

Tuesday, November 5, 1940
Prime Minister's Office
Rear of São Bento Palace
Lisbon, Portugal

It was the German envoy to Portugal's second visit to the Prime Minister's office in less than a week, a fact that made the veteran Nazi diplomat uneasy. He had begun to feel his pleasant relationship with Portugal's de facto leader had slipped in recent weeks and that made him apprehensive since he had worked for several years to bring trust and practicality to his role as envoy.

Baron Oswald von Hoyningen-Huene had wrestled with his intended approach to Prime Minister Salazar since receiving Minister Todt's instructions in Berlin to seek Portugal's permission to increase his country's orders for more wolfram. Before leaving his legation, he checked to ensure all German payments for wolfram were current so there could be no financial problems if his country's desire for more wolfram was approved. Still, he was apprehensive as he waited for Prime Minister Salazar to see him into his office.

Fifteen minutes later, Salazar's assistant stepped out of the Prime Minister's office and beckoned to von Hoyningen-Huene to enter Dr. Salazar's office. The Prime Minister stood and greeted the German diplomat with a warm smile and handshake.

"Nice to see you so soon after your last visit," Salazar reminded the German. "I hope this time our conversation will be more cordial."

Von Hoyningen-Huene paused and nodded his agreement. *He is making the point to me again and this time with a smile on his face. Damn those Abwehr people for messing up my relationship with this man.*

Salazar pointed to the divan and the pair sat down and faced each other.

"What can I do for you, Baron? I'm sure it must be important that you asked for this audience on such short notice."

"Yes, Prime Minister, the matter does possess a degree of urgency." *I must choose my words carefully or this might blow up in my face.* "As you are aware, my country has experienced a number of successful military operations and things are going quite as we have expected. Our *Wehrmacht* has expended a great deal of its munitions in doing so and our experts have forecast a need to increase our munitions production in the near future. Obviously, we will need more wolfram to fulfill those needs and your country is our most dependable supplier."

Salazar observed the veteran diplomat as he shifted slightly on the couch.

"We would like to increase our wolfram purchases as soon as possible. We are aware that wolfram has increased in value during the past year. We are prepared to pay a reasonable increase for the material. It's a simple matter, one of commerce and not political at all."

Salazar smiled and considered his reply.

In the eyes of Germany, nothing is purely political when, in fact, everything they do is political. This is a strange request but one that is not totally unrealistic. They are doing quite well from a military standpoint, at least that's what the papers say. I must be careful here; Great Britain will not look kindly to our country increasing their enemy's wolfram supplies. Now I know why Germany has been busy buying up all of my country's escudos for the past year. It is good that we only accept our own escudos for payment on the wolfram, it has been an economic boon for our country.

The Prime Minister finally addressed his visitor. "Baron, I consider your request a bit unusual. Your economists are always very adept at forecasting Germany's needs and supplies. Since we are a neutral country, I know you are aware that if your request is approved, it will be necessary to offer additional wolfram to the British as well."

Von Hoyningen-Huene nodded his understanding of the situation. *Of course, I would expect nothing less. As long as we get our wolfram, the fact that the British can also get additional wolfram is of little consequence.*

"Then, there is the job of increasing production in the mines. We are running at near capacity. I will have to check with my engineers to make sure they are in a position to increase production."

"When will you let me know, Prime Minister?" von Hoyningen-Huene inserted.

"It shouldn't take too long, Baron. If the British don't object and agree to increase their own allotment of wolfram, I can have an answer for you in a matter of days."

Much relieved with the flow of the meeting, the German envoy rose and offered his hand.

"Thank you, Prime Minister. I know you will do what you can."

"Don't thank me yet, Baron. This is not a completed deal and should not be viewed as such."

"Certainly, Prime Minister. I did not mean to interpret it any other way."

"Good. We are in agreement then."

Von Hoyningen-Huene was about to add *Heil Hitler* but stopped himself. "Thank you for your time. It is always a pleasure to talk with you."

"I feel the same, Baron."

The German envoy turned and walked toward the door. He was barely able to conceal his smile. The meeting had gone better than he expected. He must hurry back to the embassy and notify Berlin of his efforts.

Chapter Eight

Tuesday, November 19, 1940
Special Operations Executive
Iberian Desk
64 Baker Street, Westminster
London, England

The message from his Prime Minister immediately grasped the attention of the SOE's Iberian Desk's chief, Kim Philby. It was the first message Philby had directly received from him and Philby was eager to please the man in charge of Great Britain's security and well-being.

By coincidence, he was aware of the visit in London of David Eccles, another diplomat who was currently economic advisor to British ambassadors in both Lisbon and Madrid. Within the intelligence networks, Eccles was considered a most knowledgeable person in matters of Iberian commerce and had previously worked for the Central Mining Company in London and South Africa.

Philby summoned Eccles to the SOE's offices and brought him up to date on the Portuguese wolfram scenario.

After hearing details of the situation, Eccles offered his opinion on what action should be taken.

"It is obviously of great importance," he began. "Good thing the Jerries aren't aware of our *Enigma* intercepts or we would never have known about it. This chap, Dr. Schoenfeld, must be onto something big or Berlin would never have made any reference to it. He's probably figured out a way to increase wolfram's usage and that could be a problem for us."

"What can we do about it, David?" questioned Philby. "I've already alerted our man in Lisbon, Jack Beevor, to find out all he can. But, realistically, I expect it might take some time for him to come up with something."

"I know Jack Beevor, he's a good man with a good head on him. He'll get some results and I would hope sooner than later."

"Would it be possible for you to stop in Lisbon on your way back to Madrid and meet with him?"

"Certainly, my dear fellow," replied Eccles, "happy to oblige."

"Good. After your meeting get back to me on any plan you might develop. The PM seems keen on the matter and I must keep him informed."

"Of course, Kim. I'll give the matter my direct attention. I have business here for several days, but I should be in Lisbon by this weekend."

"Sounds good, David. I won't take up any more of your time."

The two shook hands and Eccles departed the office. Philby knew that David Eccles would provide a steady hand in Lisbon and was sure Jack Beevor would appreciate the help.

Wednesday, November 20, 1940
Jardim de Estrela
Barrio Alto
Lisbon, Portugal

The November morning was dry and crisp, a relative rarity for usually humid Lisbon. Izaura Ribeiro and Pilar Coehlo arrived at the lovely park named Jardim de Estrela early and easily located the benches near the park's entrance.

"I wonder what they will be like," commented Pilar. "I've never talked to or been close to any of these ladies."

"I would think they are just like everyone else, Pilar. They have probably led a hard life and have been forced into their profession.

I wouldn't expect them to be beautiful but I would imagine they are quite attractive."

"Yes, they come from the three finest houses in Lisbon, Izaura. I checked with a couple of men at the embassy."

"Good, then maybe we will be successful."

As the two friends talked, a single female approached the benches. She was a redhead, nearly full figured, and dressed in a soft print smock that covered her ample shape. As she approached the bench where Izaura and Pilar were sitting she asked in a pleasant voice, "Which of you two is Izaura?"

Izaura gestured with her hand and replied, "I'm Izaura. And who are you?"

"My name is Rosita, and I work at the Oslo."

"It's nice to meet you. This is my friend, Pilar," she said.

"Nice to meet you," Pilar responded, holding out her hand.

Rosita took the hand and replied, "Thank you both. I am happy to be here."

"We will wait for the others," Izaura said looking at the entrance to the park.

Three more young women approached the bench with apprehensive looks on their faces.

Izaura stepped forward and spoke. "I'm Izaura, the person Martin told you about. I am pleased that you decided to meet with me. This is my friend, Pilar, who works with me. Can I ask your names?"

One attractive woman of about thirty with raven black hair was the first to speak. "My name is Louisa and I work at Jamaica. These other two are cousins, Manuela and Lotto, and they work at *Roterdãv.*"

"Nice to meet you, ladies. You are as attractive as Martim said. "He believes you are also smart. That will help you with what we want you to do."

"Martim said you will pay well for our help," injected Rosita. "That's all I care about."

"Martim was correct. I will pay you for any information you are able to give me that proves to be accurate and timely. My government is interested in finding out what the Germans in Portugal are doing and what information they are sending to Berlin. This information might be about shipping, the German military or anything you think might be useful to us. We will decide on how good your information is and pay you accordingly."

"I already work for the Germans about shipping and sailors," confessed Manuela. "They don't pay us very well and we make up stories to get our money."

Izaura suppressed a smile and replied, "You can also work for us, Manuela, as long as you don't tell the Germans. If we find out you betrayed us, your services will be terminated. And, don't make up any stories for us, we're not stupid."

The four women looked at each other, but said nothing.

"To prove our good intentions, I will give each of you 2500 *escudos* to begin our relationship. The money is yours to keep. We will use a system of getting messages to me that utilizes a flower shop at the end of the *Rua Novo do Carvalho*. The shop is called *Margaridas*. Do you all know it?"

The women all shook their heads in agreement and Izaura continued. "This job is not to be disclosed under any circumstance. If you compromise the job, the PVDE will be notified and will take action. Is that clear?"

Again, the women nodded their concurrence.

"When do we start?" Manuela asked. "Tonight?"

"Yes, Manuela. By all means. I might add that if anyone gives some really valuable information, a nice bonus will be added. A really nice bonus."

"Enough to allow us to give up our profession?" probed Louisa cautiously.

"Quite possibly, Louisa. It would depend on the information you provide."

"How do we get the information to you?" Rosita questioned.

"Just write a note and put it into a sealed envelope and mark the outside with a big X. Hand it to the flower lady and she will see I get it."

"Sounds simple," Rosita added. "I'll start tonight."

"Excellent. This sounds promising. I will await your results. We will not meet again unless it is necessary. I will let Martin know if I need to talk to you."

The four ladies stepped forward as Izaura handed each a stack of escudos that were neatly tied together. No one bothered to count the bills, a trait they had learned in their profession.

The four said goodbyes to Izaura and Pilar and departed for the park's entrance. Izaura turned to Pilar and exclaimed, "That went awfully well, don't you think?"

"I'll wait and see, my dear friend. These are not your normal women and have different standards than we do. I want some results before I proclaim this a success."

"If even one of them provides us with useful information, I think it will be a success. Of the four, which one impressed you the most?"

Pilar thought for a moment and replied, "Louisa. She didn't say much but she was certainly the prettiest and best spoken."

Izaura nodded to her friend and the pair walked toward the park's entrance. In her mind, Izaura had fulfilled the need for agents within the bordellos of Lisbon. It would not be easy to wait on the results...

Monday, November 25, 1940
Testing Laboratory
Rua Padre Manuel Vaz Leal 2
Barroca Grande
Covilha, Portugal

His return flight to Portugal was anything but pleasant for Dr. Gerhardt Schoenfeld. His trip to Berlin was extended for several days when his superiors discovered errors in his calculations and experiments. He was told by the head of Germany's Ministry of Armament and War Production, Dr. Fritz Todt, that while his theory was excellent and close to fruition, it still needed additional input before it could be implemented. He was directed to return to Portugal and work out the problems as soon as possible.

His flight back was on a converted Heinkel HE 111 with improvised seating and no toilet facilities. The flight was intended for Spain but diverted to Lisbon to drop off Schoenfeld. It was a bumpy ride and the German scientist felt completely shaken when it was finally over.

He decided to forgo a stopover in Lisbon and head for his laboratory in *Barroca Grande* where he could get some much-needed sleep and return to work. The idea of seeing Louisa was inviting to the middle-aged German, but he realized he was in no shape for a strenuous evening with the Portuguese beauty at this time. Schoenfeld finally arrived at the small building that held his work area and addressed his assistant, Hans Pfeffer, in a disappointed tone.

"Hans, the Berlin people decided there must be additional work on our end before mass production can begin. Dr. Todt feels we are close to a solution, but my theory must be fine-tuned. I am too tired to start today but tomorrow we must begin early and work until it is completed. This shouldn't take more than a few days, a week at most. Please get out all the records on the studies we have conducted and all my notes on the formula. Review everything and see if you can find any flaws. We will talk in the morning, but I must get some sleep right now. I have just been on the flight from hell and I cannot concentrate on anything."

"Don't worry, Herr Doctor. I will have everything in order for tomorrow morning. Go and get a good night's sleep. You will feel much better when you wake up."

"Thank you, Hans. It is good to be back here."

"Glad to have you back, Herr Doctor. The Fatherland will be proud of our work, I'm sure of it."

Schoenfeld smiled and patted Pfeffer on the shoulder. He walked directly to the cot that was set up inside the lab. He fell immediately into a deep, deep sleep.

Tuesday, December 3, 1940
German Envoy's Office
Campo dos Mártires da Pátria 38
Lisbon, Portugal

The letter he was expecting from Portugal's Prime Minister finally arrived at the offices of Germany's ligation in Lisbon. Baron Oswald von Heyningen-Huene carefully opened the neatly typed letter that bore the official seal of Portugal. It read:

To: The Honorable Envoy of Germany
      German Ligation
      Campo dos Mártires da Pátria 38
      Lisbon

After conferring with my minister of commerce, the decision has been made to allow your country to increase its purchase of wolfram ore by approximately 50%.
This increase will be in effect on January 1, 1941 and must be paid in Portuguese Escudos on the date of shipment as per our ongoing allotments of wolfram.
I trust this decision will allow your country to utilize the mineral at its convenience.

Neutrally yours,
Dr. António de Oliveira Salazar

The veteran diplomat studied the letter and a broad smile engulfed his face. His best estimate of what Portugal would give his country had been around a 50% increase and that figure was doubled by Prime Minister Salazar's letter. This was indeed a red-letter day for the fatherland and Baron Oswald von Hoyningen-Heune was eager to share the news with his superiors in Berlin.

He pushed a button on his desk that summoned his secretary. When she arrived, he excitedly shared the good news.

"This letter is excellent news for our country and must be sent to Berlin as quickly as possible. We should use the Enigma machine. That would ensure the message reaches Berlin in a matter of minutes. You can forward the letter in the diplomatic pouch tomorrow, but I want our superiors in Berlin to receive the update as soon as possible."

"I will see to it, Herr Envoy. It will be a pleasure."

"Excellent. There is a bottle of peach schnapps in that cabinet," he gestured toward a large armoire with folded doors. "I will have a toast to our Fatherland and I want you to join me."

The secretary smiled broadly and uttered, "By all means, Herr Envoy. I will get some glasses."

"They are right behind the schnapps. I keep them for special occasions."

"This is indeed a special occasion," she answered. "I am honored to toast with you."

The envoy poured two glasses and raised his glass. "To the Fatherland."

"To the Fatherland. *Heil Hitler.*"

"*Heil Hitler,*" echoed the diplomat. He finished the drink and found the expressive flavor much to his liking. "I'll have another," he announced.

"Me too, if it is all right."

"Certainly," he replied, pouring each another glass.

Tuesday, December 3, 1940
British Ligation
Rua São Francisco Borja 63
Lapa, Lisbon, Portugal

SOE Lisbon chief Jack Beevor was directed to the British ligation in Lisbon's Lapa District for a meeting with an undisclosed visitor. He arrived on time and went to the room that served as the Board Room for the embassy. As he stepped into the room, he observed a tall figure standing next to a large picture window that overlooked the embassy's ornate garden.

As the door shut behind Beevor, the figure turned and addressed him.

"Goodness, old boy, you haven't changed a bit since you left England. Not even a glorious sunburn to mark your locale."

"David, what in the hell are you doing here?" Beevor responded.

The two shook hands warmly and David Eccles gestured for Beevor to have a seat in one of the comfortable chairs arranged around a large mahogany table.

Beevor pulled a chair and sat down. "So why do I have the honor of your presence, David? Are you slumming or what?"

"No. quite the opposite, my old friend. It seems you have become something of a celebrity around the SOE due to the wolfram thing. Kim Philby called me in and said my mining experience might be of help to you. He directed me to stop over here on my way to Madrid and feel you out. It's as simple as that."

"We are working on it at this moment, but we have very little to go on. I'm trying to locate the doctor but he's nowhere to be found. I sent one of my agents to the area around the wolfram mines to poke around, but he just left a day ago and I haven't heard back from him."

"Is there anyone inside the German ligation who might shed some light on this? Eccles asked candidly. "I'm sure they have someone spying on our people."

"Not to my knowledge. I spoke with the ambassador when this first came up but he was no help. I'm not sure he completely approves of the likes of us. The old-fashioned diplomats prefer direct contact with the enemy. They would work out everything with words."

"The word is he's about to be retired and replaced," Eccles added. "The new guy is Sir Ronald Campbell from what I've heard."

"No one around here knows about it. How did you find out?"

"I have my ways, dear boy. At times they come in quite handy if you know what I mean."

"You are an interesting person, David. I'm glad you're my friend and not my enemy."

"No worries, old boy. We've known each other since before you entered the SOE and you've always been straightforward with me. That's all that counts."

"So, what up with this wolfram cockup?"

"It's become a top priority from what I've heard. Even the PM is into it and that puts it near the top of the list."

"Interesting. Now I see why all the fuss."

"Any improvement in the use of wolfram is incredibly serious, Jack. That's why everyone is so interested. The Germans and their weapons are deadly enough already, but improved munitions are another matter. As long as our technology is as good or as equal to theirs, then the playing field is level. When one becomes superior to the other, well, that really changes things."

"I'll put everything at my disposal toward finding the person, you can assure London of that," Beevor asserted. "That area in the mountains is sparsely populated so that sort of person would stand out, wouldn't he?"

"Not if he wants to remain invisible, old boy. If I were him, I wouldn't show my face outside unless absolutely necessary."

"I see what you mean."

"Let's see what your agent uncovers, Jack. He might get lucky and locate him right away."

"And what if he doesn't? What do I do then?"

"Then, my dear friend, Plan B goes into effect."

"Plan B? I am not aware of a Plan B."

"Neither am I, Jack. Let's hope it doesn't come down to that. Unfortunately, I must return to Madrid tomorrow and resume my duties. You can update me there on your progress."

For the first time in his career with the SOE, Jack Beevor felt a chill down his back. He suddenly realized it was an unwelcome feeling.

Thursday, December 12, 1940
Izaura's Ribeiro's Flat
Rua Rodrigo da Fonseca 70
Lisbon, Portugal

With the help of her uncle João, Izaura had been able to rent a small upstairs flat on a street not far from the imposing statue of the *Marques de Pombal* at the end of the *Avenue da Liberdade*. The flat on *Rua Rodrigo da Fonseca* was small and clean and, in Izaura's mind, met her needs perfectly.

She had just returned from a visit to *Margaridas* flower shop where she picked up her first messages. There were three messages, one from Rosita, another from one of the cousins and the final note from Louisa.

She read Rosita's first, a crudely written note about a Norwegian ship's officer detailing a voyage he was making. She finished and placed the paper on a small desk she had obtained from her landlady. The second message was almost unreadable and mentioned a sailor off another ship whose name Izaura couldn't decipher with a mention of Gibraltar.

Finally, she opened Louisa's message. In a clear and slightly bent form, Louisa asked Izaura to meet her back at the benches in the *Jardim da Estrela* at noon on Saturday.

Izaura gasped. Today was Saturday, and it was almost noon. She would be lucky to make it on time and decided to hail a taxi for the trip.

She arrived at the park's entrance as the bells on the nearby *Basilica de Estrela* rang to signal twelve o'clock. She walked toward the benches and saw Louisa sitting on the same bench she had used for their first meeting. Izaura extended her hand to Louisa and greeted the woman. "Thank you for the note, Louisa. I hope I haven't kept you waiting."

"Not at all," Louisa replied. "In fact, you are right on time. I came early to enjoy the park. It's always so peaceful here, not to mention its beauty. It's one of my favorite places to visit."

"Mine, too. I started coming here to study when I was in university and I always managed to get done what I needed."

"I sometimes sit here and think about the world around me," confessed Louisa. "Particularly when things aren't going so well for me."

"We all have our special place," agreed Izaura.

"I have been thinking that I might have something really important for you," Louisa began. "I thought of telling you at our first meeting but I decided to wait."

Izaura listened closely as the attractive woman continued. "I have this customer who had been coming to see me for the past several months. He's a fairly attractive man in his mid-40's and he seems very lonely. He treats me quite well and pays me double of what my other customers pay. I believe he is German but his Portuguese is very limited. We don't talk much but I think he has developed a real fondness for me. We have never talked about his work but he mentioned the mountains once and I know he doesn't live in Lisbon. He seems to be very dedicated to his job and he travels some for it."

"Travels?" What sort of travel?"

"For instance, he is on a trip right now. He told me it would only be a matter of days but it has become a matter of weeks since I've seen him. I know he would visit me if he was back in Lisbon. He made a point of telling me that when I last saw him."

"Has he ever told you his name?"

"Not really. I always call him, *Meu Amor.* I call all my customers that."

Izaura smiled and Louisa returned the smile.

"You might well be onto something, Louisa. But we need to find out who this person is and what his job is. You can't be too direct in asking, but this will decide his value to us. Do you expect him to return in the near future?"

"As I said, he was only supposed to be away for a few days. If he's gone too much longer, I'll start to worry. He pays me well, and the extra money has been nice for me."

"You must wait for him to reappear, and you must remember not to be too interested in his name or work," Izaura reminded.

"Don't worry about me, I understand the need for patience and discretion."

"Good. I'll check with the flower lady every day in case he comes back soon."

"Fine with me. I'll let you know as soon as he appears."

Another thought suddenly materialized in Izaura's mind. "Is it at all possible that you can have a picture taken of you two, or maybe he has a picture of himself he can leave with you? Either would be a great help."

Louisa thought for a moment and replied, "I'll work on that. It's a bit unusual but I'll try."

"Great, Louisa. It would really help."

"Okay, I'll see you later."

"Bye."

Izaura watched as the woman turned and walked to the park entrance.

She is an incredible person to do what she does. I would never have expected her to be so poised. I wonder how she happened to get into her line of work. It would probably make an interesting story...

Friday, December 13, 1940
Special Operations Executive
Iberian Desk
64 Baker Street, Westminster
London, England

Kim Philby was delighted to see another *Enigma* intercept reach his desk from the lads and ladies at Bletchley Park. Less than one hour had passed since Baron Oswald von Heyningen-Heune, had sent the encrypted message to his offices in Berlin.

Philby thought to himself.

This entire scheme for lifting Germany's most secret messages is giving us a huge advantage over the Jerries. If they never find out we have all their Enigma messages, we will probably win the war. It's quite nice when your enemy lets you know their plans and what they are thinking about the future. Those Polish chaps who first broke the codes deserve most of the credit and have paid Germany back for invading their country. All's fair in war, isn't that the saying?

Philby reread the message and made arrangements to have it sent to Jack Beevor in Lisbon.

Beevor might just be heading into one of the more important situations of the entire war, and he probably doesn't even know it. And, when you realize this posting is his first real job for the SOE, it makes everything quite incredible. I hope David Eccles was able to be of some assistance to Beevor, I really do.

The Iberian desk chief then reached for a secret file he maintained in a small space between his desk and a filing cabinet. He made some notes on a piece of paper and placed them in the file. When the time was right, he would transfer them to another person in the service of the Russian Communist Party as he had been doing since his days as a student at Cambridge University. He was quite content with what he was doing and quite sure he would never be exposed or caught.

A knock on his door signaled a visitor. Philby carefully placed the folder in its hiding space and spoke in a controlled voice, "Come in."

Saturday, December 14, 1940
Testing Laboratory
Rua Padre Manuel Vaz Leal 2
Barroca Grande
Covilha, Portugal

Time since his return passed slowly for Dr. Gerhardt Schoenfeld. Work on his formula was not progressing as quickly as he expected and the sheer boredom and remoteness of his laboratory in Barroca Grande was getting on his nerves. He found himself becoming short with his assistant and he even forced himself to take long walks outside the building to calm himself.

This is totally stupid, he thought as he walked. *I'm a scientist and should be used to minor problems. I've always kept working until I find a solution, no matter how long it takes. Patience is the best friend of a true scientist and I've always adhered to that premise. I must remember to apologize to Hans when I get back from this walk, I was a bit too hard on him this afternoon. He's a good worker and an able assistant. I wonder what is causing me to feel like this...*

His thoughts continued to wonder until he approached a stream that ran along the pathway he was using. As he gazed toward the far bank, a young couple came into view, seated on a blue blanket and embraced in an ardent kiss. Schoenfeld stood still for a moment, contemplating the scene.

Suddenly, the German scientist realized what was wrong with his own world.

My god, he reasoned. *That's probably the reason I've been feeling so blue. It's so utterly simple and right before my eyes. I need to go to Lisbon and see Louisa. I should have stopped and seen her on my way back from Berlin, but I was so tired and the flight was so horrible. She would have lifted my spirits as she has done in the past. She is good for me, and I want to be good for her.*

He turned and began to retrace his steps back toward Barroca Grande and his laboratory. He felt enthused for the first time in days and felt his pace quicken through the rough woods.

Back at the stream the young couple continued their long embrace. They were oblivious to the fact that their simple embrace had produced such a perverted effect on a stranger out for a walk. People in love are seldomly aware that their actions easily affect others, usually in a most provocative manner.

Chapter Nine

Monday, December 16, 1940
Jack Beevor's Flat
Rua de São Miguel 155
Alfama, Lisbon Portugal

One of Jack Beevor's other SOE operatives returned from a trip to the area around Portugal's wolfram mining operations and was explaining what he had learned to him at Beevor's flat in Lisbon's *Alfama* District.

The man was cautiously optimistic about his findings. "I could find no real proof of any laboratory or of any Germans operating in the area," he reported. "The place is sparsely populated and everyone seems to know everyone else. They were hesitant to talk to me even when I offered them money or cigarettes for their time."

"Probably keep to themselves," Beevor interjected. "If I were them, I'd be seen as little as possible around the town."

"I agree, Jack. I did happen upon something that was a bit strange, but perhaps it means nothing."

"And what is that?"

"A merchant at the town's only store reported that one of his customers, a European he believed, came in and ordered some schnapps. Since schnapps isn't something the store usually carries, the merchant had to order it from Lisbon. The fellow ordered a full case of the schnapps and paid for it on the spot. A week later, he returned to the store and picked up the schnapps."

"Did you manage to get a description of the man?" asked Beevor.

"Not really," the agent answered. "The merchant remembered he was definitely not Portuguese and that he had a pronounced accent when speaking. I asked his age and the fellow said around 30 or so. He was also short and slightly overweight."

"It's definitely not Dr. Schoenfeld," Beevor declared. "Too young and too short."

"Perhaps he has an assistant? Another German?"

"Possibly. His work might easily require an assistant."

"Where does that leave us? Doesn't seem we've discovered anything concrete yet."

Beevor thought for a moment and decided on a plan. "I want you to go back up there and fish around again. There can't be more than a dozen or so buildings that could house a laboratory so I want all those places checked out. I also want you to see where the people from the area catch the buses for Lisbon. If Schoenfeld or the assistant, providing there is an assistant, catches a bus, we might have a starting point."

The agent nodded and prepared to depart. "Oh yes, I want you to take a day off and relax. Your journey north can stand a day's delay."

"The agent smiled and acknowledged the offer with a smile. "Thank you, Jack. I'm a bit tired from it all."

Beevor took the man's hand and gave it a shake. "Get back to me right away if you come up with anything."

Again, the agent shook his head and started for the door of the flat. The door closed quietly as the man departed.

Beevor quietly considered the situation. *Wouldn't it be just peachy if we discovered Schoenfeld's location due to a case of schnapps? Stranger things have happened, I'm sure, but not to me. We'll need some breaks to be able to cash in on all this, but it's not too much to hope for. Eccles told me to be on the lookout for anything unusual, and a case of schnapps out in the wilderness is certainly out of the ordinary. We'll just wait and see...*

Saturday, December 14, 1940
Café Chave d'Ouro
Dom Pedro IV Square
Rossio, Lisbon, Portugal

After her last unpleasant encounter with Martim Flores, Pilar Coehlo was hesitant about meeting him alone. Meeting him in a public place with lots of people was her only recourse. The Café Chave d' Ouro was perfect.

She spied Martim at his usual table and walked toward him. Martim watched saw her approach but did not rise to greet her.

"Hello, Martim. You asked to see me."

"Yes, Pilar. We need to get something straight between us."

"Us? There is no us, Martim."

"Quite the contrary, Pilar. We have become quite close in the past few months. And, after all I've done for you, I..."

"We are supposed to be friends, Martim. Just friends. Understand?"

"That's not what I had in mind, my dear. Do you think I would go to all the trouble I have on your behalf for just a friend? You are very naïve."

"I am disappointed in you, Martim. You take too many things for granted."

"I expect to be paid for my services. Nothing in life is for free."

"You are being difficult, Martim. I don't want to stay here any longer."

"You are free to leave, Pilar. Just remember this when you need help in the future."

Pilar rose abruptly and left the table.

Martim raised his glass of *aguardente* and took a sip. He was determined not to let the incident ruin his evening.

Wednesday, December 18, 1940
Special Room
Jamaica Bar
Rua Nova do Carvalho 6 – 8
Lisbon, Portugal

Madame Estella was the functioning head of nightly activities for the Jamaica Bar and Louisa Flores was her star attraction. When the call arrived from Dr. Gerhardt Schoenfeld for a reservation with the aforementioned Miss Flores for tonight, the clever woman happily pulled out all stops in preparation for his visit. Of course, the Jamaica bar's special room was selected for the couple's important reunion.

Fresh flowers were secured from nearby *Margaridas* located across the street and a bottle of Bollinger Brut 1934 was secured from a nearby wine merchant and pre-iced for exactly half an hour before the guest was scheduled to arrive. The bed linen was new and a light floral scent was added at the last minute.

Satisfied everything was in order, Madame Estella turned and faced Louisa.

"I'm sure everything is in order, my dear Louisa. I trust your man will be suitably impressed."

"He usually is, Madame. I don't believe he had ever been to a place like ours before he came here and he's told me he'll never go to another place like Jamaica Bar."

"That's nice, Louisa, but remember men tend to be very fickle and not mean what they say at the time. Later on, they conveniently forget their promises when someone new appears. I have learned that over the years and tell you this because you so dear to me."

"I understand, Madame. Remember, I'm no newcomer to this business. I know what I want and I know how to get it," she said in a calm manner.

"That's all well and good, Louisa. You have a good head on your shoulders and a great body that will age quite nicely. You are unlike the other girls here whose careers are cut short by their looks. You will be able to stay in this business as long as you wish. Maybe one day you will take my place."

Louisa hesitated a moment and replied. "What if I don't intend to stay in this business much longer?"

As the quizzical look on Madame Estella's face flashed before her, Louisa realized her question caught her boss off guard.

"Are you thinking of quitting, Louisa? Maybe getting married? Something like that?"

"Louisa smiled and answered. "No, Madame. No marriage plans or anything. I just know that I am destined for something grander than laying on my back each night and telling my customers lies they want to hear."

It was Madame Estella's turn to smile. "You are a smart lady, Louisa. You always seem to know the right thing to do. I envy you that ability."

"You don't do so badly in that respect, Madame. You are excellent at your job and all the ladies enjoy and respect you. Not many women in similar positions can say that in earnest."

Madame Estella blushed at the compliment.

"Thank you, Louisa. Your opinion means a lot."

The conversation was interrupted as a maid named Ouzie entered the room. She shook her head anxiously at Madame Estella and waited for a response.

"Your friend is here, Louisa. I told Ouzie to let me know the second he arrived.

Louisa made a final check of the room and its surroundings. Satisfied, she signaled to Ouzie.

"You can bring him up now. Everything is quite lovely."

It was several hours later and the evening had developed as both parties expected. For his part, Dr. Gerhardt Schoenfeld experienced an evening unlike any he had previously felt, and lay next to Louisa, fully spent and near sleep.

Louisa rolled over and gently stroked his arm. Schoenfeld responded with a light murmur but remained silent.

"Are you awake, my love," Louisa asked softly, her voice barely audible.

After a moment, the doctor responded, "I guess so, but I may be dreaming."

Louisa suppressed a giggle, "Did you use up all your energy, my love? There's still a lot of time left in the night and we can play some more."

Schoenfeld hesitated before weakly replying. "I don't think so, my love. I'm nearly exhausted."

Again, Louisa curbed a smile and waited for a short period.

"Is it all right for us to talk then?"

The German scientist hesitated and finally responded. "If you really want to. You don't seem to want to go to sleep."

"I never want to sleep around you, my love. But we seldomly talk and you know how much I enjoy talking. It actually breaks the boredom around here."

"Boredom? I would never have expected that from you," answered Schoenfeld. "How can you be bored in a place like this?"

"You would be surprised, my love. Same thing night after night. It gets to be monotonous after a while."

"If you put it that way, it makes sense to me. I never considered it from your point of view."

"Not all the ladies feel that way. Many don't even think about it. They go about their duties and only think about the money they are paid. They believe they have a simple life."

Gerhardt Schoenfeld was now wide awake and Louisa decided to make the most of it. "You are different from other men," she began. "You are kind and extremely generous. But..."

"But what, Louisa?"

Louisa hesitated and feigned searching for an answer.

Schoenfeld asked again, "What does *but* mean?"

Again, she hesitated and dropped her head. "It's just that..."

"What is it, Louisa?" he repeated, becoming annoyed.

"I just don't know anything about you, my love. We meet here at your convenience and enjoy each other's company, but that's all. I don't even know your name or anything about you. I don't know what business you are in, only that you seem to have a great deal of money."

"Is this about money? If so..."

"It's not about money," she interrupted. "It's about knowing the other person. You know I have feelings for you or at least you *should* know."

Schoenfeld caressed her hand and replied softly, "Sorry, Louisa. I didn't mean to..."

Louisa took the occasion to stand up and put on a sheer green robe. She walked away from the bed and lit a cigarette. She turned to her guest and offered him one but Schoenfeld declined.

"There comes a time when two people should know about each other," declared Louisa in a resolute voice. "And for us, the time has come."

Schoenfeld dropped his gaze and considered the situation.

She is right, of course. I haven't been really honest with her due to the secrecy involved with my work. The Abwehr were very specific about letting anyone know anything about my work and told me what would happen if I broke the rules. But this is Louisa, and I am quite fond of her. Shit, I'm probably in love with her if I am truthful with myself. I can't see what telling her a little about myself would hurt, whom could she possibly tell?

He lifted his head and caught Louisa's eyes. "You are right. I haven't told you anything about myself for a specific reason."

"And what would that specific reason be?" *He's about to tell me everything but I'd better be smart about this and not push him too much.*

"Well," he began slowly, "I'm not sure where to start."

"You can start with your name, my love. Is that okay?"

"Schoenfeld hesitated but gave in. "I am Gerhardt Schoenfeld, a doctor in physics."

"A doctor, really? And what is *physics*, I don't know."

"Physics is the study of energy and matter and time and how the three are related to each other. My particular field is minerals and their usage."

"I don't understand," Louisa, offering a look of frustration on her face.

"I study rocks and soils and how they can be put to better use," Schoenfeld offered, hoping to alleviate the situation. "I am in the service of my country in developing new usages for certain types of rocks."

"Rocks?" Louisa replied. "That doesn't make sense to me. What would your country want with Portuguese rocks? It's very confusing."

Schoenfeld fought for a way to explain what he was doing without disclosing the sensitive nature of his work. He tried again. "Let's say that some rocks have certain properties that make them useful to scientists like me who want to make better weapons for their countries to use."

"Weapons? I don't understand. You men you make guns?"

"Not exactly," the German hedged.

"What then?" Louisa pressed him. I don't see what you are talking about."

Schoenfeld was nearing total frustration and finally blurted out. "It's not the guns, it's what comes out of the guns. Bullets and shells and the like."

Louisa realized she had accomplished what she wanted and decided to back off. "It doesn't make any sense to me at all."

"You mustn't feel that way, Louisa. Just know I'm just a scientist working for my country and its interests."

"And what country is that. You still haven't told me."

He thought again. *Should I tell her everything? I've already gone and said too much. If the Abwehr ever finds out, I'm really in trouble. I wonder what they would do to me? Probably send me back to Germany. Then I'd never see Louisa again...*

"Germany, Louisa. Germany."

Louisa's head dropped and she hesitated. After a moment she replied, "Ah, Germany. I should have suspected so from your accent. Thank you, Gerhart, I feel I know you much better now."

"I hope so, my love. I'm not sure why you needed to know, but I feel we are closer now than before."

"Yes, my love, we certainly are."

Louisa thought for a moment and remembered the fact that Izaura had requested a picture of her lover. She turned to Schoenfeld and touched his cheek and asked demurely, "It is also possible that we can have our picture taken together? It would be a wonderful keepsake and would always remind us of this perfect night together? Please Gerhardt, I would love our picture together."

Schoenfeld considered her request and thought to himself. *I've already told her about my work and myself. What further harm would a picture do? I might as well just give in. She is so lovely and I've never felt this way about anyone in the past.*

"Certainly, Louisa. We can have it taken in the morning after we get up."

"Thank you, my love. We will be beautiful together."

"But Louisa, I am also extremely tired and need to get some sleep. Will you stay with me until morning?"

"Of course, I will. When you awake, I'll make sure that Ouzie brings us a nice breakfast like she always does. Let's go to sleep now, I am quite tired myself."

They lay down and Louisa draped her arm over Schoenfeld's shoulder and snuggled against him. In minutes, they were fast asleep.

Saturday, December 21, 1940
Secret Meeting Place
Portuguese Communist Party
Alfama, Lisbon, Portugal

The location of Portugal's clandestine Communist Party was a carefully guarded secret. It was changed whenever the need arose, frequently on the day of the scheduled meeting. Since its existence was outlawed by the ruling *Estado Novo* in the mid 1930's, the Portuguese Communist Party or, PCP, conducted its affairs behind closed doors with utmost secrecy. Even though it was popular among Portugal's lower working classes, the PCP had dwindled to its lowest number of members since its founding in March of 1921.

One of the current leaders, Júlio de Melo Fogaça, was intent on bringing the organization back to a level of respect and importance it formerly enjoyed. Fogaça was finally allowed back in Portugal after his release from the infamous *Tarrafal* concentration camp in the Cape Verde Islands after serving a five-year sentence for actions against the Portuguese government. Upon arrival in Lisbon, he immediately contacted his former PCP cadres, Álvaro Cunhal and Militão Ribeiro. The trio began the immediate reorganization of the PCP as an active force in Portugal's neutral-standing political environment.

The small gathering in a secret location owned by one of the PCP members in Lisbon's Alfama District was in full bore as Fogaça continued speaking.

"...that makes a difference. For our glorious PCP to regain its reputation and standing within our country it will be necessary for each of us to make sacrifices such as the one I have just completed. Being away from my beloved country for five long years was a blow to me and to my family, but somehow, I survived and now I am ready to do something definitive to help our party.

"The five years I spent at *Tarrafal* gave me ample time to consider our situation," he continued. "We are actually in an ideal state in that we can only go forward with our actions. The PCP has been nearly forgotten by our enemies and we must use that fact to our advantage. Each of our enemies, the Portuguese, English and Germans, yes, the Germans who remain our ideological adversaries, each have a reason to desire our demise and are prepared to use any means possible to see that we fail in our mission to convert our country to communism.

"Comrades, we must each be willing to do our part in this continuing struggle. Only when *Estado Novo* is overthrown will our people be free to choose their own political future without the fear of reprisals. Only then will we be free to conduct our lives in the spirit of the Communist Party where only the common good is tolerated. When Karl Marx and Friedrich Engels established *The Manifesto* of the Communist Party nearly a hundred years ago, the first steps were taken to establish a new world order."

Several people in attendance greeted Fogaça's statements with vocal support. The PCP leader acknowledged their efforts and continued his dialogue. A thin smile crept onto his face as he continued speaking from memory. He had rehearsed this speech many times and knew its contents by heart.

"It is important that we increase our numbers as quickly as possible. No one should be excluded from our ranks, there are jobs to be done by everyone involved. We want people who see themselves as oppressed or those who simply want a better life. Portugal is full of common people who are all seeking order and a more fulfilling role for themselves and their families.

"I have set a goal of two hundred new members over a two-month time period and you all must see that we meet this goal. As our numbers increase, so does our status and power. You must reach out to your fellow workers and friends; they are the best source of new membership. I do not expect much help from the international communist party, they have never really helped the PCP in the past. If we are to accomplish anything, it must be done internally with the blood and sweat of each of you here. I wish you the best and want you to know that I am available at any hour should the need arise. You will be contacted in the usual manner when we need to meet again. At this table," he pointed to a square table off his left side, "are the tools you need to convince our countrymen that our cause is just and plausible. Feel free to take as much of the material as you want, there is ample supplies for everyone.

"If no one had questions, please pick up your supplies and get right to work. The CPC is again alive and functioning. You all are its beating heart and your efforts will be rewarded. Comrades, fulfill our destinies and help reestablish the PCP as a viable force."

The assembled comrades stood and applauded their leader. For the PCP, it was a good start to a most difficult undertaking. Júlio de Melo Fogaça was fully aware of the problems he faced and the difficulties involved. He had nurtured his ideas for the past five years during his imprisonment. It was now time to put his ideas to work.

Saturday, December 21, 1940
Jack Beevor's Flat
Rua de São Miguel 155
Alfama, Lisbon Portugal

Some eight blocks from the CPC gathering, Lisbon's SOE chief was in an earnest conversation with his agent Izaura Ribeiro. Beevor was both delighted and amazed by what Izaura was telling him about her conversation with Louisa Flores.

"...and she managed to get a great deal of information on what he does even though the information meant nothing to her. She just repeated what he told her and I put two and two together. I believe we are on the right track and Dr. Schoenfeld is Louisa's wealthy client. They had a picture taken but it is still being developed. She will bring it to me the minute she has it in her hands."

"You have been incredibly successful, Izaura. For an agent working on her first real mission, you have performed admirably," assured Beevor.

"Thank you, Jack. Coming from you the compliment means a lot to me."

"Jean-Paul Benoit, the Free French attaché assigned to our unit thinks he might have the doctor's laboratory location in the mountains around Barroca Grande. He received information about another foreigner in the area who ordered a case of schnapps."

"Are you sure it wasn't Dr. Schoenfeld?" Izaura inquired.

"No, that person had the wrong build. Too short and the wrong hair color."

"Maybe he is an assistant. You would think that anyone as important as Dr. Schoenfeld would rate an assistant to carry on the dirty part of their work."

"My assessment totally," Beevor agreed. "It's a good bet the pair is holed up somewhere so as to not attract any attention. As far as I can tell, the schnapps thing is their first major mistake."

"What about Louisa? Schoenfeld's relationship with her is also a mistake, isn't it?"

"Sure, it is, but the poor chap's probably in love. From what you have told me, Louisa is a really beautiful woman that would be easy for any man to fall in love with."

"She is certainly that, Jack. I'll bet she has broken many hearts in the past and will probably do so again in the future."

"I'm glad she's on our side. If her information is accurate and I don't believe there's any reason to doubt her, she could be the key to our handling this matter."

"I'll see her again tomorrow when she delivers the picture."

"Excellent. We have no time to waste and as soon as London concurs, we will begin to take actions to interrupt or even cancel his work."

"If you have nothing else for me, I need to go and meet my friend Pilar. We want to go shopping on the Rossio and today is the day for sales in some of the better shops."

"Off you go, young lady. Buy yourself something nice to celebrate. If all this pans out, you will have an attractive bonus waiting for you."

"Really? I wasn't aware that the SOE gave bonuses to its agents."

"Well, actually they don't. I have a discretionary account that allows me latitude in certain matters. I use it whenever the situation calls for it. Understand?"

"Yes, I do," Izaura smiled. "I certainly do. What London doesn't know won't hurt them, right?"

It was Beevor's turn to smile. "You are wise, well beyond your years, Izaura. You learn fast."

Izaura turned and left the flat. Beevor went to the window and watched her disappear down the narrow Rua de São Miguel. *She is proving to be an excellent agent and has a nose for getting to the facts. I made a good choice with her and she can be even more valuable to us in the future.*

He returned to his small desk and continued preparing his report for London. He was sure his superiors would be happy with his Lisbon group's success. He would bet his last quid on it.

1 4 3

Sunday, December 22, 1940
Testing Laboratory
Rua Padre Manuel Vaz Leal 2
Barroca Grande
Covilha, Portugal

The trip back to *Barroca Grande* was a blur for Dr. Gerhardt Schoenberg who spent most of the time in the rustic, crowded, smelly bus thinking of his time with Louisa Flores. The interlude infused the German scientist with a new fervor and he determined to push ahead and finalize his formula for improving wolfram in the cause of his Fatherland.

He greeted his assistant with a smile and shook his hand energetically.

"Hans, I must tell you this trip was the best thing that has happened to me in months. I feel like a new person and I'm eager to get our work here concluded. You should make a visit to Lisbon in the future. It will refresh you like nothing else."

"Thank you, Herr Doctor," Hans Pfeffer replied. "But not until our work here is done. I've been too busy to even consider such a trip. I think you will be happy with my recent findings. If my calculations are correct, we are quite near a breakthrough in our process."

"Let me see what you have done," Schoenfeld remarked. Pfeffer handed his superior a folder with several pages sticking out of the sides. Schoenfeld opened the folder and began reading."

After five or six minutes, he stopped and addressed his assistant. "Remarkable work, Hans. I agree that we are on the verge of something important."

"Will you let Berlin know of our progress? I'm sure they are eager to get this matter resolved."

Schoenfeld considered his answer and finally spoke. "No, Hans. I don't think so. Something else might come up and then Berlin would insist on the fact that we told them it was almost over. I'd rather wait until we are sure of everything before we speak to Berlin. They have a nasty habit of recalling every conversation, every communication to their benefit. No, this time I will wait until we are sure of the results."

"How much longer do you think, Herr Doctor?"

Again, Schoenfeld pondered his answer. "A week, two at the most."

A broad smile crossed the face of Hans Pfeffer. Although he thoroughly enjoyed his work, he knew his sojourn in the steep and precipitous mountains of Portugal was nearing its end. He vowed to remember this work for the rest of his career.

Sunday, December 22, 1940
Jack Beevor's Flat
Rua de São Miguel 155
Alfama, Lisbon Portugal

Izaura Veigas Ribeiro hurriedly knocked on the door to Jack Beevor's flat. She had taken a tram and marveled at its noisy and swaying motion as it negotiated Lisbon's cobblestone streets. Two near misses with taxis highlighted the short ride that always promised a thrill.

Beevor greeted his agent and motioned her inside. She immediately handed him an envelope that contained an oversized photograph of a happy couple.

"So that's what he looks like," commented Beevor. "Not too bad looking in a scholarly sort of way. But your Louisa is a real beauty. I can see why she has his interest."

"And she is smart, too. Look at what she has already accomplished."

"Righto. I am totally impressed."

"So, what will we do next?"

"I will take this over to the embassy and have it duplicated at once. Then you can have the original and get it back to Louisa."

"That's fine. She was a bit worried Schoenfeld might come back soon and would expect the photograph to be there."

"Once we have the duplicate, we will include it in the diplomatic pouch for London. We'll let those chaps do their thing and get it verified. I believe they are already working on getting a picture of him from an old yearbook or something. Anyway, that's their problem. We have done what was needed on our end."

Izaura took a deep breath and studied the photo. Then she handed it back to Beevor.

"You will continue to stroke your ladies and see if we can come up with anything useful. They all seem eager to please."

Izaura raised her eyebrow as Beevor realized his gaffe. "Sorry Izaura, I didn't mean..."

Izaura smiled and said, "That's okay, Jack. I know what you intended to say."

Jack Beevor relaxed his sheepish grin and took the photo back, placing it inside the envelope.

"I'll get right over to the embassy. I don't want to miss the pouch."

Again, Izaura cracked the briefest of smiles. It was pleasant to see her boss squirming a bit.

Chapter Ten

Monday, December 23, 1940
Prime Minister's Office
Rear of São Bento Palace
Lisbon, Portugal

The head of Portugal's PVDE was once again shown into the offices of Prime Minister António de Oliveira Salazar located around a cozy garden in the rear of São Bento Palace. Captain Agostinho Lourenço was dressed in civilian clothes and bundled up to stem the effects of the cold and windy weather that Lisbon was experiencing.

As was the case during past visits, Portugal's prime minister was deeply engrossed in a file that was spread out across his plain oak desk. Salazar continued reading and finally turned to face Lourenço.

"Good morning, my dear Captain. What brings you here on such a blustery day?"

"A matter of importance, Prime Minister. At least I believe it to be of importance."

"It probably is, Agostinho. I've seldom seen you wrong in such matters. You have an instinct for abnormal happenings and the good sense to act on them as soon as possible. What is it this time?"

"I got a call from my nephew Tomás about a conversation he had with one of his friends. It seems the friend works at a broom factory in Lisbon and was approached by someone from the outside about joining the Portuguese Communist Party. A number of ideas were discussed and the man was promised a gun if he agreed to join the PCP."

"A gun, really?"

"Yes, a gun. The communist organizer indicated the PCP was reestablishing itself and intended to carry out some operations that would place them in the public's eye."

"I was under the impression the PCP was almost non-existent," Salazar offered. "It's probably been years since I've even heard their name mentioned."

"Yes, four or five. We put their leaders in prison at *Tarrafal* and the organization basically fell apart."

"Why would they attempt to reorganize now?"

"One or two of their leaders were recently released so I figure they are behind this attempt."

"You were quite right to come to me with this, Agostinho. These people have proven to be dangerous in the past. If they succeed in getting help from their Russian counterparts, such as guns or explosives, they could create a problem for us."

"That's exactly what I thought, Prime Minister. I instructed my nephew to entice his friend into joining the PCP so he can report their activities to us. In fact, he might already have become a member. We will pay him a little something for his trouble. I'm told his family can use the extra money."

"That's the case with so many of our citizens, Agostinho. They are good people and willing to work hard but our country is poor and the opportunities are limited."

"I know, sir. But the war has helped many of our countrymen. In Lisbon, the great number of visitors who spend freely has perked up our economy. I see happier people on the streets who seem to have a new purpose in their lives."

"You are quite right, Agostinho. Our country's finances are finally headed in the right direction. If this war lasts a few more years, our economy will be healthier than it has been in decades."

"All due to your leadership, Prime Minister."

"Thank you, Agostinho, but I'm just a part of it to be honest."

"The most important part," Lourenço declared emphatically. "Without you our beloved country would be lost."

"Possibly, Agostinho. But there are a great many Portuguese involved in our struggle and most of them go unnoticed. They work for small pay and put in long hours."

"It's always been like that and I don't think it will change anytime in the near future."

"You might be right, but I will never stop trying."

"I will keep you informed about the PCP, Prime Minister. If they are up to anything, I'll stop it before it begins."

"Yes, Agostinho, I know you will."

Lourenço did an about-face and departed the office. Salazar took a moment to contemplate the man who had just left. *We need more people like him in key positions in our government. I am extremely lucky to have a man of his character and drive that I can always count on. I know that if the situation becomes intense, he will always be there for me...*

Monday, December 23, 1940
Special Operations Executive
Iberian Desk
64 Baker Street, Westminster
London, England

The diplomatic pouch containing the photograph of the person supposed to be Dr. Gerhardt Schoenfeld reached the SOE's Iberian Desk the following day. It was sent to another office at 64 Baker Street where a careful scrutiny and comparison was made of an existing photograph that the SOE had acquired from a yearbook acquired from Schoenfeld's former school in Germany.

The analyst peered intently at the two photographs. Even with the five-year difference between the two objects, it was clear to his eye that the subject in the recent photograph was surely Dr. Gerhardt Schoenfeld, former professor at *Munich's Technische Universitat*

Munchen. A report was quickly prepared and sent directly to the SOE's Iberian Desk and its chief, Kim Philby.

Philby took the good news in his usual, controlled fashion and considered his alternatives.

First of all, I must get this information to the PM and await his orders to act. I'm sure he will act quickly; it seems of great importance. I also think this warrants my sending David Eccles back to Lisbon to assist Jack Beevor in finding this fellow's whereabouts. Not that Beevor hasn't done a first- class job, he has actually exceeded my expectations. For a first-timer in the field, he has already shown the qualities of a seasoned intelligence officer.

Philby then added a series of comments to the two photographs and sent them by courier to the War Rooms and Prime Minister Winston Churchill. He then sent instructions to David Eccles to head to Lisbon as soon as possible to assist Jack Beevor. He decided to use Great Britain's diplomatic pouch to Madrid for the orders sending Eccles to Lisbon. *No point in trusting this to a cable or such, no telling who might have access to our communications. After all, we have all the Enigma codes so it is reasonable to assume our enemies have some of ours.*

Satisfied he had fulfilled all his responsibilities covering the Portuguese operation, he now considered what he should send to his Communist contact. Maybe nothing for now and see just how everything develops. No point in raising everyone's hopes, particularly in Russia. If things don't pan out, they might not look favorably on my reports...

He looked about his desk and for the first time in a long while, there was nothing new and not much else to do. He decided against heading home to his home on Carlyle Square in Chelsea and opted instead to visit the Leconfield House on Curzon Street in Mayfair and their excellent bar, the Pig and Eye. The place was just off Hyde park and was the favorite haunt of MI5 agents. It was also a perfect setting to get caught up on the events of the day.

He stepped outside and was lucky to catch a vacant cab. The 5-minute ride was without incident and Philby stepped inside the large building that houses a number of offices along with the noisy bar. He pushed open the door and was greeted by a good deal of smoke and noise. He spied a pair of MI5 agents he was friendly with and made it over to their table.

"What's new, blokes?" he asked definitively.

"Grab yourself something to wet your whistle," came the reply. "We'll talk after you have something in your hand."

Monday, December 23, 1940
Room 248, Hotel Palacio
Rua Particular
Estoril, Portugal

Juan Pujol Garcia, about to enter his 29th year, didn't consider himself a particularly intelligent man, but he did pride himself for possessing one outstanding attribute, a high degree of cleverness. His combination of ingenuity, shrewdness and smartness made him one of Great Britain's most valuable assets—a double spy.

While he stayed in Lisbon, Garcia decided to live life to its fullest. He took a room at the magnificent Hotel Palacio in Estoril and continued supplying the German Abwehr with fictitious accounts of British shipping from a phantom network of agents he created from his imagination. He utilized British travel magazines, railroad schedules and anything else he could find that would lend credence to his plan. His code name, Garbo, had become increasingly important to Britain's SOE in that his German handlers considered him a first-rate spy and continued to pay him handsomely for his efforts. They increased the payments to his non-existent assortment of made up spies and Garcia gracefully pocketed the additional money. This currency windfall allowed Garbo to lead an expansive lifestyle since no one in the *Abwehr* sensed the fact that he was actually living in Portugal when all his reports and communications indicated he was perfectly embedded in England.

Garbo continued to press Jack Beevor for some local field duties whenever the opportunity arose, without any success. He argued that his value to Britain's SOE would increase if given the chance, but Beevor had many fires to put out and Garbo's pleas fell on deaf ears.

This all changed when Beevor received a communication from London about a possible revival of Portugal's PCP, and its possible effect on Beevor's work. One aspect of the communiqué was that London fully expected the revived PCP to attempt some sort of armed confrontation to reestablish itself and attract new members.

Beevor immediately thought of Garbo and his completely believable resume, ingeniously fashioned to show he was a person who fought for his beliefs and was prepared to do anything for a cause he believed in.

Beevor pondered the situation. *Garbo would fit in perfectly with the communists. He seems a true idealist and willing to do what it takes to succeed; both traits the PCP will devour. He is always asking me to assign him some field work here in Lisbon and this might just be the assignment. If I can have an insider within their organization, no telling what could come of it. It shouldn't be all that dangerous for him, he's way too cunning for the likes of the PCP. I'll ask around the embassy and see if anyone knows about this PCP and how we might contact them. After all, we are already paying Garbo a good deal of money so some additional duties, duties that he has asked for, would make good sense. I'll send a note to his hotel and have him meet me here. With any luck at all we should have something working within a few days.*

Beevor's handwritten note arrived at the Hotel Palacio the following day and was met with keen interest by the Spanish spy. *This is the first time I have been asked to meet with Beevor. I am usually the one who does the asking, so maybe something has changed. I'll wait and see what comes of it and try not get too excited about it...*

Tuesday, December 24, 1940
Outskirts of town
Barroca Grande
Covilha, Portugal

Jean-Paul Benoit, the Free French attaché assigned to Beevor's unit was in a foul mood. It was just before Christmas Day and he was walking in a wooded area which seemed to be devoid of any human life. He spent another morning scouring the mountains surrounding the town of Barroca Grande searching for a possible laboratory. He had spent the past two days with no success and was considering abandoning the mission. He decided to make his way back to Barroca Grande and grab a bus to Lisbon.

He chose a shortcut across a narrow stream and stumbled on a rock as he crossed the water. He looked up and noticed a strong odor coming from the stream. He scooped a small amount into his hand and brought it up to his nose. A strong smell resembling diesel emanated from the water and assaulted his nostrils.,

It's not diesel but definitely contains some other substances I can't identify. It's coming from upriver and is worth a look.

He started up the stream that turned north and curved toward the nearby mountains. After a few minutes walking, he came to another curve and was surprised to see a small building partially hidden from view accessible by a path leading to the south in the direction of Barroca Grande.

What is this? I've never even noticed this building before. I didn't know it existed until I came around that bend in the stream.

Benoit crouched down as a figure emerged from the building. He was short, a bit overweight, was wearing a white apron and carrying a bottle of liquid. The figure made his way toward the creek and Benoit flattened himself behind some bushes. The man approached Benoit's hiding place and came within a few feet of the Frenchman's position. His gaze was fixed on the bottle he carried and he passed Benoit and knelt down by the stream. He carefully poured the liquid into the stream and stood up, assessing his work. Satisfied the liquid was headed downstream, he replaced the cork on the bottle and began his way back.

Benoit tried to not move a muscle as the figure approached. Again, the oncoming man's gaze was straight ahead as he passed the prone figure and continued toward the building.

The Free French attaché waited a few moments and finally stood erect. He reached the stream and bent close to the water. The same acrid smell was present, but much more defined and incredibly nasty to the nose.

He decided to make his way back to Barroca Grande by another route but took out his area map and marked the spot of the building's location. He was sure he had stumbled on something important and was excited to get back to Lisbon and inform Jack Beevor of his find. He also realized that his mood had suddenly changed for the better.

Thursday, December 26, 1940
Martim Flores Residence
Rua da Galé 3, Old Jewish Quarter
Alfama, Lisbon, Portugal

Martim Flores was fast asleep after a long night of haggling over jewelry prices when a series of loud knocks on the door to his residence jarred him into a state of semi-consciousness.

He moved toward the door and opened it a crack.

"Who is it?" he demanded. "What do you want?"

"PVDE," an authoritative voice responded. "Open the door."

Martim considered the situation and opened the door. Two men, similarly dressed in suits and fedoras stepped into the house.

"Are you Martim Flores?" one asked.

"Of course, I am. Who else did you expect to be here?"

"No need for that, senhor. We only want to ask you some questions."

Martim nodded and waited as the second man spoke.

"Do you know a Monsieur Chaisson, a Jewish refugee from France in our city?" the officer asked.

Martim hesitated and responded, "No, I don't think so. What's this all about?"

"Senhor Chaisson was found with his throat cut near the docks two nights ago. Our investigation placed him at the Café Chave d'Oro the same night and witnesses said he was sitting with you and that you had a heated discussion."

Martim looked downward and eventually spoke. "Oh yes, I remember the man. I never really knew his name."

"What were you discussing?" the second PVDE officer probed.

"What I discuss with all my customers," Martim replied cautiously. "The sale of some jewelry he had in his possession. That's not against the law is it?"

"No Senhor Flores. It isn't. Why was your conversation so spirited? Several people at the café said you were both on the verge of shouting."

"He didn't like what I offered him for the jewelry. He felt I was cheating him and he got mad about it. I tried to explain a great deal of jewelry is for sale in Lisbon and the prices on many items have fallen. I told him to take it or leave it. He finally calmed down and we departed on good terms."

"Did he accept your offer?"

"No. He wished to think about it before deciding. I told him to return to the café if he changed his mind and we could work it all out."

The two officers looked at each other and one signaled their departure.

"We'll get back to you, Senhor Flores," one said coldly. "Please don't attempt to leave Lisbon without informing us until this matter is concluded."

Martim Flores acknowledged the order and walked to the door.

"Always happy to assist the PVDE in its work," he declared.

The two men departed and Martim closed the door. He thought on the matter.

That was too close. I must find a way to keep out of public places and definitely keep from getting into an argument. The PVDE has no real evidence to connect me to the murder so I don't have anything to worry about. Still, I must be more careful in the future.

Friday, December 27, 1940
British Ambassador's Residence
Rua São Francisco Borja 63
Lapa, Lisbon, Portugal

Sir Ronald Hugh Campbell took over the duties of British Ambassador the day before with little fanfare other than a formal reception at the British Embassy. A tough diplomat with an impressive record, Campbell was the British ambassador to France when the armistice between Germany and France was signed at Compiègne on June 22, almost six months ago. He was part of a massive escape from France through Saint-Jean-de-Luz on the light cruiser *HMS Galatea* in an evacuation operation Great Britain labeled *Operation Ariel*. The remaining British Expeditionary forces were evacuated during the operation, effectively ending Britain's military presence in that country.

Campbell was in his 58th year and was given the post over some more experienced diplomats and brought some much-needed vigor to the embassy. In London's eyes, Sir Ronald Campbell who was awarded CMG in 1917, was a person who got things done and was the perfect person to guide Great Britain through Portugal's fragile position of neutrality during the war.

Campbell attacked his duties with the same vitality and drive he displayed in both Yugoslavia and France. He scheduled individual meetings with everyone on the British embassy staff and meticulously reviewed their responsibilities and assignments. He listened patiently to each person and offered advice if he felt it was necessary.

His meeting with SOE chief Jack Beevor was a bit touchier than most of the others. Beevor was assigned to the military attaché but acted alone under the parameters set by London for its agents.

He brought up this point to Beevor during their discussion. "So, Mr. Beevor, you have the run of the country and have no one to report to other than London. Is that correct?"

Beevor sensed a potential difference in interpreting his orders and answered with caution. His training as a lawyer prior to joining the SOE helped him immensely.

"No, Sir Ronald," he began. "I am assigned to the military attaché and report to him whenever the need arises. I don't bother him with small issues, but I do keep him in the loop with anything I consider important."

"And how often would that be, Mr. Beevor? Once or twice a week?"

Again, Jack Beevor chose his words carefully. "There's no set schedule, Sir Ronald. I report to him whenever I consider it necessary."

"So, Mr. Beevor, I must repeat myself. You have the run of the country and report only when the feeling moves you."

"Not really, Sir Ronald. London has..."

"Mr. Beevor," interrupted the ambassador. "I am fully aware of what London imparts and also the fact that the PM is fully vested in your organization. Rules that apply to most intelligence operations don't seem to apply to the SOE. Am I correct?"

"I don't know about all that, Sir Ronald. I just do what I am ordered to do and utilize whatever means possible to accomplish those orders," replied Beevor defensively. "I certainly don't want to upset the proverbial apple cart and am willing to act in any manner you see fit."

"Well, Mr. Beevor," the new ambassador said as he adopted a more docile tone, "we both have the same objective as far as I can tell. Our country is in a messy situation at this moment and little Portugal has emerged as a major player in this nasty war. Their neutrality is of prime importance to Great Britain and to me personally. I want nothing to interfere with that neutrality and in particular the actions of your SOE. I realize there is a fine line concerning your operations and I respect the fact that London has given you specific orders. But I must insist you come to me with anything important you decide. And, I would ask that your parameters in establishing that importance be bent in my direction. Am I making myself clear, Mr. Beevor?"

"Certainly, Sir Ronald. Perfectly clear."

"Then we understand each other, Jack. May I call you Jack?"

"Of course, Sir Ronald. I would be delighted if you did."

"Good. I will expect to hear from you whenever. Are you working on anything really hush hush at this time?"

Beevor considered his position and decided to inform the new ambassador of his quest to locate Dr. Gerhardt Schoenfeld. After giving him the original details, he brought Campbell up to date.

"And, our Free French attaché thinks he has located the laboratory that Schoenfeld is operating from. I am waiting for London to positively identify the photograph we sent them as Dr. Schoenfeld. Once I receive the confirmation, I want to develop a plan to neutralize the good doctor."

"Not without my permission, Jack. Something like that could have negative reactions from the Jerries. We must be very careful how we handle all this. Remember Mr. Shakespeare penned in Henry IV, *Caution is preferable to rash bravery.* I feel that applies to this matter; don't you agree?"

Beevor smiled and responded. "It most certainly does, Sir Ronald."

"Then let's shake hands and you go and find some spies or whatever it is you do. I'll look forward to your next report."

"Thank you, Sir Ronald. It has been a pleasure to meet you."

"Likewise, Jack. Best of luck to you and your staff."

Jack Beevor turned and left the room. He was convinced he had held his own with the exceptionally skillful diplomat.

Saturday, December 28, 1940
Jack Beevor's Flat
Rua de São Miguel 155
Alfama, Lisbon Portugal

The confirmation of Dr. Gerhardt Schoenfeld's identity reached Jack Beevor about an hour after the diplomatic pouch arrived on the daily BOAC flight from London. Beevor happened to be in the embassy on other business and quickly opened the letter from Kim Philby. His face broadened when he read the contents. He decided to make good on his promise to Sir Ronald Campbell and inform him of this latest development. He inquired as to an appointment but was told that the ambassador was on a short trip to Gibraltar and would not return until the following day. He asked for the earliest appointment possible and was given a 9 o'clock slot Monday morning.

Satisfied he had fulfilled his agreement with Campbell, he immediately sent word for Izaura Ribeiro and Jean-Paul Benoit to meet him at his flat at 6 o'clock this evening. He then treated himself to a lunch of *petiscos,* the Portuguese cousin to Spanish tapas that caught his attention upon arrival in Lisbon. These tasty snacks mirrored the various regions of Portugal and were generally seafood-based. His favorite luncheon place was *Petiscos Coimbra* and Beevor visited it whenever he found it possible. Inexpensive and flavorful, the petiscos had become Jack Beevor's favorite lunchtime fare and he delighted in taking his friends with him to share the experience of the cozy place.

While he finished his second round of *petiscos,* Beevor washed down the delicacy with a Sagres, the beer of choice for most Portuguese. He also considered his options for the upcoming meeting with Izaura and Jean-Paul later that day.

I must plan this carefully; the ambassador will want to know all the details. We must not do anything that would infuriate the Germans, that would be politically incorrect. Yet we must find a way to stop the doctor's experiments or whatever he is doing in that laboratory. London has made this a high priority and I am right in the middle of it all. Think, Jack. What is the most expeditious course of action? Damn if I know right now, but it might come to me later.

Beevor paid his check and returned to his flat. He reread the note from Philby and finally placed it on the kitchen table.

Jean-Paul Benoit and Izaura Ribeiro arrived within minutes of each other and took a place around the kitchen table. Jack Beevor produced a bottle of Malmsey Madeira and some small glasses. The bottle was passed and the three agents poured themselves a swig. The pleasant taste took the edge off the evening's conversation as Beevor began the conversation.

"The fact that Jean-Paul has been able to locate Dr. Schoenfeld's laboratory is a main advance in our work. London has positively identified the doctor from the photo I sent them so you both should be congratulated."

Izaura smiled at Jean-Paul who acknowledged the praise.

"Now we must come up with a plan that puts this information to good use. We must find a way to put an end to the doctor's work and we must do it without pissing off the Nazis. I have tried to come up with something but am at a loss what to do next. Whatever we come up with must be a team effort so I thought you two should have a say. Izaura, you must see Louisa continues her relationship with Schoenfeld. He cannot suspect we are on to him under any circumstances."

"Why can't we just go in and destroy everything?" Jean-Paul asked. "How would the Germans know it was us who did it? Maybe it could be made to look like an accident. God knows there are always accidents around laboratories, explosive chemicals and the like."

"We would have the most to gain from something like that and the Germans would suspect us from the beginning. The political aspects of that in a neutral country like Portugal could be disastrous," Beevor replied. "Besides, the British ambassador would have to approve such a plan and I don't believe for a minute he would agree to it. We would have too much to lose if I knew his thinking."

"Yes," Jean-Paul agreed. "The word around the embassy is that his reputation from other embassies is one of a tough but fair-minded boss. He does not take undue chances in most matters and has a firm grip on what the situation calls for."

"That's right, Jean-Paul. I've already had my sit-down with him and he laid his stance on the table. He goes by the book and doesn't care who knows it. He's obviously got friends in high places or he wouldn't have landed the job here."

Izaura took it all in and finally spoke. "Why not do it and find a way to blame it on someone else? It would have to be carefully planned down to the last detail, but we have the element of surprise on our side. And, Dr. Schoenfeld is not expecting us to do anything, right? He doesn't know we are on to him."

Beevor's first inclination was to reject Izaura's idea, but as he poured himself another glass of madeira a possibility began to emerge from deep within his imagination.

"You might be onto something Izaura. I must think about it before I believe it plausible. Anyway, it's something to consider and there's nothing else on the table at this point." He raised his glass toward Izaura and toasted, "To your plan young lady. May it develop and prove beneficial to our cause."

"To our cause," resounded throughout the kitchen. Jack Beevor was already deep in thought as the voices faded. He returned to the present and poured himself another glass of the incredibly friendly wine. His planning could wait until the bottle was empty.

Saturday, December 28, 1940
Burnay Palace
Rua da Junqueira 87
Alcântara, Lisbon, Portugal

The Patriarch of Lisbon, Cardinal Manuel Cerejeira, was busy attending to some improvements to his summer home at centuries-old Burnay Palace in the Alcantara section of Lisbon when one of his parishioners asked for an audience. Cerejeira knew the man and told an assistant to show him in.

The man arrived and kissed the cardinal's ring.

"What brings you to see me, António?" the prelate asked. "How did you know I was here?"

"I went to your office and your assistant directed me here, Your Eminence," António Fares responded. "I wanted to tell you something sooner rather than later."

Cerejeira smiled and touched his friend's elbow. "It couldn't wait until Sunday, António? It must be really important."

"I believe so, Eminence. It concerns my son Rodrigo. One of his friends was approached by the Portuguese Communist Party about becoming a member. The fellow told Rodrigo's friend that the PCP was reorganizing and promised him a job in the future that paid him good money. He was also guaranteed a gun and told that the PCP would become very militant in the near future in order to get their message out to all the people in Portugal.

"Since I know how much the PCP hates the Catholic Church, I believe it is possible they might intend to hurt and destroy some churches and I immediately thought of you."

"You are very thoughtful, António. I will ask God to bless you in a special way."

"Thank you, Eminence. I am honored for your blessing."

Cardinal Manuel Cerejeira again extended his hand to António Fares who kissed the ring and started to depart. "Thank you, António. I will put this information to good use, you can rest assured."

The cardinal watched the man depart and thought to himself.

This is a serious matter. I must go and see the Prime Minister as soon as possible. He walked to a nearby phone and picked up the receiver.

"Please connect me with the prime minister's office," he said evenly.

In a few moments, a familiar voice came on the other end.

"Hello, Manuel," Dr. António Salazar uttered. "What can I do for you?"

"We need to meet as soon as possible, António. Something has arisen that needs your attention."

"What is it my old friend? You seem a bit shaken."

"Not over the phone, António. I'd prefer we speak in person."

"Then by all means come right over. I'll alert my staff."

"It will take me some time to get there, I'm over in Alcântara at the moment."

"I'll be waiting when you arrive, Manuel."

"Thank you, António, I'm sorry to bother you."

"Nonsense, Manuel. I always enjoy our meetings."

"As do I, my dear friend. I'll be there shortly."

Lisbon's religious patriarch placed the receiver down and turned to leave the palace. His short ride into Lisbon would provide him with ample time to prepare for his talk with the country's Prime Minister.

Chapter Eleven

Saturday, December 28, 1940
Jack Beevor's Flat
Rua de São Miguel 155
Alfama, Lisbon Portugal

An unexpected visitor arrived at Jack Beevor's flat in the person of Juan Pujol García, a member of Beevor's SOE unit also known as Garbo.

Beevor greeted the Spaniard with a friendly smile and extended his hand as he closed the flat's front door behind them. He noticed his agent was carrying a large rectangular object in one hand that was wrapped in a blanket.

"What's that you're carrying?" inquired Beevor.

Garbo placed the object on a nearby chair and carefully unfurled the blanket covering the object. The barrel of a gun emerged followed by the remainder of the rifle.

"What have we here?" Beevor said with great interest. "This thing is a beauty. From the looks of it, it's never been fired."

"It's my new semi-automatic self-loading rifle," replied Garbo with pride. "The PCP gave it to me when I signed my letter of agreement to join their organization. They give one to each new comrade who joins."

"Really? Beevor replied incredulously. "They have the resources to give one to each new member?"

"It seems so. One of the leaders told me they received a shipment from Mother Russia that amounted to 200 new *Svetas* so they intend to grow the PCP's numbers to at least that amount."

"*Svetas?*"

"Yes. The actual name is an *SVT-40* but everyone refers to it as a *Sveta*. I haven't had the chance to fire it yet but I thought you might be interested so I brought it with me."

"You did great, Garbo. London will jump when they hear about this. So, this means you are a full-fledged communist, my devious friend. What name did you use to join?"

Garbo looked at Beevor with disbelief. "You don't trust me to be discreet," Garbo countered.

"It's not that, I just..."

Garbo smiled. "I had fake papers made by a friend who happens to be a printer. He believes I'm on a special mission for the government to thwart the communists and was willing to help me. I used the name of an old colleague in Spain who was killed during the war. It was sort of a memorial to his memory and our friendship."

Beevor was in awe of his agent's resourcefulness. "I'll see you get a bonus for this, Garbo. You deserve one."

"No need for that, Senor. I am well paid for my services by your government. I did it because you included me in this operation and for that I am grateful."

"On behalf of the King and our country, I thank you. Your services are greatly appreciated."

"I am happy to oblige, Senor."

"Excellent. I must make some notes and take some measurements for my report to London."

"I also anticipated that, Senor. I have prepared this for you." He handed Beevor a page with all the measurements that included the type of ammunition and some specifics the PCP had included along with the rifle.

"Also," Garbo added. "All the serial numbers have been removed from the guns. The PCP doesn't want any of the rifles traced back to them. I think that was unnecessary since they are the only ones in Portugal and Spain who possess these rifles, but if they wanted to remove the markings, I guess the rifles belonged to them, right?"

"Yes, my friend, you are correct." Beevor held the rifle up and remarked, "Light, good balance. Seems like a potent weapon."

"I'll let you know. We are scheduled for some practice in a few days to become familiar with it. I'll let you know after the session."

"You do that, Garbo. I'll pass that on to London after we talk."

"I must be going, Senor. I promised to meet some friends at the Estoril Casino. I don't want to be late."

"Be on your way, Garbo. And, many thanks."

The pair shook hands and Garbo departed the flat with his weapon.

Jack Beevor shut the door and thought, *with men like him on our side we can't possibly lose the war. I wish I had more like him, it would make my job all the easier. What am I thinking? My unit has some excellent people and I'm proud of what they have accomplished. Garbo just adds to our prowess. I should be thankful I have him with us, that's all...*

Sunday, December 29, 1940
British Ambassador's Residence
Rua São Francisco Borja 63
Lapa, Lisbon, Portugal

Jack Beevor was excited to meet with the new British ambassador and share the good news concerning the location of Dr. Schoenfeld's laboratory in *Barroca Grande*. He related the details of Jean-Paul Benoit's findings and shared the news that London had positively confirmed the doctor's identity.

He slowly became concerned that Sir Ronald Campbell didn't react to the news with much enthusiasm. Beevor finally asked the British diplomat, "Is there something wrong, Sir Ronald? You don't seem too enthused with these new developments."

"No, Jack, that's not the case at all. My lack of enthusiasm stems from my trip yesterday with the Portuguese head of his country's business development. We took a trip up north and actually visited the largest wolfram mine in Portugal.

'The reason I was invited was because Prime Minister Salazar wanted to inform me that Germany has increased its next order of the mineral by 50%, the maximum Portugal will allow. Of course, we can also increase our order by the same percentage but, if I read the situation correctly, the Jerries have found a new usage for the wolfram. They had asked for even more, but the Portuguese limited the increase to only 50%. I also feel, given what you have just told me, that this increase in purchasing is directly tied into Dr. Schoenfeld's research. If he has indeed discovered something new, it could easily give the Germans a leg up in the arms and munitions race."

"Then we must take some action to stop Schoenfeld from achieving any further results, shouldn't we Sir Ronald?"

"My thoughts exactly, Jack. But if we do something drastic, it could be the end of our chummy relationship with Portugal. We cannot afford any scenario like that; my orders from London are quite specific."

Beevor fought the urge to tell the ambassador what he had in mind and considered his eventualities.

No, I shouldn't mention my plan to blame the communists, I haven't even developed it fully. I can always let him know when I know exactly what I want to do. This new development about the Boche increasing their wolfram shipments throws another wrench into the mix. Such an increase can't possibly be put into effect immediately since almost all of the mining is done by hand. I would think another two or three weeks before any increased shipment can be made ready and that gives me some time to craft some sort of plan. Is it possible we might be able to accomplish both ends of the problem at one time? I must give this some serious thought. And, I might surely want to consult with David Eccles on this; thank goodness he's scheduled to come here in a day or two.

"...and, I must have your absolute word on that." continued Sir Ronald.

"Absolutely, Sir Ronald. "I would never hide anything I develop from you."

"Good, my dear boy. I expected such a reaction from you."

Beevor chose not to reply and waited for the ambassador to continue.

"You will just keep doing what you have started, you seem to have things under control. If anything breaks in our favor or against us, I need to know immediately."

"Understood, Sir Ronald."

"Excellent. I see we are on the same wavelength and that makes for a good team effort. I'll query London and see what they have to say. My belief is that they will allow us to deal with the problem on our end."

"I certainly hope so, Sir Ronald. It might be awkward if they decide to get involved."

"Leave that to me, old boy. That sort of larking about is my type of business and, quite frankly, I'm sort of well-established in the field," the diplomat smiled broadly as he spoke. "Now, I must get about the King's business, so I will ask you to leave me. Please notify me as soon as anything develops any further."

"Will do, Sir Ronald. Thank you for your time."

"All in a day's duties, Jack. All in a day's duties."

Jack Beevor stood and walked briskly from the ambassador's office. He was already contemplating his upcoming meeting with David Eccles.

Monday, December 30, 1940
Benches at Entrance to Park
Jardim de Estrela, Barrio Alto
Lisbon, Portugal

Izaura Ribeiro had passed a note to Louisa Flores to meet her at the *Jardim de Estrela's* convenient benches and was happy to see Louisa appear on time for their meeting.

"Hello, Louisa," greeted Izaura with genuine feeling. "I hope you are doing well."

"Thank you Izaura. I'd be doing better if the money you promised me was in my hands," returned Louisa with the same genuineness.

"It's in the works, Louisa. The sum is large enough that we had to get London to authorize it and send us the money. I hope it doesn't take much longer; I really do."

Louisa nodded but remained silent.

"That's not the only reason I asked you to meet me here," Izaura continued. "It is very important that you continue seeing Dr. Schoenfeld for the near future and ensure he does not suspect anything. We are developing a plan but it will take time to put it into place."

"Will I be paid additional money for that?" Louisa replied coldly.

"Yes, Louisa. You will always be paid for your work on our behalf."

"That's good, Izaura. I hope you don't take this personally. I like you and I admire the way you conduct your work."

"I try, Louisa. I'm not always sure I am doing the right thing."

"We all have the same problem, Izaura. My line of work is much simpler, with few real problems. I perform a service and am paid for my work. Simple, right?"

"Yes," replied Izaura with a broad smile. "If you look at it like that."

"I have no other way to look at it if you consider what I do. I'm in an old business, probably one of the oldest on record."

Again, Izaura smiled at her contact. "Yes, you are."

"So, I need to get back to the Jamaica Bar if you have nothing else for me."

"Nothing else, Louisa. Thank you for meeting me."

"I'll let you know if and when he comes back. See you."

Louisa got up and walked toward the entrance. Izaura followed her movements until she was out of sight. *I am fortunate to have her helping us. She is certainly one of a kind.* Izaura stood and headed toward the park's entrance. Her meeting came off as expected and she intended to inform Jack Beevor of Louisa's itching to be paid for giving up Schoenfeld. She silently hoped the money would be soon forthcoming. She had to take care of her informers.

Monday, December 30, 1940
Prime Minister's Office
Rear of São Bento Palace
Lisbon, Portugal

The Patriarch of Lisbon was quickly shown into Prime Minister António de Oliveira Salazar's office. Salazar rose and greeted his old friend warmly and kissed his ring.

"What's so important you had to see me at once, Manuel? My secretary said you sounded in a panic when you called. Has something terrible happened?"

"Sorry to have alarmed everyone, António, but I felt this news was critical. I knew you would want to know about it if you haven't already been informed."

"Please sit down and tell me all about it. Can I get you something to drink?"

"Cold water would be fine. It will calm me down a bit." Manuel sat down uneasily on the sofa.

Salazar pushed a button on his desk and ordered two glasses of cold water.

"I'll join you, Manuel. My throat is also dry. Darn humidity!"

A minute later, the secretary arrived with a tray that contained two glasses and a sweating pride. Cardinal Cerejeira took one and the prime minister the other. Each took a sip and the prelate began talking.

"António, a parishioner whom I respect and have known for years came to me with a story about the communists reorganizing.

This concerned me about the church and its relationship with our country. I have no idea what the communists will do but it is entirely possible they will exert their wrath on our churches and clergy. I'm not worried for myself, but there are many convents and churches with no means to defend themselves. The man who brought me the news was upset and afraid for all Catholics. I'm sure he represents the feelings of many Portuguese. I don't know if you are aware of the communists' plans but they are better organized than they were in the past. They are even giving guns to new members and I believe they intend to use those weapons." The cardinal's head hung slightly as he considered the dilemma facing his people.

Portugal's prime minister saw the anguish in his old friend's face and sought to console him. "Manuel, we are aware of what the communists are doing and the PVDE is trying to infiltrate the organization. Everything they do is totally clandestine. We don't know where they are meeting. But we will find out and you can rest assured that we will deal with this new menace. Since there are still many refugees here in Lisbon attempting to flee the Nazis, the PVDE has its hands full. I have told Captain Lourenço to add more staff, but that takes time to implement."

"So, what can I tell my priests so they can relay a message of hope to their parishioners?"

Salazar thought a moment and answered. "You must renew your views on the communists and their record of persecuting the catholic church around the world. Remind your people of their disruptive tactics and the fact they have been unsuccessful in their previous attempts. Tell them to pay attention to anyone they know is a communist and to report anything they feel is out of the ordinary. Thousands of people acting as spies will only make the communists' job that much harder. Anytime they hear of a planned communist attack or the like, tell them to call the PVDE and report it. If the information proves reliable, the PVDE will take immediate action."

It was Cardinal Cerejeira's turn to pause and contemplate his friend's words.

"What you propose makes great sense, António. I will have my bishops prepare sermons to read this Sunday at Holy Mass. I hope our followers will take the words seriously. Their lives could easily be at stake."

"Let's pray it doesn't come to that, Manuel. The PVDE can be very productive in handling the communists."

"I certainly hope so, António. For all our sakes."

Tuesday, December 31, 1940
Ante room of Board Room
British Embassy
Rua São Francisco Borja 63
Lapa, Lisbon, Portugal

David Eccles finally made his way to Lisbon and a meeting with Jack Beevor. He was held up by refugee problems along the Spanish-French border and was able to resolve the problems without bloodshed.

"You look tired, David, and unwashed," Beevor commented on his friend's appearance. "Have a hard go of it?"

"Too many angry people and a lack of a peaceful sleep," Eccles answered. "There's no easy solution to problems these days and tempers on both sides are extremely short. Somehow you manage to find a way to appease everyone, but it all takes time and the willingness to compromise. These poor refugees are in a terrible position. They can't go back to their homes or countries and lack the proper paperwork to go any further. The Germans have demanded the Spanish enforce their border laws to the letter of the law and General Franco isn't willing to confront his former allies on the matter. Most of the Spanish border guards are willing to look the other way, but are afraid they will be held accountable and removed from their positions. I was finally able to find a compromise and a number of refugees were allowed to pass into Spain. The agreement won't last long and more problems will develop with new refugees arriving every day."

"We have the same issues here, David. There aren't enough ships or planes to get everyone out. The fact the refugees have made it this far is to their credit, but getting out is another matter. Since I must still put in time here at the embassy, I am forced to deal with some of these people. Money isn't the problem in most cases, the refugees sold everything they owned to get this far. Spaces on departing ships are booked for weeks in advance and unless something happens to the original ticket holder, the others are out of luck."

"Nasty situation," Eccles agreed. "The poor blokes have few real options."

"Exactly, David. We can't help them all but the embassy does its best."

"So, what's your situation here, Jack? London says you have some interesting developments to share with me."

Jack Beevor spent the next fifteen minutes bringing Eccles up to date on the Schoenfeld matter and laid out his plan. He finished his account and waited for comments from his colleague.

David Eccles took his time considering the options Beevor put forth and finally spoke in a level tone.

"Jack, I am not at all opposed to your thinking on this matter. Fact is, we must find a way to stop the next large German shipment and deal with Dr. Schoenfeld at the same time. The acts must be almost simultaneous since one will alert the other and we might not get a second chance. Putting an end to the good doctor will be easy, but halting the shipment could get quite tricky. A shipment this large would have to be made by rail and would pass through Spain on its way to Germany. Under no circumstances should this train be allowed to cross the Spanish border. We simply cannot risk a confrontation with Spain. Hitler met with Franco back in October in an attempt to get him to enter the war on the Nazis side, but so far Spain has resisted and I don't see them committing to Germany even though Germany was their ally in the Spanish Civil War."

"So, what's next, David? I have been waiting for your input before going any further."

Eccles deliberated in his mind and eventually responded. "We must plan this carefully, very carefully, my friend. One slip and everything is in the shitter. What are our assets for use in the field? I'm sure you have a limited number of personnel at your disposal."

Beevor listed all of his unit's personnel along with a few lower level embassy people he believed he could borrow from the military attaches. The total came to eleven or twelve, depending on who was available.

Eccles considered the number and remarked positively, "If these people know what they are doing, that might be enough to do the job. We had better get crackin' on this, our timeframe is fairly limited. We need to study the train schedules and routes such a train would utilize to locate the optimal attack point.

"I particularly like the idea of blaming everything on the communists. They deserve some exposure even if they haven't actually earned it. It will keep the authorities off our backs and provide a valid explanation for both actions."

Jack nodded in agreement and asked, "What about Sir Ronald? Should we keep him in the loop?"

"Not right now, Jack. I'll handle him when the time comes. It's probably best we keep all this to ourselves."

"I know who to put on the train schedules," asserted Beevor. "Izaura is quite clever and able to extract information in a short time that would take others much longer."

"Whatever you say, Jack. This is your show and you have to make most of the important decisions. I'm just here to add a bit of glamour to the mission."

Jack Beevor looked at his friend and broke into a huge grin. "Whatever you say, David. It's good to have you here."

"Likewise, old boy. This should be a bloody hoot. Excellent way to start a New Year."

The pair exchanged glances and returned to their planning. Jack Beevor's plan to combat the wolfram shipment and deal with Dr. Schoenfeld had suddenly become a reality.

Tuesday, December 31, 1940
Gentlemen's Bar
Hotel Palacio
Estoril, Portugal

Jean Pujol was very satisfied with his permeation into the ranks of Portugal's PCP. His ruse had become something personal to him and he reveled in his early success. He sat at the Hotel Palacio's Gentlemen's Bar and rehashed his involvement with the PCP so far.

He realized his prior experience as a soldier in Spain's civil war gave him a distinct edge over his fellow recruits who were mostly younger, from poor backgrounds and simply wanted to improve their family's existence. His recent expertise with his new rifle brought a contented smile as he recalled the events of that day earlier in the week.

A group of a dozen recruits were trucked to a deserted farm area outside Lisbon to become acquainted with their weapons under the supervision of a former policeman who was the instructor.

A series of crude targets had been set up in the fields and hills around the farm. The communist recruits were instructed how to hold the rifles and the correct posture required to keep the weapon steady to hit the target.

The first few attempts ended in failure so the instructor stepped in and fired a series of shots at the closest target. He did better, but still failed to inflict any serious damage to the target.

When it became Pujol's turn, he calmly stepped forward and fired a series of bullets that hit squarely in the middle of the target. His fellow recruits let out a loud cheer and patted him on the back for his effort. The former policeman joined in the celebration and took some of the credit for having instructed Pujol in how to handle the rifle. He promised to make a report to the PCP's leaders to insure Pujol's feat would not go unnoticed.

To Jean Pujol, or Garbo as he now preferred to be known by his British handlers, it was all in a day's work. At the next party meeting, he was singled out by Álvaro Cunhal as the type of soldier who would lead the PCP to greater heights than it had ever seen. Cunhal was only 27 and the possessor of a law degree and was currently a teacher in the City of Lisbon. He had been chosen to attend the Seventh World Congress in Moscow five years earlier and was recognized as the PCP's future leader. Paroled from Tarrafal Prison along with other communist leaders, he was again involved in the PCP's plans and actions against the *Estado Novo*.

Cunhal, along with Júlio de Melo Fogaça, was determined to bring the PCP back to its former status prior to its banishment in 1935.

After the meeting, Cunhal waved at Garbo to come with him into another room. He informed Garbo that he had been selected for promotion within the PCP and would serve as his assistant. "We need more dedicated comrades like you," Cunhal asserted. "People with skills who are not afraid to use those skills in our cause. If we are to grow and succeed, we must utilize the best people we have to make sure everything is done correctly."

"I will try my best, Senor," replied Garbo, accepting Cunhal's hand and squeezing it firmly. "I think we have some good recruits who just need more detailed instruction to become good at what they do. They all seem willing and that's a good start."

"I agree. It's up to our leadership to provide the training and expertise necessary to become a true fighting unit," added Cunhal. "With your help, we can achieve our goals."

Garbo took another swig of his white port and resumed his contemplation. He was indeed a lucky man to finally be allowed to be a part of the SOE's field work. He vowed never to disappoint Jack Beevor or his superiors.

Tuesday, December 31, 1940
Offices of Comboios de Portugueses
Lisbon Portugal

Izaura Ribeiro took the news of her new assignment with the same fervor and determination that she displayed in all her prior assignments. She went at once to the offices of the *Comboios de Ferro Portugueses,* the company that controlled all of Portugal's train service.

She had entered the offices a half-hour earlier and requested a map showing all the rail services around Barroca Grande and the surrounding area. When the clerk hesitated about providing the maps she had requested, Izaura knew she was in trouble with her assignment.

Another man approached the counter and asked. "Miss, I'm the office manager here and I am wondering why you are requesting these maps. It is unusual for someone to ask for specific maps and I need to know why you need them."

Izaura was ready for the question and quickly blurted out, "I'm a reporter for *O Século,* and we are doing a story on Portuguese mines and ore exports. Is there a problem in getting these maps? It seems to me they should be provided to anyone who asks for them. Is this not the case?"

"No, Miss. It's just that these are strange times with the war and all, and we just want to be careful. The PVDE has given us instructions about the information we give out and I certainly want to follow their orders."

"That's all well and good," Izaura replied. "But if I don't get what I asked for right now, I intend to call my editor who just happens to be my uncle and tell him you are refusing to give me the maps I asked for. I'm sure he will not be happy with your refusal. Are you willing to take that chance?"

The manager thought for a moment and conceded, "There's no need for that Miss. I was just following the rules. You may certainly have the maps you need and my clerk with assist you in any way possible. I am sorry for the inconvenience; I assure you it won't happen again."

"Thank you, Senhor. You are making the right decision."

"Of course. Santiago, please give this lady whatever she has requested."

The clerk acknowledged his boss's directive and stepped up to where Izaura stood. "Now, Miss. Exactly what is it you wanted?"

Izaura replied to the clerk and repeated her request. About five minutes later, the man returned with a series of maps, neatly bunched and tied together with a ribbon.

"They're all here, Miss. Will there be anything else?'

"No, thank you for your help. Happy New Year."

Izaura gathered the maps and walked toward the entrance to *Comboios de Ferro Portugueses.* She was pleased with the way the experience unfolded and happy to have had the foresight to clear with her uncle, João Ribeiro, the cover story about an article for *O Século.*

It is always better to be prepared before your start, she reflected. Thank God my uncle understands what my job entails.

She hopped a trolley in the direction of Jack Beevor's flat on *Rua de São Miguel.* She knew he would be pleased with her efforts in this most important mission.

Chapter Twelve

Tuesday, December 31, 1940
Jamaica Bar
Rua Nova do Carvalho 6 – 8
Lisbon, Portugal

The short announcement that Dr. Gerhardt Schoenfeld would arrive within minutes caught Louisa Flores off guard. She wondered if something had happened to her client to make him change his way of notifying her of an impending visit. He had always given a day's warning, but this time was different.

Louisa quickly bathed and put on some makeup and was combing her hair when an excited Ouzie burst into her room. "He's here, Louisa."

"I'll be right down, Ouzie. Offer him a drink and let him know I'm coming."

"Yes, Louisa," exclaimed the maid. She hurried off and Louisa finished combing her hair.

Minutes later, Louisa Flores swept into the Jamaica Bar's ante room as fresh and lovely as Dr. Gerhardt Schoenfeld had ever seen her. She flashed a congenial smile to the man who stood as she entered.

"Welcome back, *Meu Amor*" she offered openly. "I never expected to see you on such short notice."

"It couldn't be helped," Schoenfeld responded. "The lines were down where I was and I had to wait for a stop near Lisbon to call you. I had to bribe the driver into stopping long enough for me to make the call."

"You are so thoughtful, you really are."

"You are worth it, Louisa. Are you okay?"

"I'm fine. Same as usual. Not much changes around here, but I don't think that's of great interest to you. Madame has planned a New Year's Eve party, but they're usually boring."

Schoenfeld disregarded her comment and asked, "Louisa, is there someplace we can go and talk?"

She looked upstairs but the German shook his head. "No, I didn't mean that. I just want to talk to you for a while."

Louisa sensed something was different and motioned for him to follow her. "Come with me, I know just the place."

The two moved to a small room adjacent to the one where they met. A small couch and a single table were the only pieces of furniture in the room.

"Yes, this will do," Louisa asserted. "No one will bother us here."

"Good, Louisa. I have something important to tell you."

Louisa acknowledged his words and nodded her head for him to begin.

"I have just received word from Germany that I must begin my preparations for returning to Berlin. My work here is almost completed and my superiors want me to finish it in my original workshop. I hadn't expected to be ordered back to Germany this soon but I must make the best of it."

"That's quite exciting news, *meu amor.* You must be pleased that your work is so well regarded."

"Yes, but that's only part of it. I have no assurance I will be allowed back in Portugal once all this is completed. I might be assigned another project that requires me to stay in Berlin."

Louisa thought for a moment before answering. "Then, what are you to do? It doesn't sound as if you have any choice."

"I have one choice, Louisa. I can take you to Germany if you will come with me."

Louisa was stunned by the doctor's statement and fought to respond correctly. "That's a wonderful offer, *meu amor.* But..."

"But what, Louisa. You would love Germany. You would be

treated like royalty and have everything you could ever want. It would be a great adventure for both of us."

Louisa fought for the correct response and finally said, "I would have to think about it, *meu amor*. It would mean changing my life and leaving my family and my country to go to a place I've never seen that is involved in a war."

"A war we are winning," inserted Schoenfeld with confidence. "Some experts are predicting the war will be over in a matter of months and then everything will return to normal. My Germany is a beautiful place and we could have a wonderful life there."

"But it's terribly cold there in the winter, isn't it?" Louisa responded with little emotion. She was still looking for a way out of what had suddenly become a major predicament.

Schoenfeld sensed her hesitancy and asked plainly, "Don't you love me, Louisa? I thought you would be overjoyed with my suggestion. You don't seem too enthusiastic about it."

Louisa sighed and weakly reacted, "Of course I love you, *meu amor*. It's just this is so unexpected. I must think clearly about how my decision will affect me and my family."

"We can't take your family, Louisa. That would be impossible."

"That's not what I meant. I simply feel if I would leave and go with you, I might never see my family again. I love them dearly and would miss them terribly. Besides, I don't speak any German and wouldn't know how to reply to anyone."

"I would teach you, Louisa. After all, I have learned Portuguese since I came here."

Louisa chose not to answer Schoenfeld and continued contemplating her situation. *I'm not sure what to do about this. I'm certainly not going to pack up and move to Germany, that's out of the question. Too bad he feels this way, he's really a nice fellow and is also very generous. Shit, I'm not in love with him or anyone else, but Izaura wants me to keep him here as long as possible. I don't know why this is necessary but she hasn't paid me yet and I can't do anything without that money they promised me. Shit! This is ridiculous and I don't see an easy way out. I guess I should tell him I'll think it over. That should buy me some time. What else can I do. If I turn him down flatly, he might just bolt away from here with his heart broken. I've seen stranger things happen before. I guess I have no other option than to tell him I'll think about his offer.*

She returned to the moment and took Schoenfeld's hand. "Look, *meu amor,* this is simply too much for me to consider all at once. I need time to sort everything out and to talk to my family. I know this isn't what you want to hear but it's the best I can do for the moment. If this answer doesn't suit you, I'd understand if you wanted to change your mind. I'd still care for you, no matter what happens."

It was Schoenfeld's turn to consider the situation. *I will do anything to get this woman to leave with me. She is something special and I am a better person around her. If she needs time, I'll certainly give it to her, it's the least I can do. Maybe I shouldn't have sprung it on her like this, after all it would be a life-changing decision. If she comes with me to Berlin, no one there will ever hear a word about her past, for both our sakes.*

He emerged from his thoughts and looked directly at Louisa Flores. "My sweet Louisa, you may have all the time you need within reason. I'm not exactly sure when I will be recalled to Berlin, so you must take that into consideration. If you need a few days, a week, even two, that will be okay with me. I just want you to say yes, that's all that matters to me."

Louisa was moved by his gesture and spoke again. "You are a kind man, *meu amor.* And I know your offer comes from your heart. I will give this my serious thought and talk to members of my family. I will have an answer for you, only not just now. I hope you understand.'

"I do, Louisa. I do."

"Good. Then let's go upstairs and express our feelings for each other. I feel we've learned to do that quite nicely."

She took Schoenfeld by the hand and let him up the nearby stairs. It wasn't quite the evening she expected, but was pleased it would end on a happy note. She also knew it was important to notify Izaura Ribeiro of this latest development. And, she couldn't help feeling if her decision would put her life in danger.

Tuesday, December 31, 1940
Prime Minister's Office
Rear of São Bento Palace
Lisbon, Portugal

Following the visit from Cardinal Cerejeira, Prime Minister António Salazar called the head of the PVDE to his office.

Captain Agostinho Lourenço was acutely aware that a summons on short notice the day before a holiday from his leader involved something special.

As soon as Lourenço was seated, the Prime Minister got right to the point. "Captain, Cardinal Cerejeira just left my office in a troubled state. One of his parishioners approached him with news that the PCP was reorganizing and that his churches and clergy might be targets of this organization.

"I agree with his assessment since the Catholic Church and the Communist Party are bitter enemies. Catholics might well be targets for the PCP and I don't want that to happen. You must step up your efforts to disrupt these fanatics and ensure the churches and clergy are safe. Some of our country's historical churches could be their first targets in order for the PCP to make a definitive statement," concluded Salazar.

Lourenço calmly replied, "We are aware of the situation, Prime Minister. After I met with you previously on this matter, I put extra men on the case. We now have three agents who are members of the PCP as well as the young man I mentioned to you earlier. If and when the PCP plans something definitive, these men should be able to let us know."

"Excellent, Agostinho. I hoped you would be on top of this. We can't afford to let them operate freely in our country."

"Prime Minister, I'm also beginning to believe these people aren't as well-armed as I first thought. Only two of the four agents we planted were given rifles, the others were promised weapons when the PCP's next shipment arrived. I think the PCP was given a limited number of rifles and they have already exhausted their supply."

"You might be right, Agostinho. But I don't want to take them lightly. I have directed the head of our Army to organize his troops produce a plan for guarding our great old churches as well as our historic buildings. We are in the process of developing three additional Army divisions with emphasis on national defense and the defense of Lisbon in particular. You will see the results of these actions immediately. I believe the PCP will think twice before attempting to attack these buildings with the Portuguese Army on guard. The first soldiers will start their duties the day after tomorrow. In a month, we expect to have all the important churches and buildings fully protected."

"That's good news, Prime Minister. We are doing the right thing."

"Agostinho, it is vitally important we have inside information on the PCP's future plans. It would only take a few of them to cause us problems. And, if they are successful in their efforts, their organization will attract additional followers and encourage their Russian counterparts to provide them additional arms and monies."

"Yes, Prime Minister, that has also occurred to me. I will do everything possible to thwart these people."

"I'm counting on you and your people, Agostinho. So is our country."

"Thank you, Sir. I am aware of the gravity of my position and I will use all of my resources to get the job done."

"Very well, Agostinho. Just keep me notified whenever anything happens or you develop any plans."

"Certainly, Prime Minister. You have my word."

The pair shook hands and Lourenço turned and departed. The heavy load on his shoulders had suddenly taken on weight.

Thursday, January 2, 1941
Testing Laboratory
Rua Padre Manuel Vaz Leal 2
Barroca Grande
Covilha, Portugal

Dr. Gerhardt Schoenfeld was back in his laboratory but realized his work wasn't as focused as usual. He experienced short periods of mind wandering that mostly concerned his latest visit to Lisbon and Louisa Flores.

I am unsure as to why Louisa wasn't excited! I thought she would be when I talked about our going to Germany. I thought she would jump at the chance to leave her profession and come with me to my beautiful Germany. Maybe I was wrong in popping it out to her in the way I did. I know she cares for me but is that enough? I haven't had all that much experience in dealing with women and I assumed the best way to ask her was directly. Perhaps that wasn't too smart and my offer simply overwhelmed her. I know we haven't known each other that long, but that doesn't really matter to me. I just want her near me for the rest of my life.

I know she would be made welcome in Germany, many of my friends would take to her at once. They would be happy for me to have found someone after the terrible time I had with my former wife. I just don't understand why Louisa was so hesitant. At least she agreed to think it over and discuss it with her family. At least there's hope for the two of us in the end. I want to go back to Lisbon and see her again but my work is too close to completion for any interruption. I'll just have to wait it out and hope she finally makes up her mind. If she says yes, it will be the best thing that has ever happened to me. Even better than the honors our Führer will bestow on me for my work. I'll be a hero in Germany and my country will enjoy a definite advantage in our munitions cause.

He sighed and concluded, *I'll just have to wait and see what happens. It won't be easy, but I have no other choice.* He returned to his work and was soon lost in his calculations.

Friday, January 3, 1941
Jack Beevor's Flat
Rua de São Miguel 155
Alfama, Lisbon, Portugal

The pro-British agent known as Garbo waited patiently for Jack Beevor to return to his flat. The day was cold and windy and Garbo chastised himself for not wearing sufficient clothes to ward off the inclement weather. He sat in his car across from Beevor's flat and finished what was now his last cup of cold coffee. He chided himself for not ensuring the SOE chief would be at home when he arrived.

A half hour later, a taxi arrived and deposited Jack Beevor at the entrance. Garbo opened the car door and quickly headed for the front door.

Beevor saw him coming and looked around for anyone hanging in the area. Satisfied they were not observed, he then welcomed his agent. "Garbo, it's good to see you, old man. Do you need a chat? It must be important for you to just come over without notice."

"It is, old man," Garbo answered sarcastically. "I don't want to waste your time or mine."

"Then come on in," Beevor offered. "It's much warmer inside. How long have you been waiting?"

"Too long," Garbo replied. "I was getting really cold out there. I didn't wear enough clothes."

Beevor took off his coat and gestured for Garbo to sit down. "So, what do you have for me? I've just put some tea on the stove for us."

Garbo hesitated a moment, then began. "As I told you, the PCP made me a second officer in my unit. Last night we had a meeting and decided we would develop a plan to attack and destroy one or more of Lisbon's historic churches or buildings to bring our presence and the cause of communism to everyone's attention. I tried to talk the leaders out of it by saying it was too early for such a move, but they called me a defeatist and told me to be quiet."

"Did they decide on the which buildings or churches?" Beevor questioned.

"Several were mentioned but the leaders said they needed to study the places to see which ones would be the easiest to attack.

They intended to visit several locations, then decide which ones would make the most vulnerable target. I'm not sure they will tell us the mark until right before the attack. If they do it that way, it would be almost impossible to stop."

Jack Beevor pondered the situation and finally remarked. "We have to be really careful about this Garbo. We don't want these fools blowing up priceless buildings. But we can't risk them finding out you are on our side or your life would be in peril. You must somehow discover which places are targets and I will talk with my ambassador about developing a warning system for the Portuguese government. I'm not sure what he will do about it, but at least we can try."

"Then I'll be leaving, Senor. As soon as I learn anything, I'll get back to you. Hopefully in time to stop the attack."

"Thank you for coming, Garbo. Your help has been invaluable."

"No problem, Senor. You are paying me well for my time."

Monday, January 6, 1941
Secret PCP Meeting Place
Alto Barrio, Lisbon, Portugal

Álvaro Cunhal and Júlio de Melo Fogaça were deep in discussion about the choice of targets for their initial attack on the Catholic Church and the Republic of Portugal.

"We are facing a difficult decision, Álvaro," Fogaça said uneasily. "We are limited to the few meager explosives we have been able to find or steal. Unless we suddenly secure more explosives, we only have enough to destroy one building. We have been promised a shipment from Russia, but they promised us before and the shipments never materialized. I can't put my trust in the Russians even if they are loyal comrades."

Cunhal nodded his agreement and responded, "So we have to decide if it's the government or the church we want to strike."

Fogaça nodded this time and thought, *While the Catholic church is our oldest and most problematic enemy, it is the government and dictator Salazar that imprisoned us for the past five years and collapsed the PCP. We must send a message to them and to the people of Portugal that we intend to reestablish ourselves and the PCP as a major political factor in this country. By destroying a symbolic structure, the government owns and the people of Portugal admire, we will accomplish more than just destroying a Catholic Church.*

Júlio de Melo Fogaça looked up and faced his friend and co-conspirator. "The decision is easy for me, Álvaro. We need to show the government we mean business and are capable of destroying something it owns and occupies."

"Which building do you have in mind, Júlio?"

"Well, of the three buildings on our initial list, only one seems suited to our needs. I went by yesterday and there is only minimal security. An old army pensioner seemed the only guard and he wasn't even armed. I don't feel we will have any resistance when we attack."

"So, tell me, comrade," Cunhal said impatiently.

"The *Palace Fronteira*. You may recall it's a 17th Century Building and its sits away from downtown Lisbon."

"I remember visiting it when I was in school. It was very pretty inside and contained a collection of spectacular tiles. It had a nice garden area and was near the Lisbon Zoo."

"You have a good memory, Comrade. I can see the place made a good impression on you."

"It would be a shame to destroy something that beautiful, but if the cause..."

"The cause is the most important thing to us right now. We are fighting for our very survival and what we believe in. An old building that could be rebuilt provides us with an excellent target. We need to make plans to destroy the *Palace Fronteira* as soon as possible," continued Álvaro Cunhal.

Fogaça gathered some maps and other papers he had brought to the meeting. In his mind, the PCP was finally ready to act on behalf of world communism. His years of imprisonment and futility were about to come to an end.

"If that's what you think best, Comrade. I'll start planning and assign the men to the mission. It shouldn't take more than a few days to set up. Who should I assign to this?"

"The Spaniard we recruited has prior military experience during the Spanish Civil War. He would be perfect for the job."

Fogaça gathered some maps and other papers he had brought to the meeting. In his mind, the PCP was finally ready to act on behalf of world communism. His years of imprisonment and futility were about to come to an end.

"Begin the preparations. We don't want to waste this opportunity."

Fogaça smiled at his co-leader and left, eager to begin his mission.

Tuesday, January 7, 1941
Board Room
British Consulate
Rua São Francisco Borja 63
Lapa, Lisbon, Portugal

Izaura Ribeiro and Jack Beevor bent over the assortment of maps spread out over the magnificent cork oak table that graced the elongated room. The British embassy's board room was commandeered for this part of Beevor's upcoming mission to thwart Germany from receiving an extra-large shipment of wolfram it had purchased from Portugal for its munitions programs.

Izaura explained to her boss that the wolfram ore mined around Barroca Grande was initially transported to a martialing yard in Coimbra and then connected to another train bound for Salamanca in Spain.

"We have a choice of before or after Coimbra," commented Izaura. "Once the ore reaches Spain, I don't feel we have much chance to destroy the shipment."

"We can't risk offending the Spanish," Beevor replied. "We have reports that a number of ranking government officials have put pressure on General Franco to enter the war on Germany's side. An incident like we are planning would be beneficial to those arguments if it occurred on Spanish soil."

"There are numerous possibilities in Portugal for an attack," Izaura informed. "We just need a very steep grade with a deep gorge and hopefully a deep creek or river. The entire area is very sparsely populated and shouldn't be a problem for us to operate in."

"You need to find someone familiar with the area as soon as possible, to tell you the best place to blow up the train. But be careful, I'm sure the Germans have eyes and ears everywhere, even in our consulate. We can't let on about what we are doing."

"Ask the military attaché, he knows about us and our mission here. He might know someone we can trust."

"I'll do it right after we are finished this meeting. His office isn't far from this room."

"You have done well, Izaura. These maps and schedules are essential to the success of our mission."

Izaura smiled at the compliment. This job was turning out to be far more exciting than she could have ever imagined. She reminded herself that her uncle João was responsible for her being at the British embassy and she vowed to thank him again at the next opportunity.

Wednesday, January 8, 1941
Secret meeting place
PCP cell
Alfama, Lisbon, Portugal

Juan Pujol García, or Garbo to the British SOE, was summoned on short notice to one of the PCP's secret houses in Lisbon's *Alfama* District. He arrived and found several members of his cell along with Comrade Álvaro Cunhal, the CPC's acting leader. The wizened Garbo suspected this meeting involved the upcoming attack on a Portuguese target and found out quickly that his supposition was correct.

"Our Spanish comrade," he said pointing to Garbo, "will be in charge of this most important assignment. He has prior military training and I feel good about placing this job in his hands."

Garbo lowered his head and thought.

This is insane. I don't want to blow up any buildings but if I fail, I might easily compromise my standing in the PCP. Nobody said this was going to be easy, I'll just have to figure out a way to get through it. I bet Cunhal has instructed one of the other comrades to shoot me if I act strangely and don't succeed. Well, I asked to be in the field and this is all part of it. I'll just have to think clearly and find a way...

Cunhal finished reviewing his instructions and signaled to Garbo to follow him. The pair entered an adjacent room where Garbo observed a number of boxes.

"Here are your explosives, Comrade. I want you to become familiar with them before you leave on the mission." He pointed to several boxes in the rear of the stack of boxes.

Garbo moved to examine the explosives.

My god, these are as old as me. I wonder where the PCP got them. Do they work?

"Have you checked these out, Comrade?" he asked Cunhal.

Cunhal looked at the boxes and replied, "No, we haven't had time to test any of them. The person I got them from assured me they were good as new. He also said he would return my money if they didn't work."

What would you expect him to say? surmised Garbo. These might work or they might not. I can see why the PCP had problems in the past. These leaders might be good politicians, but as far as military planners, they have a great deal to learn.

"They don't look very fresh to me," Garbo stated. "The boxes are so old they are falling apart. We'll have to tape them up before we leave."

"Do whatever necessary, Comrade. I just want you to make sure you succeed. Important people are watching our actions and I don't want to disappoint them."

"When it this supposed to happen? And, exactly what is our target."

"All in good time, Comrade. Your mission is scheduled for tonight. You and the others assigned will remain here until it is time. I will give you a map and tell you the target when you leave."

"I must have time to study the surrounding area, Comrade. Surely you realize the importance of being aware of the surroundings. Harming innocent civilians will give our cause a black eye."

"All that has been taken care of, Comrade. I made the surveillance myself and I will brief you in detail before you leave. Why are you so insistent on knowing where the target is?"

"It is my intention to survive this mission, Comrade Leader. I learned from my experiences in the war that one must be prepared for any eventualities. Surely you understand."

Cunhal thought a moment and answered, "Yes, I do, Comrade. But you must realize security is incredibly important to the PCP, and since this is our first mission, the security surrounding it is doubly important."

Garbo realized it would do no good to push the matter any further and declined to comment. He knew it would require all his skill and cunning to get out of this delicate situation. He also had to admit he was enjoying himself even though the dangers he faced seemed to be increasing by the minute.

Chapter Thirteen

Wednesday, January 8, 1941
Jack Beevor's Flat
Rua de São Miguel 155
Alfama, Lisbon, Portugal

Jack Beevor peered at the map Izaura Ribeiro had lain across his kitchen table. It contained the Portuguese railroad routes essential to his plan of destroying the upcoming shipment of wolfram ore intended for Nazi Germany.

Izaura was explaining her research to him and the attack point she considered prime for the SOE's mission.

"This spot here," she pointed to an X she had penciled on the map. "It's a crossing of the Côa River almost two-thirds of the way between Coimbra and Salamanca. The Côa is a tributary of the much larger Duero and flows south to north, a rarity in Portugal.

"I checked with someone from that area who works at my uncle's newspaper and the fellow doesn't recall much about the railroad bridge, except it seemed old. He believes the Côa is quite deep at that point and if this is true, would be perfect for our plan. I would like to go there and check it myself, but there aren't too many other choices. There's nowhere before Coimbra and only one other possible river crossing, but this spot seems better suited to our needs."

"You must leave immediately, Izaura. I'll get you an automobile along with a driver from the embassy for your trip. Since we aren't sure of the shipment date, we need to have all our facts in order, or as the Australians say, 'Ducks on the pond.'"

"You make the call. I'll be ready within a half-hour."

"Excellent, Izaura. We should have our assets in place by tomorrow or the day after."

"I would prefer tomorrow," answered Izaura with passion. "The sooner the better."

Beevor smiled at his young agent. *She is dedicated and driven, the attributes of a top flight agent. Let's see what she comes up with; we might even have the solution to our plan.*

He returned his attention to the map on the table. The area around the Côa River was sparsely populated with only one road traversing the entire area. It seemed perfect for the plan.

Wednesday, January 8, 1941
PCP secret house
Alfama, Lisbon, Portugal

Álvaro Cunhal listened patiently as Garbo discussed the quality of the explosives that had been secured for the PCP bombing.

"...and, there's no telling how old these are," an exasperated Garbo declared.

"Probably from the Great War if I had to guess. The printing on the boxes is even faded."

"This is all we could manage to procure," countered Cunhal. "You will just have to make do. I'm sure you will figure out something. You seem to be very resourceful, Comrade."

Garbo hung his head in disgust. A plan was slowly taking shape in the back of his mind, a plan that would satisfy everyone concerned.

"I will try, Comrade Leader. Maybe I can make all this work."

"Good, then it's settled. You will leave here in one hour. I have assigned several comrades to assist you. They are already in the next room."

"And will you tell me now what our target is? I'd really like to know before we leave here."

Cunhal considered the request and answered. "Yes, I will tell you. You can't possibly tell anyone in the next hour and this place is heavily guarded.

"I have chosen this target carefully. There is practically no security around the place and it's not too far from here. You and your men can come right back here and report your success. The whole operation shouldn't take more than an hour."

"That's if we have no problems," corrected Garbo.

"Yes, that's true. You must be resourceful."

Garbo acknowledged the words with a nod.

"What about the place? What is it?"

"The building is called the *Palace Fronteira*, a historic building that was built in the 17th Century. It's only a 10-minute walk from here so you should have no trouble finding it. I have a map for you to follow"

Garbo took the map in his hand and studied it. "This should be easy, Comrade." He folded the map and put it in his jacket.

"Then everything is set. Come and meet your other comrades. They too are eager to serve our cause."

Garbo followed the leader into the next room. Four other men were present, armed with their *Svetas* they held tightly.

"Here is your leader for this mission," Cunhal announced. "You must follow his orders without fail, only he has the experience to lead you."

The men observed Garbo but said nothing.

"I will leave you to get acquainted, Comrades. Do your best for Communism and the PCP tonight. We will be very proud of you all."

The men nodded but remained silent. They continued to stare intently at their new leader. It was up to Garbo to gradually gain their trust.

Wednesday, January 8, 1941
PVDE Offices
Governmental Complex
Lisbon, Portugal

Captain Agostinho Lourenco's undistinguished offices within Lisbon's governmental complex was perfect for the PVDE head of Portugal's intelligence service.

The door to the offices had a simple number and no lettering designating the country's powerful security and intelligence gathering unit responsible only to Prime Minister António Salazar.

Lourenco was seated behind his desk reading reports submitted by his field agents when a young man appeared at the door to his office.

"What is it, Cornelio? Have you any news?"

"Yes, Captain. I'm afraid I do," the young man answered nervously.

"That's why I had you join the PCP, Cornelio."

Cornelio Scelfoes shrugged his shoulders and nodded.

"So, let's have it. What have you learned?"

"The PCP is planning on bombing a public building tonight," Scelfoes blurted. "I wasn't able to find out anything more, only that it is tonight. The PCP's security is tight and I only heard bits and pieces of a conversation."

"Without the location, there is little we can do to prevent it, Cornelio. I will have security increased at a few important buildings, but that's all."

"I have failed you, Captain. I should have gotten more information."

"Nonsense, Cornelio. I had you placed in the PCP to get us information. You will not always be successful, but every bit of information you gather helps us. Return to the PCP and see what develops. Some time you will hear something valuable to me and we will act on it. Now, return to the PCP before they miss you."

"As you wish," Cornelio sighed. "I'll let you know if anything develops."

Lourenco picked up the phone and asked for the nearby Army base. He explained to the officer in charge the need for deploying soldiers to some of several of Portugal's most important buildings. After a brief discussion, they agreed on the most likely targets. He thanked the officer for his help, sat back and pondered.

If the PCP is successful in their attempt tonight, I will have to do something specific to combat their presence. I must arrest their leaders and send them away again. This will not be easy to do, they are very clever people...

Wednesday, January 8, 1941
Approaching the Palacio Fronteira
Alfama, Lisbon, Portugal

Garbo's night had become progressively more complicated. Of the four men assigned him, only one displayed any sense of attentiveness or competence. Jamie Preto was twenty-one and a college dropout who had turned to communism as a means to an end. He saw in the PCP an opportunity to help himself and his country. When he discussed the plan with Garbo, he displayed a sense of purpose that caught Garbo's attention. Jamie was willing to do what it took to see the PCP would be successful. The other three comrades were simply along for the ride.

The small group arrived at the Palacio Fronteira and fanned out according to the plan Garbo devised. It was deadly silent around the area and there was no sign of a watchman or anyone moving.

Garbo studied the scenario and felt everything was in order for his team to proceed. He made a sweeping motion with his hand, the signal for the men to take assigned positions around the building. He then motioned to Jamie Preto to come with him. Garbo had placed Jaime in charge of the box of explosives intended to destroy the building.

"Come with me," he directed. The pair stepped forward toward the palace's front entrance when an elderly man in uniform appeared. The man's head was down and he carried a flickering torch that provided a degree of light in the darkened night.

Garbo froze and touched Jaime's shoulder. They knelt down behind a small bush and observed the guard as he approached their hiding place. Garbo looked over at another comrade who had leveled his rifle and shook his head. The man frowned and lowered his rifle.

Garbo and Jaime crouched as low as possible as the man shuffled by. In a matter of seconds, he was gone around another corner of the building. Garbo gave the thumbs up and approached the entrance.

"We'll place the explosives here, Jaime. Carve out several holes and I will place the charges. Make sure you leave long fuses; I don't want these damn old charges going off while we are still around."

Jamie acknowledged the instructions with a nod, took out a medium-sized knife and began scraping holes in the exterior plaster of the building. Fifteen minutes later, he signaled Garbo he was finished.

Garbo stepped forward and began inserting the explosives. His concern about their effectiveness increased as he handled the soft, mushy tubes.

This stuff is really the shits. I don't know if I could make them work under the best of circumstances. The fuses are frayed and I'm not sure they will make good contact. I tried to explain this to our leaders, but they were insistent we proceed.

Garbo and Jaime inserted fuses into the explosives that were all attached to a master fuse. Garbo finished his labor and turned toward Jaime, some ten yards away. He motioned for the youth to join him.

"We'll see how they work, Jaime. Go ahead and light the master fuse."

Jamie stepped forward and lit the main fuse that spiraled toward the charges imbedded in the building. The caterpillar of light crawled along the lines sputtered

So far so good. Now we will see if these charges work, surmised Garbo.

Ten seconds later, the fuses seemed to sputter and go out.

"Merda," commented Garbo. "This is ridiculous."

"I'll go see what's wrong," Jaime offered, moving quickly toward the front of the building.

Garbo tried to catch him but Jaime was already on his way. Out of the corner of his eye, Garbo saw another of his comrades advancing toward the explosives. He waved frantically at the man but was unable to catch the fellow's eyes.

The two arrived at the front of the building within seconds of each other. Jaime signaled the other man away but the man was intent on staying and ignored the signal. Jaime knelt down and began examining the charge. He wiggled the fuse and attempted to reinsert the line. Nothing happened. He turned to the next charge along the front wall and attempted to do the same thing with the fuse. In a split second, the charge exploded in Jaime's face, killing him instantly. The second comrade who had followed Jaime was also bleeding profusely from wounds to his arm and legs. He cried out in agony. A tone the forecast his imminent death.

Garbo signaled the two other men to leave the area and surveyed the scene. The watchman appeared around a corner carrying his torch and with his eyes wide open in amazement.

This is asinine, rationalized Garbo. *Amateurs, that's what we are. One man killed and another in a bad way. I need to get out of here right away.* He thought briefly about not returning to the PCP house but dismissed the idea.

I must keep up the charade at all costs. I will tell them exactly what happened and get myself out of this heap of crap. He retreated from the area and made his way back to the PCP safe house. By this time a number of local residents had emerged from their homes and were making their way toward the site of the explosion. Garbo made sure not to make eye contact with anyone along the way.

He arrived at the house and made straight for the room where he knew Álvaro Cunhal was waiting. He banged the door open and shouted in an angry voice, "Your explosives weren't worth a shit and we have lost one of our comrades, and maybe another."

"Calm down, Comrade," Cunhal replied. "Tell me exactly what happened."

Garbo tried unsuccessfully to control his emotions. "Those explosives were old and unreliable," he began wildly. "We attached several of them to the front of the building and..."

Wednesday, January 8, 1941
Park Benches
Jardim de Estrela
Barrio Alto
Lisbon, Portugal

Izaura arrived at the Jardim de Estrela several minutes before her scheduled meeting with Louisa Flores. The day was drizzly and a cold wind blew that made for an uncomfortable setting for the two women. Izaura had put off the meeting as long as possible but Louisa continued to press the issue and Izaura finally relented.

She carried a small bag that contained Louisa's payoff and held the bag tightly as she pulled her coat up around her neck. Days like this were rare in Lisbon and Izaura chided herself for not making the meeting indoors.

When Louisa poked her head through the park's entrance, Izaura forced a big smile and waited until Louisa arrived at the bench.

"Prompt as usual," remarked Izaura. "I got here a little early and had to sit out in this wind and drizzle."

"It isn't too bad," Louisa attempted to comfort her. "We can do our business and get out of this wind."

"Of course, Louisa. That would be fine with me." Izaura produced the bag and handed it to Louisa. "It's all there if you want to count it."

"I trust you, Izaura. If I didn't, I would never have done what I did for you. I betrayed someone who I cared for and I will probably regret that for the rest of my life."

"This is war, Louisa. We are all asked to do certain things for our beliefs and sometimes we must do what we don't like, no matter the consequences."

Louisa considered her words but did not respond.

"So, what will you do now, Louisa? Have you made any plans?"

"Yes. I have talked with my mother and sister and we intend to move to the south of Spain, somewhere along the coast. I will try and open a small business with the money and start my life over. I won't make any of the mistakes I made the first time around, at least I'll try not to."

"I envy you, Louisa. Not many people have the chance to start over."

"Thank you, Izaura. You have been kind to me during all this."

"Your information has proven quite valuable to the British and they intend to make the most of it."

Again, Louisa chose not to reply. She stood and extended her hand.

"Good bye, Izaura. It was nice meeting you."

"Same to you, Louisa. I wish you the best of everything."

Louisa turned and walked toward the park entrance. Izaura knew it was the last time she would see the beautiful lady who became her best agent.

Wednesday, January 8, 1941
Jack Beevor's Flat
Rua de São Miguel 155
Alfama, Lisbon, Portugal

Word was received from the British Consulate of an impending shipment of wolfram ore to Nazi Germany. The information was relayed to Jack Beevor who quickly called his team together to discuss its upcoming mission.

"The consulate has an insider at the German Embassy who is privy to key information and the military attaché believes the intelligence is accurate," Beevor explained to the group. "We now have a specific date the ore will depart the mines and when it should arrive in Coimbra."

"And we have the freight schedules out of Coimbra into Spain," Izaura interjected. "We can estimate when the train will cross the bridge we have selected with reasonable accuracy."

"These schedules even include water stops along the way," Beevor pointed out. "There's one just before the bridge and that's where we will plant our Nobel 808 explosives under the ore cars on the train. We will detonate every other car so I am assigning five royal marines from the embassy to accompany Izaura. She will be in charge and the soldiers will all know something about explosives. Prior to that, the group will plant charges at a point on the bridge that will ensure all the ore cars are affected. The shock waves will set off the detonators under the cars as they reach a precise point on the train trestle."

"How do we know the water stop won't be guarded?" asked Jean-Paul Benoit, the Free French attaché.

"Glad you asked, Jean-Paul. You will accompany Izaura and wait at the water stop for the train. If there are any guards, you will deal with them accordingly. I really don't expect any problems."

Benoit nodded at Beevor's statement and studied the map. "It's workable," he acknowledged.

"Good, we are all agreed. The ore leaves the mines day after tomorrow and so do we. I want to be in position well ahead of the train so there will be no slipups. Any questions?"

No one spoke and Beevor signaled the end of the meeting. "Go home and get some rest, I want everyone fresh when we leave. I have secured a furniture van for our use on the trip. It's very nondescript and should not attract attention."

The group rose and started to leave. Beevor motioned for Benoit to stay as the others filed out.

"Jean-Paul, I intend to lead the mission to blow up the laboratory in Barroca Grande. I want you to go with me tomorrow and scout out the place. We will take the charges with us and find a suitable hiding place for them. We should be able to go and return before nightfall."

"Whatever you say," Benoit replied. "The trip is not that difficult provided we don't run into any trouble."

"Good. Best way to handle trouble is avoid it."

Benoit nodded and continued out of the room. Beevor again studied the map. His first real field mission was in sight. He hoped he had thought of everything.

Wednesday, January 8, 1941
German Envoy's Office
Campo dos Mártires da Pátria 38
Lisbon, Portugal

Germany Envoy to Portugal Baron Oswald von Hoyningen-Huene was engrossed in a conversation with visiting SS Major Cecil Adolf Nassenstein, one of the SS's top espionage experts. The two were involved in a conversation when von Hoyningen-Huene's secretary knocked on the door to his office.

She entered and handed the diplomat a sealed envelope bearing the seal of the Portuguese Government.

"I thought you would want to see this at once, Excellency. It just arrived by courier and I feel it might be important."

"You were right to interrupt. I was expecting such an envelope."

Von Hoyningen-Huene tore open the envelope and read the contents.

"I didn't think we had a chance, Major. The PVDE is too clever to allow us to use guards on the ore train. Their precious neutrality makes them over cautious. We will have to send agents to the Spanish border and board the train as soon as it reaches Spanish soil."

"You mean *if* it reaches Spanish soil, Herr Envoy. I think there is a good possibility that any action against the train would take place in Portugal. Somewhere in those steep mountains, if you want my opinion."

"Thank you Major, we have already considered that. We will deploy an engine with a small car attached that will precede the actual ore train. I would expect them to spot any problems on the tracks and have time to warn the train. They won't be armed, but at least it offers a small degree of protection."

"If the saboteurs are clever, they won't be easy to spot or stop. I don't have a good feeling about this."

"There is little else we can do, Major. I considered shipping the wolfram out of Portugal, but there were logistical problems in getting a ship at the right time to carry the ore. Plus, the British Royal Navy is constantly harassing any ship that seems bound for Germany. It is too much of a risk for us to take."

"I agree, Herr Envoy. This is a most delicate situation and the Fatherland needs the ore as soon as possible. The Spanish route is the only viable method of shipping the wolfram. Once the train reaches Spain, our worries are greatly reduced."

"Let's get back to our business, Major. I want to know what the SS intends to do about the situation here in Lisbon. A great number of refugees have escaped from Germany and other countries and wind up here. The number has increased over the months and it seems to me that nothing has been done to prevent this mass exodus."

"Herr Envoy, the SS is doing all we can to stop this flow. All the borders are fully staffed and our men are experts in weeding out Jews and undesirables. There are simply too many for us to deal with. The French underground established several escape routes through the Pyrenees and many of the Spaniards on the other side of the border are sympathetic to the escapees. Plus, most of the escapees, mainly Jews, have money to pay for their exodus. The Spanish government has tried to stop these crossings but their resources are spread thin and their efforts haven't resulted in many arrests."

"You must add more men to your force, Major. I can't be responsible for all these people escaping. Berlin has sent word there will be dire consequences if these departures are not halted. I've also instructed our local *Abwehr* chief to put a number of his men on it but that doesn't seem to have had any effect. The numbers indicate there are more people arriving each day."

"As I mentioned, Herr Envoy, we are fully staffed," replied Major Nassenstein, his voice rising. "There is nothing more I can do. You can call Berlin if you wish, but I am powerless to do any more."

Von Hoyningen-Huene was now exasperated, but saw no alternative.

"I will wait and see how all this works out," the veteran diplomat finalized. "If Germany intends to survive this conflict, we had better have Lady Luck on our side. If she deserts us, we will be in trouble."

He signaled the Major to leave and returned to paperwork on his desk. The Major uttered a shrill, *"Heil Hitler,"* saluted and left the room.

Thursday, January 9, 1941
PCP Safe house
Alfama, Lisbon, Portugal

The following morning, Álvaro Cunhal verbally vented his frustration at the failure of the PCP to bomb the *Palace Fronteira* that also resulted in the loss of two comrades. Moments later, he turned to Garbo and said apologetically, "You told me the explosives were out of date and I didn't listen. Now we have lost two of our comrades and the action has alerted the government that someone is attempting to destroy one or more of their buildings. That will mean increased security and make our job even more difficult. I must find a way to get new explosives that work, no matter the cost. I will not send another team out on a mission until I have succeeded."

"Good, Comrade Leader," Garbo agreed. "Our comrades will be happy to learn of your plans for our future. We must have fresh vitalities in our group."

"But we must not stop planning," insisted Cunhal. "The explosives Russia promised could arrive any day. We must be ready."

Garbo acknowledged his leader with a head nod and spoke in a low tone. "We have another problem, Comrade Leader."

"What else could there be?" asked Cunhal.

"Our comrades who were killed were carrying their *Svetas* when the charges exploded. The PVDE will be able to identify them as *Svetas* and place the blame directly on the PCP. I think we should lay low for a while until this all blows over. We wouldn't want any of our comrades to fall into their grasp."

Cunhal considered Garbo's suggestion and commented. "Perhaps you are right, Comrade. The finger will point at us and we don't need any added pressure at this point in our development. I will give orders for everyone to stand down and return to their former duties until I feel comfortable, we can succeed."

Garbo took a deep breath and patted Cunhal on the shoulder. "That's the right thing to do, Comrade. In the end it will make the PCP all the stronger."

Cunhal sighed and said plaintively, "I certainly expect so, Comrade. We have many goals before us and a great deal is expected from us by Moscow. I must send them a report and I hate having to tell them of our failures."

"No need to tell them anything, Comrade Leader. Tell them we are still developing our plans and are in great need of explosives. Implore them to help us begin our great mission against the capitalists and our enemies."

Cunhal considered Garbo's suggestion and nodded. It might be better to withhold the facts about the botched bombing until there was something more concrete to report. He looked at the Spaniard who thought the way a natural leader should. He was glad the man was his comrade.

Chapter Fourteen

Friday, January 10, 1941
Prime Minister's Office
Rear of São Bento Palace
Lisbon, Portugal

Captain Agostinho Lourenco waited patiently for Portugal's Prime Minister to enter his office. When the solitary figure arrived, the PVDE head stood and greeted his country's leader.

"Sorry to have kept you waiting," Salazar exclaimed, "I had another meeting outside the office. There was an accident involving a tram and the traffic was completely stopped."

"I didn't mind waiting, Prime Minister. I have news of the bombing of the *Palace Fronteira* and I thought you would want to hear about it as soon as possible."

"Certainly, Agostinho. What have you learned?"

"Two things, Prime Minister. First of all, the explosives that were used were old and practically useless. Most of the charges didn't go off and we removed them from the building's outer wall. Only one detonated and killed two of the perpetrators."

"Interesting, Agostinho. Any idea where the explosives originated?"

"Somewhere outside the country, but exactly where there's no telling. Thank God these didn't work any better, they could have easily done great damage to the *Palace Fronteira*. As it is, there is only minor damage to the front wall that can be easily repaired."

"What about the two bodies?"

"Nothing yet, Prime Minister. No one has inquired or shown up to claim the bodies. I'll let you know if anything changes. But there is something else we discovered."

"What is it?"

"Both men were carrying rifles with them, almost new. The rifles weren't badly damaged and we were able to identify the model."

"And?"

"The rifles were *Svetas* or *SVT-40's*. These are the newest Russian battle rifles and were probably used by members of the PCP. Our sources within the PCP indicate each new member of the organization is given a *Sveta* when he joins and this is the first instance, we have seen them used in an operation."

"The PCP, huh?" It seems they have reorganized in record time."

"Yes, Prime Minister. I think the attack on the *Palace Fronteira* was intended to show everyone in Portugal they are back on the political scene."

"I think you are right, Agostinho. Their leaders are fanatics and will stop at nothing to overthrow our government."

"I have notified the military to increase security around our important buildings and churches; if they attempt something like this again, they will face a ready challenge. I'll go over the plans with the head of the army and make sure everything possible is protected from attack."

"You do that, Agostinho. If the army general has any qualms about helping in this, ask him to give me a call."

Captain Agostinho Lourenço smiled at his country's leader.

"As you wish, Prime Minister. It will be a pleasure."

Salazar smiled back at his police chief. He knew his country's security was in capable hands.

Saturday, January 11, 1941
Approaching watering station
Guarda District
Central Portugal

Izaura Ribeiro and Jean-Paul Benoit and their retinue of Royal Marines made excellent time in their furniture van and arrived nearly a half-hour earlier than had been planned.

Izaura sent the marines to scout the immediate area and selected a secluded spot to park the furniture truck.

"When the marines return, they can unload the explosives and hide them over there."

She pointed to a patch of bushes and small trees adjacent to the railroad tracks just before the watering station. Jean-Paul acknowledged the site and stared at the scene. The setting was serenely pastoral, pleasing to the eyes, and provided good cover. A sound choice.

Izaura went over a prepared checklist in her mind, mentally continuing aspects of the mission. She was determined that nothing would go wrong on her first field mission for the SOE under her charge.

The royal marines returned and reported finding nothing out of the ordinary on their scouting expedition. Izaura directed them to unload the explosives and place them behind the bushes near the tracks.

This was accomplished in about fifteen minutes and the truck moved clear. As the furniture truck disappeared from view, a sound of a locomotive emanated from an easterly direction.

"That can't be the train," Izaura exclaimed. "It's too early."

"Maybe they made excellent time," countered Jean-Paul.

As the sound grew closer, an engine pulling a small caboose appeared in the distance.

"What's that?" Izaura questioned, her tone rising.

"It's just an engine pulling a caboose," replied Jean-Paul. "Nothing to worry about."

"Well, it worries me. It's not supposed to be here. Could be a decoy."

"Let's just wait and see. No need to be alarmed."

Izaura nodded and crouched down behind some bushes.

The engine slowed down and prepared to take on water. The engineer and another man in overalls jumped down from the cab and lit cigarettes. The engineer pointed to the water spout and the other man moved toward the tower and reached for a cord that dangled from the arm. He pulled the arm toward the engine and began filling the engine's boilers.

"See, they are simply filling up with water. No worries."

Suddenly, three more figures materialized from the caboose and began talking with the engineer.

"What are they doing here?" Izaura asked impatiently. "Three more men to deal with."

"I don't know. Maybe they are just hitching a ride on the engine."

"Not likely," Izaura countered. "That's too many people for just hitching a ride."

"We'll see. They seem to be nearly finished with the watering."

The tower spout was replaced and the men returned to the caboose. The engineer and his helper remounted the engine cab and started turning up the power. A minute later and the engine began pulling away from the water tower.

Izaura gave a relieved sigh and looked at Jean-Paul.

"You were right, Jean-Paul. Thank goodness."

"Our train should be along soon, Izaura."

"I hope so. It's so hard waiting..."

Less than ten minutes later, a deeper whistle announced the arrival of another locomotive. As it turned the bend, Izaura could see a string of cars following behind the engine and coal car.

"That's our train," she pronounced. She signaled to the marines who were already aware of the train's presence. They all crouched low as the engine pressed closer. It passed their position and came to a stop under the water tower. A man alighted and prepared to pull the water spout down.

Izaura gave a signal to the marines who took off toward the ore cars that were some 100 yards away. Izaura looked toward the rear of the train but there was no sign of any activity.

The watering action took about ten minutes to finish. During that time each marine was able to attach explosive charges to the undercarriage of the ore cars. Their job finished, they returned to where Izaura and Jean-Paul waited.

For some reason, the train sat in its position and didn't move. Jean-Paul looked closely and observed the engineer who had alighted from the cab and was relieving himself directly under the water tower. A smile crossed his face as he turned to Izaura.

"Nature calls," he stated. "The train should be moving soon."

Minutes later, the locomotive belched and the train started moving slowly forward.

A relieved Izaura Ribeiro spoke softly to Jean-Paul. "You were right. Nothing to worry about."

She signaled to the marines who remounted the nearby truck. The train had not cleared the water station as the truck sped away toward its next stop.

Saturday, January 11, 1941
Testing Laboratory
Rua Padre Manuel Vaz Leal 2
Barroca Grande
Covilha, Portugal

At the same time more than 100 miles to the south, Jack Beevor and Royal Marine Sergeant Trevor Goodfellow made their way through some dense undergrowth to a spot marked on a map by Jean-Paul Benoit.

"It should be around here," Goodfellow announced, "if the map is correct."

"Jean-Paul was very exact with his description," replied Jack Beevor. "I'd stake a month's pay that the place is somewhere around here. We just have to look a bit harder. You go around there and I'll head this way," he continued pointing in another direction.

"Aye, sir," Goodfellow answered and started off.

Beevor looked at the extensive growth around him and conceded the Germans had chosen their laboratory location well.

No telling where the place is. It could be right under our noses and we still couldn't see it. Just have to keep looking, it will turn up soon.

Three minutes later, Beevor heard a shrill sound from the area where Sergeant Goodfellow had gone. He started in the direction of the sound and came upon the Royal Marine crouched behind some thick bushes.

"What kind of sound was that, Sergeant?"

"It was my best imitation of a wild bird," Goodfellow responded. "Didn't you like it?"

Beevor smiled but didn't reply. He looked in the direction that the royal marine was facing and noticed a building nestled between the trees that was mostly hidden from view.

"I'll bet that's what we are searchin' for," Goodfellow exclaimed. "It fits the description and is certainly well concealed."

Beevor acknowledged the comment with a nod and looked around. A small opening on a nearby hill caught his eye. "Let's look over here," he said in a low tone. He signaled the royal marine to follow.

The opening proved to be the entrance to a small cave, almost completely covered with vegetation that made it difficult to spot.

Beevor peered inside the cave and pronounced, "We'll hide the explosives here, Sergeant. Be careful not to disturb the vegetation. We don't want to alert anyone who might wander by."

Goodfellow looked at the SOE leader but refrained from answering. He carefully placed the pack containing the plastique charges and fuses inside the cave's opening and stepped back.

"There. Like it's never been touched," offered Trevor Goodfellow.

"Our plan better work," answered Beevor. "There's a lot riding on this part of the mission. Let's lay low for a couple of hours and then we can set the charges. It's important this place gets blown up around the same time as the train."

Goodfellow agreed with a nod and settled into a comfortable position that allowed him to see the laboratory. Beevor sat next to him and contemplated.

This will be the hardest part for me. Waiting, it's not something I enjoy very much. So far, no movement from around the laboratory. I wonder if anyone is inside?

Twenty minutes later two figures emerged from the building, each carrying several vials that seemed filled with liquid. They made their way away from the laboratory and disappeared around a bend not far from the building.

Probably going to the stream to dump some chemicals if Jean-Paul's description was accurate. Shouldn't take them too long, the stream should be fairly close to the laboratory.

A few minutes later the pair returned. Beevor was able to identify Dr. Schoenfeld from the photograph Louisa had provided, a perception that made him extremely happy.

Blimey, that's the bloke himself. I couldn't ask for anything better. The other fellow must be his assistant; he fits the description. Not bad if I don't say so myself.

Beevor reached over and tapped Sergeant Goodfellow on the shoulder. The marine turned and Beevor gave a thumbs up. The marine immediately agreed with a thumbs up of his own.

The two men then settled down to await the timing of their mission. So far everything was going as expected.

Saturday, January 11, 1941
Watering station 4
Guarda District
Central Portugal

The furniture truck carrying Izaura Ribeiro, Jean-Paul Benoit and their royal marine contingent made good time on the oft-bumpy road that led them to the bridge crossing the Côa River.

They arrived only a few minutes behind schedule and were pleased to find the bridge and the surrounding area deserted.

Izaura signaled the marines to begin setting the plastique charges. Two marines went to the ridge closest to their truck and the other two to a position near the far side of the bridge. The marines scrambled across the bridge and disappeared under the structure's wooden staves. They had been thoroughly briefed on placement of the explosives to achieve maximum effect when the charges exploded.

The marines on the far side of the railway bridge finished their task first and began scrambling back across the crossing. Upon reaching the others, they quickly assisted in finishing the placement of the gray claylike charges.

When they completed their work, they all returned to the furniture truck. Izaura motioned them into the rear and Jean-Paul drove the vehicle toward a wooded rise that commanded a full view of the bridge and surrounding countryside and was concealed from the railroad tracks.

"We're all set," Jean-Paul remarked. "Now we wait."

Izaura nodded agreement and sat back in the cab of the truck.

What seemed like hours was actually less than 30 minutes.

A puff of smoke and a distant noise from the west signaled the arrival of a locomotive chugging up the incline.

Izaura and Jean-Paul craned their necks in the direction of the sound. Jean-Paul produced a pair of binoculars from his backpack and adjusted the view. Moments later he exclaimed, "It's just the engine and caboose we saw back at the water stop."

"What are they doing here?" Izaura pondered.

"Probably scouting the tracks for trouble," offered Jean-Paul. "That's what I'd do if I was in the Germans' place. Put an engine ahead of the train to ensure the tracks are clear."

"That makes sense. I hadn't thought of that."

"You can't think of everything, Izaura. You've done quite well so far if you ask me."

"They seem to be slowing up," Jan-Paul observed. "The bridge is the perfect spot for explosives, a fact that hasn't escaped their scrutiny."

"But they can't see what we planted, can they?"

"Not if our men were thorough. You'd have to be right on top of the charges to see them, and I don't see anyone getting off the caboose to check."

The engine crawled its way slowly over the bridge in what seemed like an eternity to Izaura and Jean-Paul. In the rear of the truck, the royal marines crammed to see what was going on.

"Blokes are takin their blasted time, they are," one of the marines offered.

At the same time, a louder noise and more smoke announced the arrival of the freight train.

"The train made up some time," observed Jean-Paul. "Probably on purpose. They want to arrive at the bridge just after the span has been cleared by the locomotive."

"I can't believe this is happening," exclaimed Izaura.

"Don't fret yet, Izaura. They haven't discovered anything so far and chances are they won't. Just wait and see."

"Easy for you to say," she returned. "You have more experience than I."

Jean-Paul smiled at his compatriot but did not reply.

The train with the wolfram cars came into view as the scout train continued its slow progress across the bridge.

"Now it gets interesting," Jean-Paul observed.

The train approached the bridge and reduced speed as it got closer to the wooden structure. It reached the bridge entrance and began to slowly traverse the crossing.

Benoit refocused his binoculars on the first locomotive that appeared to have stopped just before exiting the structure. He saw that several men had alighted from the caboose and were scrambling onto the bridge.

"Oh, damn. It looks as if they've spotted something on the far end. Three of them are climbing into the structure. If they find the charges, it might ruin everything."

The Frenchman's fears were realized when one of the men on the bridge emerged and began waving his hands. The engineer sounded a shrill whistle and kept repeating it every few seconds. The man who emerged began running toward the ore train and waved his arms for the train to go backwards.

Meantime, the train had now made its way onto the bridge and wasn't able to stop its forward progress all at once. It crept forward as the engineer applied the brakes.

"Just a few feet more," agonized Izaura. "They are almost to the spot where we planted the charges. Please Lord, let them continue."

The locomotive' brakes squealed on the steel rails but still continued forward.

As it crossed the spot where the plastique rested, the first charges exploded with a loud bang. Several more followed in quick succession as the timbers on the bridge began to crack. Suddenly, several loud explosions rocked the air as the charges attached to the ore cars began detonating. The engine and coal car slid gracefully off the bridge followed by the remains of a number of ore cars that followed. After a few moments, the entire section of the bridge collapsed into the Côa River as the locomotive made a last gasp of life as it belched and slipped beneath the water. The other engine, seeing what was happening, quickly made it to the end of the bridge and safety. The men on the locomotive stood frozen, watching the demise of the bridge and the ore train.

Izaura turned to Jean-Paul and hugged him to the surprise of the Frenchman.

"We did it," she shouted. "We did it."

Jean-Paul smiled at her as the royal marines exited the back of the truck and joined their leaders in the celebration.

One of the marines spoke in a loud voice, "I counted twelve explosions from the ore cars. That means we got every one of them."

"Great work," Izaura pronounced. "The Jerries will be without their wolfram for some time."

"Let's get out of here," suggested Jean-Paul. "No telling who else in around that might be interested in the train."

Izaura made a last sweep of the scene and was delighted to see at least two swimmers heading back to shore. At least the engineer and his coalman would be spared.

No reason innocent Portuguese railway men should be killed or injured for just doing their jobs.

She turned to Jean-Paul and gave the order to re-board the truck. She couldn't wait to see Jack Beevor and tell him of their success.

Saturday, January 11, 1941
Testing Laboratory
Rua Padre Manuel Vaz Leal 2
Barroca Grande
Covilha, Portugal

Jack Beevor looked at his wristwatch and decided it was time to act. He signaled Sergeant Trevor Goodfellow to follow him. The pair stopped, picked up the charges they had hidden and made their way toward the laboratory that was the workplace of Dr. Gerhardt Schoenfeld.

They arrived in a few minutes and took up a position about thirty yards from the building.

Beevor leaned over to the royal marine and whispered, "You take the far side and I'll deal with this side. I'll give you a couple of minutes to make it over there and signal you to start."

Goodfellow nodded and took off around some overgrown bushes that saturated the entire area.

Beevor waited and eventually started toward the building. He knelt beside a wall and started to attach the plastique to the wall. He heard a door open and a figure stepped out. It was Dr. Schoenfeld's assistant who was carrying two vials of liquid. The man turned away from Beevor and started toward the creek.

I must finish this quickly. He will be back in just a minute.

Beevor took out another charge and placed it several yards further along the building. He took out a lighter and lit the fuse. He retreated quickly and managed to get out of sight as Hans Pfeffer reappeared. Beevor squatted down and was relieved when Sergeant Goodfellow arrived and knelt beside him.

"We should have our explosion soon," Beevor stated. "The fuses were set for four minutes and that is only a minute away."

Goodfellow nodded and remained crouched beside him.

A moment later the door opened and Dr. Schoenfeld stepped out. He carried a notebook and a pencil and continued writing. He stopped, thought a moment, and stepped back inside the building. Beevor looked at Goodfellow and shrugged his shoulder.

Goodfellow nodded negatively and continued to observe the building.

Not long after, a series of blasts brought the laboratory building down in a burst of flames and debris. The pair waited a long minute and slowly approached what remained of the edifice.

"I want to make sure they are both dead," declared Jack Beevor. "I need that information for my report."

Sergeant Goodfellow probed the remains and eventually pointed to two partial corpses among the ruins.

"They've had it," he exclaimed with finality.

"Good show," replied Beevor. "Let's get out of here. I don't want to leave any traces."

"Righto, I'm right behind you."

The two disappeared into the bushes and began their journey back to Lisbon. So far, it was a good day for Great Britain and the SOE.

Chapter Fifteen

Saturday, January 11, 1941
Jack Beevor's Flat
Rua de São Miguel 155
Alfama, Lisbon Portugal

The second bottle of *aguardente velha* was still about two-thirds full when Izaura Ribeiro knocked softly on the door of Jack Beevor's flat in the Alfama. Beevor motioned to Sergeant Goodfellow to open the door and downed a small amount of the precious liquid that remained in his glass.

The look of accomplishment on Izaura's face said it all.

"So, you succeeded in your mission," Beevor questioned.

"It was wonderful," Jean-Paul Benoit answered as he stepped forward. "We managed to get the entire train. The marines counted twelve explosions from the wolfram cars themselves, one for each car. I'm sure there's very little left for anyone to salvage."

"Yes, it was nice," added Izaura. "We almost had a problem but by the time they realized what was going on, it was too late. The plan worked perfectly, if I don't say so myself."

"Good job to you both. I will let London know about your heroics in tomorrow's diplomatic pouch."

"What about you? How did you do with the laboratory?" asked Izaura.

"Let's just say that the dishonorable doctor and his assistant have departed this earth and are conducting their experiments elsewhere," Beevor returned. "We blew the place to smithereens. We checked and nothing of value was left there. We also saw both bodies in the rubble."

"So, this was quite a day for our little group," Izaura added.

"Help yourself to the *aguardente velha*," motioned Beevor. "There's another bottle after we finish this one."

Neither Izaura nor Jean-Paul needed any urging. Both felt they had earned the drinks after their most rewarding day.

Tuesday, January 14, 1941
PCP Safe House
Alfama, Lisbon, Portugal

Lisbon's newspapers carried the train bombing on the front page for several days following the incident, with various theories as to who and why the ore train and bridge was blown up. No one came forth to claim responsibility for the act and political theorists had a field day by proposing various possibilities.

Naturally, Nazi Germany's main enemy, Great Britain, got more than its share of the blame, but with no actual evidence, those views were at best speculations with little actual substance.

At the clandestine headquarters of the PCP, Álvaro Cunhal was involved in a deep discussion with the other leaders of the Communist organization. Included in the group was Pujol, aka Garbo.

"It is necessary for the PCP to gain the respect of the Portuguese people," one of the leaders said. "To do that, we need to provide the people with something they can identify with. Something that makes us equal or superior to the other parties. Salazar gets his name in front of everyone by simply doing his job. We have no such luxury."

"Our last mission failed miserably," interjected Cunhal. "Through no fault of our Spanish comrade, we failed to destroy our target and lost two loyal comrades in the process."

"How can the Spaniard not be at fault?" another leader asked. "Wasn't he in charge of the mission?"

"Yes," Cunhal answered defensively. "But the fault lay in the condition of the explosives we provided. They were old and failed to detonate properly. I have sworn to provide new explosives for our next mission."

"I applaud Comrade Cunhal's dedication," another leader chimed in, "but that does not help our present situation. We need to do something now. Make a statement of the greatness of the PCP."

Garbo saw the opportunity and stood up. "Comrades, I'm not sure the answer isn't right in front of us. Everyone is talking about the detonation of the Côa River bridge and the loss of the freight train. It's been on the front page of every newspaper since it happened. No one has any idea of who planned or fashioned the attack, and I don't think the government has any idea either. It would be very simple for the PCP to claim we were responsible and no one would be the wiser. The Portuguese public would think twice about the PCP and its prowess in pulling off a major incident."

The room became suddenly silent as the PCP leadership considered Garbo's words.

Álvaro Cunhal spoke evenly. "In my mind, our Spanish Comrade has an excellent idea. It will cost us nothing to lay claim to the attack and everyone will take the PCP more seriously in the future. Our own comrades will take pride in our accomplishment and volunteer for other hazardous missions. I believe this would be good for us and I believe Moscow will take note and maybe be more responsive to our needs."

A voice then called for a vote.

"All in favor of the PCP taking credit for the bombing, raise your hand."

Every hand around the table raised their hand. All believed their decision was about to give the PCP new life in the eyes of many Portuguese.

Cunhal went to a phone booth he knew could not be traced and dialed the number for *O Século*. He knew if Lisbon's leading newspaper ran the story, all other Lisbon periodicals would soon follow. The reputation of the PCP as an organization to be respected had gained needed luster.

Wednesday, January 15, 1941
Prime Minister's Office
Rear of São Bento Palace
Lisbon, Portugal

Captain Agostinho Lourenco considered Prime Minister Salazar's comment almost comical, but concealed his amusement as Portugal's head finished his question.

Is my Prime Minister kidding? The PCP responsible for the attack on the bridge and train? Preposterous! They couldn't organize anything like that if they had five years to do it. The people who pulled this off were trained professionals and good at their job. No evidence was found, nothing to connect any organization or person to the attack.

I feel it was probably the British, they had the most to gain. I put out some feelers, but no one seems to know anything about it. Since the British are our ancient allies, I don't want to stir the pot too much.

Lourenço realized that Salazar was waiting for an answer.

"Prime Minister, I do not feel the PCP is organized well enough or capable of pulling off an attack as complicated as this. There is also the matter of the explosion outside Barroca Grande that no one is paying any attention to, particularly the newspapers. We've identified the dead men as German citizens and one as a respected doctor of physics. Since the two incidents occurred at approximately the same time of day, it is easy to assume they might be connected. What were two Germans doing in such an isolated area that just happens to be near the wolfram mines?

"These questions must be answered before we can make any assumptions as to who perpetrated these attacks. If the British are involved, we must be sure we can prove that fact because the old treaty between our country and Great Britain becomes involved.

"The only thing I am completely sure about is the fact that the PCP did not attack the train. They botched the simple job of bombing the *Palace Fronteira* and wound up losing two of their men in the process. I have a person inside the PCP and I will learn more about them in the future.

"As of right now, I would say to the newspapers that the matters are under investigation and not much else. The stories will lose interest in time and maybe we will catch a break as to who pulled off these incidents."

Salazar considered his subordinate's thoughts and responded.

"Agostinho, I believe you are right about the PCP and possibly everything else you spoke of. Since our neutrality is of prime importance, I feel a thorough investigation is in order and I know you will get to the bottom of it. Please refer any questions the newspapers might ask to my office and I will ensure they are handled properly. If the British went to all this trouble to stop the ore shipment, the real answer might lie in the explosion at Barroca Grande. Perhaps the doctor had discovered something quite important that would help the Nazis in the war. I don't know, but it seems to make sense to me."

"To be sure, Prime Minister. It makes sense to me too."

"Then go ahead with your investigations, Agostinho. As soon as anything develops, let me know."

"As always, Prime Minister."

Salazar rose and extended his hand to the security chief. He knew the events of the past few days were in good hands.

Friday, January 17, 1941
British Ambassador's Residence
Rua São Francisco Borja 63
Lapa, Lisbon, Portugal

Jack Beevor was once again seated in front of British Ambassador Sir Ronald Campbell. The two were discussing the fallout from the bridge attack and laboratory blast that Beevor had engineered for the SOE.

" ...and, ... you must realize your actions placed our embassy in a most delicate position, Jack. So far, no one has come to me with any accusations, but I know the Portuguese aren't very happy it happened on Portuguese soil. You are fortunate no one was killed on the train attack, that would have made it worse."

Beevor acknowledged the ambassador's point with a slight nod of his head.

Campbell continued. "You must cease any similar actions you might have in mind for the present, and possibly for your entire stay in Portugal. I think the PVDE suspects us, but they have no proof and that's in our favor. Prime Minister Salazar hasn't summoned me to his office of yet, and that means he has no proof.

"I expect the PVDE to begin following certain members of our staff here at the chancellery and that includes you, Jack. You must be extremely careful in where you go and to whom you talk. Don't take any unnecessary chances or the whole thing might just blow up in our faces."

"I understand, Sir Ronald. I don't believe I had any other choice in the matter. London..."

"I am not interested in what London thinks or wants," Campbell interrupted. "I care about Portugal, Lisbon and Dr. Salazar, not necessarily in that order."

"I understand, Sir Ronald. It won't happen again."

"It had better not, or you will be the proverbial cooked goose. Am I perfectly clear?"

"Perfectly."

"Then get your arse out of here and do something constructive," Campbell uttered with a wry smile. "I don't want to see you in here again."

Jack Beevor stood, turned and departed. He too had a wry smile that broadened as he exited the room. Working for the SOE was even more fulfilling than he could have ever imagined.

Chapter Sixteen

Saturday, February 1, 1941
Café Chave d'Ouro
Dom Pedro IV Square
Rossio, Lisbon, Portugal

Izaura Ribeiro's duties returned to normalcy following the destruction of the ore train some weeks earlier. She busied herself with several small projects and returned to the British Embassy one day a week to assist the staff processing the ever-increasing flow of refugees.

A particular case caught her attention. A Polish man and woman in their seventies arrived in Lisbon after escaping the ghetto in Warsaw. All the couple's relatives were killed and only a kind gesture by a German priest allowed them to escape. Their only possessions were the clothes on their back and an incredibly ornate necklace that was a family heirloom. The woman showed the necklace to Izaura as tears flowed down her cheeks.

"It's all we have," she sobbed. "We must sell it to get to a safer place. Can you help us?"

Izaura thought of Martim Silva and nodded to the couple.

"I know someone. I'll contact him and see that he helps you. Come back tomorrow and I'll give you the details."

The couple agreed and Izaura finished the processing. She then called Pilar and made a date to see Martim at the Café Chevre d'Oro later that evening. Pilar was somewhat hesitant to accompany her, but agreed to meet her friend.

Izaura arrived first and took a table near where Martim usually sat. Minutes later, Pilar arrived and greeted her friend.

"It's been awhile since we last met, Izaura. Have you been busy?"

"You could say that. My duties have taken me out of Lisbon several times. But, I'm back now and we can get together more often."

Pilar looked apprehensive so Izaura inquired about her mood.

"You look distressed, Pilar. Is anything wrong?"

Pilar hesitated, then answered, "It's nothing really."

Izaura probed her friend a bit further.

"Then why the apprehensive look on your face? It must be more important than you let on."

Pilar hesitated again, but finally spoke.

"It's about Martim. He's changed a lot in the past weeks. He's short and lets his temper get the best of him. I don't know what to make of it."

"Some type of pressure," Izaura remarked. "Maybe it's his job. Things might not be going so well for him."

"No, Izaura. He has more money than ever. He tips the waiters with large bills and carries a large roll. It's not the money."

"I don't know, Pilar. I haven't seen him for some time."

"When he arrives, observe his words and actions. You might learn something. He seemed a nice person but now I have second thoughts. Something is different about him, I'm sure of that."

The discussion ended as Martim Flores approached the table.

Good evening ladies," he said flatly. "Izaura, it's good to see you again."

"Likewise, Martim. How have you been?"

"I'm okay. My business is also okay but the competition is fierce. Too many people trying to buy jewelry and the prices have fallen. And the police have stepped up their surveillances. I have to be much more careful now than I was before. I don't want to end up in jail."

"I guess so. But these people will be alone. Why such an obscure location?"

"If they want to meet me, that's the place," Martim said cheekily. "I must not take any chances."

"A taxi can find it. I'll make sure they are there."

"Good. Now we can have our drinks." Martim motioned for a waiter.

Izaura sat back and observed Martim.

Pilar is definitely right about Martim. Something is bothering him and he seems a different person. I don't like the smell of this and will make it my business to be at the meeting when the Polish couple arrive.

She continued to watch Martim Flores until it was time to leave. Something was definitely different about Pilar's friend.

Sunday, February 2, 1941
Corner of Rua dos Cordoeiros
a Pedrouços and Travessa Torrinha
Restelo, Lisbon, Portugal

Izaura Ribeiro borrowed a 1939 Ford Anglia from the embassy car pool and arrived at the corner a few minutes before nine. She was happy the color of the car was black and the fact it blended into the neighborhood nicely.

I'm not sure why I felt the need to be here, Martim has always been open with me. His recent behavior has been off, but there's probably a reason for it. If all goes smoothly, I'll just chalk it up to bad woman intuition.

Izaura sat low in the front seat with her head just above the steering wheel. At five minutes to nine, a city taxi arrived. The Polish couple got out and waited under a dim corner light fixture.

Ten minutes later, a solitary figure walked onto *Rua dos Cordoeiros a Pedrouços* and made its way toward the couple. Izaura recognized Martim and forced herself even lower on the seat.

Martim stopped next to the couple and looked around in all directions. Satisfied they were alone he turned and introduced himself. The Polish man offered his hand but Martim disregarded the gesture and continued talking.

Martim continued talking and eventually held out his hand. The man looked at the woman and shook his head affirmatively. She reached into her bag and produced an object wrapped in cloth and handed it to Martim. He unwrapped the cloth and held up a necklace Izaura recognized from the day before. He studied it under the hazy street light for several seconds and then handed it back to the woman. A conversation began that suddenly turned argumentative. The Polish man shouted at Martim and the woman began crying. Martim shouted back and pushed the older man who fell to the cobblestones of the street. The woman shouted at Martim and pulled him away.

Izaura was perplexed as to what to do next. She opened the door to her car and took a few steps toward the corner. At the same time, Martim produced a knife from inside his coat and pointed it at the woman. She shrieked and put both hands toward him. Martim muttered something and continued toward the woman. He reached her and slashed her throat. The woman gasped again as she fell backwards on the street.

The Polish man struggled to get up when Martim reached him. A swift slash to the man's throat sent his back to the cobblestones.

Izaura couldn't believe her eyes. She screamed at Martim, "What are you doing? Are you crazy?

Martim Flores turned toward Izaura, "What are you doing here?"

"I was uneasy about this location and about you. Your actions of late were uncertain and I made it my business to see this through."

"You made a bad decision, Izaura. You should have minded your own business. Now I have to deal with you." He turned to the two elderly refugees bleeding out on the cobblestones. "I offered them money for the necklace. The man thought it was too little and then he insulted me. I have had enough of these refugees with their sordid stories. These people had no relatives, no one to miss them. I am tired of this whole situation. With this necklace I can get out of this business and go somewhere and live like royalty. No one will know."

"I will know, Martim," Izaura said somberly.

"Yes, that is unfortunate. I must take care of you in the same manner." He stepped toward Izaura who was still ten yards away.

Izaura reached inside her jacket for the Webley .455 caliber MK.VI that Jack Beevor had provided her for her safety. As Martim approached, she leveled the pistol and said calmly, "Not so fast, Martim. I'm not as defenseless as those poor people."

Martim stopped and considered his options. "I have no other choice, Izaura. It's you or me."

"Don't be a fool, Martim. I know how to use this pistol."

Martim hesitated and began to turn his back. About halfway through he turned and lunged at Izaura. She stepped back and fired the pistol, hitting Martim in the chest. He groaned and fell to the cobblestones.

"You have killed me," he gasped.

"You deserve it, Martim. You killed those helpless people."

A siren in the distance marked the arrival of a police car that had been alerted by a neighbor on the *Rua dos Cordoeiros a Pedrouços*.

Izaura stood in the street and lowered the pistol. She knew she had done the right thing in stopping Martim Flores' rampage. She now hoped the police would agree.

Wednesday, May 7, 1941
Avenida Mediterráneo, 127
Porto de Sagunt, Spain

The four months since leaving Portugal for Spain flew by for Louisa Flores. She decided on a location some 20 miles above Valencia, Spain, that was complete with a marvelous beach and friendly people. Port de Sagunt was a sleepy, seaside town on the Mediterranean that served as a getaway spot for bored citizens of Madrid, Sagunto and other Spanish towns and cities.

Louisa found a perfect location the first week she and her family arrived in Port de Sagunt. The space was on the main street, the Avenida de Mediterráneo, and was large enough for Louisa's new business as well as providing a small living space for the family.

It was Louisa's dream to open a flower shop in the space and the money she received from Izaura Ribeiro was sufficient to cover the costs for the first year.

The name chosen by Louisa reflected her fondness for the local flower shop she frequented in Lisbon. *Margaridas à beira-mar* was her tribute to the flower stand and woman so important to her work for the SOE.

The shop opened and was successful from the start. Louisa's excellent talent for flower combinations and colors was genuinely praised by the local Spaniards and her shop began making money right away. Her sister helped with the arrangements and waited on customers while her mother took care of the living space and did all the cooking for the three women.

At times, Louisa thought about Gerhardt Schoenfeld and his offer of marriage, but these thoughts became fewer and fewer as time passed. She was sure she had made the right decision and while she wished her former client no harm, did not desire to know what had happened to him.

Three months later, Louisa found a small cottage not far from the flower shop and moved her family into larger quarters.

The run of good luck continued for the beautiful lady from Lisbon.

Wednesday, June 4, 1942
British Embassy
Rua São Francisco Borja 63
Lapa, Lisbon, Portugal

Jack Beevor understood the unfortunate circumstances of his meeting this April morning with Ambassador Sir Ronald Campbell. In his heart, he had hoped it would never come to this.

He thought back over the events that had led to this luckless meeting.

It all started back in March. My MI5 friend here in Lisbon came to me and asked for a simple favor. He asked me if I knew of an apartment away from the chancery where he could interview someone whom he did not want to meet on embassy grounds. The request was simple enough and the fellow had worked closely with me on several occasions. Since I had the unoccupied flat on Rua de São Miguel down the street from my flat available if I needed it, I saw no reason why I shouldn't oblige my MI5 associate so I gave him the key to the flat and thought nothing about it.

Three weeks later the man whom the MI5 agent interviewed was arrested by the PVDE. After some intense grilling the man disclosed the fact that he had met with a British man whose name he did not know at a certain address on the *Rua de São Miguel.* The PVDE raided the place and found nothing, but a review of the lease on the flat turned up Jack Beevor's name as the lessee.

The PVDE then incorrectly concluded that Beevor was the person who interviewed the detainee and reported the matter to Prime Minister António Salazar.

A few days later, Salazar called Sir Ronald Campbell to his office and asked him if there existed a secret British intelligence operation in Lisbon and was a member of the embassy staff named Major Jack Beevor a part of that operation. He provided an address, *Rua de São Miguel 9* along with a copy of the lease with Beevor's signature.

Campbell was taken back by this assertion but was aware of the fact that Jack Beevor had two flats on that street. Moreover, he knew that Beevor lived in the one at *Rua de São Miguel 155.*

The ambassador realized that Beevor was in a pickle and decided to be frank and truthful with Prime Minister Salazar. The competent diplomat had worked hard to gain the prime minister's trust and some sensitive negotiations were ongoing at that very moment.

"Yes, Prime Minister, Mr. Beevor serves as the assistant military attaché at my embassy but to my knowledge he had never performed any duties that were in any way harmful to Portugal or to our Portuguese/British alliance," vowed Campbell.

Salazar considered the answer and spoke in a low voice. "Then Mr. Ambassador, can you tell me why this man needed two flats on the same street; one for living and the other for exactly what?"

Campbell knew he was in a corner and reluctantly answered, "No, Prime Minister, I don't know why. I am prepared to question Major Beevor at once and report back to you with his answer."

"That won't be necessary, Sir Ronald. The PVDE has determined that this Beevor falls into the category as some *Abwehr* agents who have been expelled from Portugal for their activities. I'm afraid Mr. Beevor must depart Lisbon at the first opportunity."

Campbell thought quickly and responded, "Prime Minister, I would ask Major Beevor be given enough time to prepare for his successor and to prevent any undue publicity arising from Major Beevor's departure."

Salazar considered the ambassador's request and granted him appropriate time to conclude the matter.

Before his exodus, Jack Beevor decided to write a report on German intelligence activities he had witnessed in Portugal to give to Salazar. It would include German penetration of several governmental departments that even extended to the prime minister's office. Bribes on a considerable scale to numerous officials across the country were included. Also, *Abwehr* activities involving the ownership of Lisbon brothels to provide intelligence information from visiting seamen as well as the black propaganda activities of several *Abwehr* operatives became part of the report.

The commentary was finalized. The chancellery head edited the final report and sent it to London for approval. The SOE quickly accepted the report and Ambassador Campbell was directed to send it straight to Salazar.

The Portuguese prime minister was surprised and elated over the report he called, *"sincero e leal"* and even considered lifting Beevor's expulsion from the country.

In view of the fact that three weeks had passed and Beevor's replacement was due in short order, the ambassador called Beevor into his office for this meeting. "Jack, I have decided it would be best for you to head back to London. I want you to rest assured your record of service while in Portugal will be exemplary and, on behalf of the King, I thank you for what you have accomplished. Some of your exploits, and you know of what I refer, will never be known except by the highest authorities but that is the nature of intelligence work. I personally feel you did a remarkable job here with limited staff and inadequate funding. You are a credit to the SOE and to Great Britain. I wish you the best in your career and subsequent activities."

Beevor considered the ambassador's statement and concurred with his judgement. He was eager to get back to London and had been told an excellent opportunity awaited him on his return. He enjoyed his tenure in Portugal and in particular his interaction with a number of Portuguese citizens who supported his work. He would miss Izaura Ribeiro and his Lisbon staff and their contributions to the British cause, but his intrusion by the *PVDE* had basically limited his efforts as an intelligence agent.

He did not realize at the time the effect his report would have on the Portuguese government. Several important departments were shaken up and a number of proven loyal officers replaced those who were on the German payroll.

Jack Beevor's report severely limited the actions of *Abwehr* agents in Portugal and proved to be a great help in strengthening the alliance between his country and the government of Portugal.

The young intelligence office threw a good-bye party in his flat for all his staff and several friends from the embassy. To say a good time was had by all would be a gross understatement.

Afterword

This novel is a work of love for me since I am of Portuguese extraction. At an early age my grandfather made me aware of the former greatness and beautiful customs and cuisine of Portugal that I have tried to display in Lisbon.

If you ever have a chance to visit the country, please do. Portugal is magical in many respects and offers a unique insight into a people and way of life that have not changed a great deal in centuries.

The country itself is also quite beautiful and an average Portuguese is delighted to share his or her country's personality with you.

I sincerely hope this work gives you an insight into what makes Portugal and the City of Lisbon so important to me.

Jack DuArte
Lexington, KY.

Heroes and Adversaries

Portuguese

Cardinal Manuel Cerejeira — Salazar's roommate at the University of Coimbra became a priest and much respected intellectual. He was the cementing fixture between the Catholic Church and Portugal's governments throughout his career. He was named Patriarch of Portugal in 1929 and served in that capacity for 48 years. He was an integral part of Estado Novo and Salazar often sought his consul when making difficult decisions that affected the country. He died August 2, 1977 at age 88 and is buried in the Monastery of Monastery of São Vicente de Fora, Lisbon.

Consul Aristides de Sousa Mendes — After his efforts to assist refugees to escape the Nazis through Bordeaux proved his undoing, Sousa Mendes was recalled to Portugal for disregarding his instructions as consulate. He was demoted and his pay cut in half. Blacklisted and almost insolvent, he suffered a stroke in 1945 that left him partially paralyzed and unable to work. The former diplomat died at age 68 on April 3, 1954 in Lisbon's Franciscan Hospital. Decades later, in 1988, his children were finally able to clear his name. He was recognized by several Jewish organizations for his humanitarian work and, in 1995, Portugal held a week-long National Homage to Sousa Mendes where Portuguese President Mario Soares declared Sousa Mendes to be "Portugal's greatest hero of the Twentieth Century."

Captain Agostinho Lourenço — Salazar's right-hand man as head of the PVDE was to become the president of Interpol in 1956, a position he held for five years with the international police organization. Always pro-British in his views, he had close ties with MI6. He died on August 2, 1964 at the age of 77. There is a street in Lisbon named in his honor. He remained a close friend of Salazar until his death.

Prime Minister António de Oliveira Salazar — Served as Portugal's prime minister for 36 years until a stroke left him disabled in September of 1968. He was replaced without his knowledge and died two years later at the age of 81. Tens of thousands paid tribute to the popular leader at a Requiem at the Jerónimos Monastery, the place that was the backdrop for Salazar's successful World Exposition some thirty years before. He was buried in a plain grave in his birthplace of Vimieiro. During his lifetime, he never left his beloved Portugal.

Ricardo Espírito Santo — Portuguese banker who entertained the Duke & Duchess of Windsor was also heavily involved with German banking institutions. In April of 1945, he was involved in a nasty incident in France and the story was misreported by the Times of London. This caused a run on his bank that nearly forced its closure and Espírito Santo sued the Times for £250,000. The case was settled and the Banco Espírito Santo slowly regained its health.

British

John Grosvenor "Jack" Beevor — After his ill-fated and unfortunate tenure in Lisbon, Beevor was recalled to London where he eventually held a stellar career with the SOE. He returned to London as assistant to SOE chief Sir. Charles Hambro. In 1944 became general staff officer at the Italian Headquarters of Special Operations Mediterranean. After the war he held various banking positions and high management positions with a number of important corporate companies. While in Lisbon, he met and later married his wife Carinthia. He died on February 26, 1987 at age 82. Their son, Sir Anthony Beevor, is a celebrated military historian responsible for numerous works on World War II.

Sir Ronald Ian Campbell — Veteran British diplomat was placed in volatile Lisbon embassy when Sir Walford Selby retired. An able boss, his work was praised by London and the United States during World War II. He served as Envoy Extraordinary and Minister Plenipotentiary (deputy head of mission) at Washington, D.C., until 1944. He became Assistant Under-Secretary of State at the Foreign Office in 1945, and served as the United Kingdom's ambassador to Egypt from 1946 to 1950. He died on April 22, 1983 at the age of 92.

Prime Minister Sir Winston S. Churchill — Arguably the greatest world leader of his generation, Churchill was inexplicably ousted from office in 1946 only to be re-elected in 1951. He was voted Great Britain's greatest person ever, defeating Shakespeare and other well-known personages of the past. He was knighted in 1953 and received the Nobel Prize for Literature with his History of the English-Speaking Peoples the same year. His exploits have been featured in numerous films including the recent Darkest Hour (2017) with Gary Oldman as a particularly enticing Churchill.

Churchill died at his London home on January 24, 1965 of complications from a stroke at age 90 At his request, he was buried in his family's plot at St. Martin's Church, Bladon, not far from his birthplace at Blenheim Palace.

David McAdam Eccles — The dapper graduate of New College, Oxford, left the intelligence service in 1943 and became a member of the British Parliament where he held a number of ministerial positions including Minister of Works and President of the Bord of Trade. He was raised to peerage in 1962 and was made a viscount in 1964. His governmental career lasted until 1999 when he died on February 24, at aged 94, while he was still a member of the House of Lords. His honors include Order of the Companions of Honor (CH), Royal Victorian Order (KCVO) and Privy Council of the United Kingdom (PC).

Sir Samuel Hoare — Held various top posts in British governments and served as ambassador to Spain during WW2. A nobleman by birth, he was elected to the House of Commons in 1910. He later fought in WW1 and entered diplomatic service in 1922 as Secretary of State for Air. An excellent writer, Hoare used that skill as a diplomat on numerous occasions. He was made a Commander of the Order of St. Michael and St. George in 1917 and received similar awards from both Russia and Italy for his actions. He died in May 7, 1959 at age 79.

Harold Adrian Russell 'Kim' Philby — Philby was perhaps the most notorious double agent in British history. He was lured into Communism in the early 1930's during his time at Cambridge and acted as a Russian agent until he was unearthed in 1951 by Bill Harvey, a former FBI agent and then a member of the CIA. He defected to the Soviet Union in 1963 and remained there until his death on May 11, 1988 at age 76. He is buried in Kuntsevo Cemetery in Moscow.

Sir Walford Selby — Had been in Great Britain's diplomatic service for 36 years when he served as his country's ambassador to Portugal. He was envoy to Austria from 1933- 1937 during that country's hectic period prior to German annexation of its neighbor. He was an old school diplomat nearing retirement but held a firm hand to matters affecting his embassy and country. He was knighted in 1931 for service to his country. He authored an autobiography, Diplomatic Twilight, to critical acclaim in 1953. Selby died on August 7, 1965 in Salisbury, the capitol of Zimbabwe.

Duke and Duchess of Windsor — The Duke served as Governor of the Bahamas from August 1940 to March 1945. After the war, the couple moved to Paris where they stayed in self-imposed exile. They later shuttled between Europe and the United States as society celebrities. The former King Edward VIII died in Paris on May 28, 1972 at the age of 77. His Duchess, the former Wallis Simpson, also died in Paris on April 24, 1986 and was buried five days later in the Royal Burial Ground, Frogmore, Berkshire, England, alongside her husband.

German

Baron Oswald Theodor von Hoyningen-Huene — Career German diplomat was Ambassador to Portugal from 1934-1944. His close ties to the country and its people made German diplomatic activity an important factor in many of the Portugal's important pre-war and wartime decisions. After the war, Prime Minister Salazar allowed him to live in Lisbon after his retirement. He died in Basel, Switzerland on August 26, 1963 at age 78.

Walter Schellenberg — Held various positions in Nazi Germany's *Schutzstaffel,* Hitler's personal bodyguards. His ideas gave birth to the formation of the Reich Security Main Office (RSHA) and he was instrumental in developing Germany's plan for the occupation of Great Britain Informationsheft G.B. (Operation Sea Lord). Considered one of the brightest and most devoted Nazis, Schellenberg had a hand in numerous clandestine activities and was a part of the highest tier of Nazi leadership. Captured in Denmark after the war, he was tried at Nuremberg and sentenced to six years in prison of which he served only two, due to illness. He died in Turin, Italy in 1952.

Spanish

Prime Minister Francisco Franco — The Caudillo ruled by decree until 1973 when he relinquished the title of Prime Minister. Even though Franco considered joining the Axis in 1940, his basic demands of Germany included control of Gibraltar and French North Africa that Hitler opposed and caused Spain to remain neutral during WWII. Before his death in 1975, he restored the monarchy of Spain to Prince Juan Carlos de Borbón (Juan Carlos I) who then led the country into democracy. On October 30, 1975 he was taken off life support while in a coma. He was interred at the Valle de los Caídos, the only person buried there who did not die in the Spanish Civil War.

Juan Pujol García — One of the best-known double spies in the war, code name Garbo. King George VI made Pujol a member of the most excellent order of the British Empire (MBE) and Germany awarded him the Iron Cross, Second Class, for his work as code name Alaric in their service. A number of documentaries about his life and efforts have been made and shown. Pujol died in Caracas, Venezuela, at age 76, on October 10, 1988, and is buried in Choroni, Venezuela.

Ramon Serrano Suñer — Second most powerful figure in Post-Civil War Spain, Suñer was pro-Nazi and attempted to guide his country toward Germany's causes. He became minister of foreign affairs and developed a hatred for Joachim von Ribbentrop. He was instrumental in sending Spain's Blue Division to fight alongside the Wehrmacht in 1941 in Russia and was ousted from his position when a Falangist extremist attempted the assassination of a Spanish general at Begoña. Franco used the incident to oust the Falangists from power including his brother-in-law. Suñer lived to be 101 and died in Madrid on September 1, 2003, just eleven days before his 102nd birthday.

Jack DuArte is a native New Orleanian who began writing at age fourteen. He served in the US Air Force during Vietnam and was awarded the Bronze Star. *Lisbon* is DuArte's 9th novel in his WWII Series. DuArte resides in Lexington, KY, with his Havanese Cisco, his minature horse Darleigh and German Shepard Chase.

Preview all eight at:
<u>jackduarte.net</u>

Best possible prices and
volume discounts

The Resistance *(Revised)*

Early World War II, and the newly appointed head of the French Resistance, Jean Moulin, formulates a plan that will safeguard some of France's greatest art treasures that are being sought by Nazi Reichsmarschall Hermann Goring. The action moves in rapid-fire sequence from London to France as England's Special Operations Executive (SOE) aids the French Resistance in its prodigious mission. The story takes an unexpected twist when an agent of the Vichy government's hated Milice secret police inadvertently stumbles upon the treasures. The story reaches its incredible conclusion in the holy City of Lourdes amid gunfire and heroic acts on the part of Resistance members and their allies.

---

jackduarte.net

Singapore

In 1940, England's great island fortress of Singapore sits placidly behind its great array of guns, seemingly unaware of Japan's intent to conquer that part of Southeast Asia. British Naval lieutenant William Elliott is assigned to the Special Operations Executive (SOE) and soon becomes a key element in alerting his superiors to Japanese intentions. When the invasion begins, Elliott is thrust into a series of events that makes him choose between his duty to his country and the captivating Singaporean doctor he loves. Singapore's final chapters are a life and death struggle for survival and freedom for the island's inhabitants.

jackduarte.net

Spitfire

Spitfire is the third installment of Jack DuArte' World War II Series. The setting is Great Britain in 1940, immediately before and during the epic Battle of Britain. Fighting a superior number of Luftwaffe bombers and fighters, the valiant Royal Air Force wages a desperate air battle to save their country from certain defeat. Flight Lieutenant Anthony Nelson and his younger brother, Fletcher, are pilots of 54 Squadron Spitfires, the great British fighter plane that is Britain's only hope for survival. Through a suspenseful series of events, both find they are in love with the same woman. A hair-raising set of circumstances brings Spitfire to a spellbinding conclusion that will keep the reader glued to the final pages.

jackduarte.net

Malta

The Island of Malta and its strategic location in the Mediterranean has made it a prime target for the Axis powers. In early 1942, the German Luftwaffe decides to concentrate on Malta and begins a horrendous bombing attack. A handful of heroic British RAF pilots brave the odds and begin ferrying new Spitfire Mark VI's to help defend the island. Once there, their troubles begin in earnest. Malta is best-selling author Jack DuArte's fourth installment in his WWII series. Malta features incredible action over the skies of the Mediterranean and Sicily as well as the remarkable story of what Malta's defenders faced in their struggle. Malta was called 'the most bombed place on earth' during this period and was awarded the George Cross by King George VI. Malta mirrors the lives of a number of these honored British aviators as they battle heat, dirt, the 'Malta Dog' and deplorable conditions to help save the vital island.

---

jackduarte.net

The White Mouse

The White Mouse was the name given by the Gestapo to Nancy Wake, an Australian woman setting up escape routes from France during WWII. After fleeing to England, the White Mouse joins the British Special Operations Executive (SOE) and returns to occupied France around the time of the Normandy invasion in 1944. Through sheer determination, along with the help of other SOE operatives, she manages to bring together a number of Maquis unites in the Auvergne to harass and delay German reinforcements attempting to reach German coastal defenses. Aided by an American Army Captain on loan to the SOE, The White Mouse reunites US Army Captain Brian Russell with his French Resistance love that was brought to life in Jack DuArte's first novel, the best-selling, The Resistance.

Kidnap the Pope

Adolf Hitler is maddened when his ally and friend Italian dictator Benito Mussolini is ousted from power. Believing that nothing happens in Italy without the consent of the Catholic Church and the pope himself, the German Fuhrer decides to avenge Mussolini. He orders a high-ranking SS General to develop a plan to invade the Vatican and kidnap the pope. SS General Karl Wolff is placed in a dilemma... follow his personal feelings on the disturbing order or directly disobey a direct order from Hitler. Kidnap the Pope follows the non-stop action of World War II and the countries involved. Can the Vatican be saved and can Pope Pus XII continue his diplomatic efforts on behalf of his church and its followers?

---

jackduarte.net

The First James Bond

As WWII draws to a close, Winston Churchill orders a super-secretive M Section British Commando unit to remove Martin Bormann, Hitler's secretary and the key to Nazi Germany's banking system. Utilizing the River Spree, these commandos use kayaks to defy the odds and snatch Bormann from under the noses of advancing Russian forces in downtown Berlin. Bormann is taken backt to London where he provides Great Britain's Intelligence Services vital information to help alleviate Great Britain's horrendous war debt. From start to finish, The First James Bond unveils this masterful scenario and its spell-binding ending.

---

jackduarte.net

The Shetland Bus

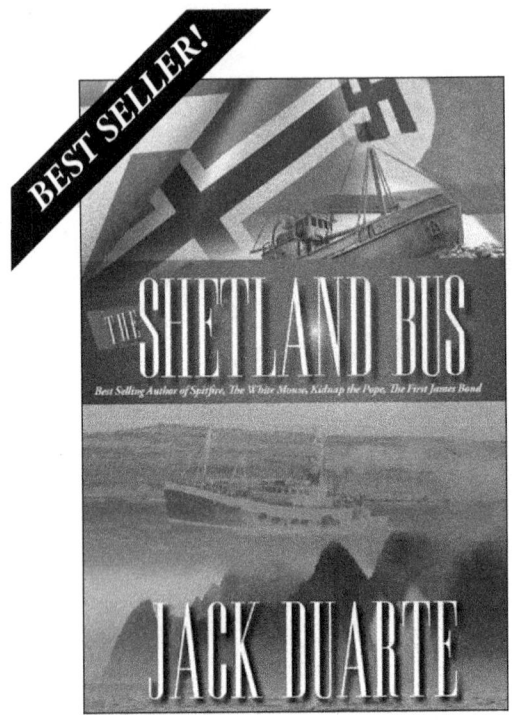

At the start of WW II, Germany overruns Norway and occupies the great northern country. Many Norwegian fisherman flee and some even take their fishing boats to nearby Scotland. Britain's Special Operations Executive (SOE) sets up a base in the Shetland Islands and these boats and crews begin systematic supplying and ferrying to aid the Norwegian Resistance. These trips are only made when the dangerous North Sea is at its worst; when nighttime offers a tiny measure of safety. The Shetland Bus is the heroic story of these boats and men and their efforts to outlast perilous seas and a demonic enemy. From start to finish, The Shetland Bus is filled with action-packed sequences of this masterful attempt to thwart Nazi Germany.

jackduarte.net

CPSIA information can be obtained
at www.ICGtesting.com
Printed in the USA
FSHW020423160121
77678FS

9 781733 459754